THIS
LOVE
KILLS
ME

Also by A.B. Whelan

14 Days to Die

As Sick as Our Secrets

If I Had Two Lives

THIS
LOVE
KILLS
ME

A.B. WHELAN

BURBANK BOOKS
PUBLISHING

This Love Kills Me: a novel / A.B. Whelan
   ISBN: 9780983472971
   ISBN 13: **978-0-9834729-7-1**
   1.   Psychological thriller
   2.   Suspense, Thriller, & Mystery
   3.   Domestic suspense
   4.   kidnapping
   5.   Sexual abuse
   6.   Dysfunctional family

"Sooner or later everyone sits down to a banquet of consequences."

— *Robert Louis Stevenson*

PROLOGUE

Los Angeles Times
Acclaimed Fantasy Writer Vanishes from Cruise Ship

BY EDUARDO MONTOYA | STAFF WRITER MARCH 14, 2017 | 7 AM

As an annual tradition, the Rose family gathered in Los Angeles to celebrate William and Barbara Rose's 35th wedding anniversary. The couple boarded the Princess Royal cruise ship to Cabo San Lucas, Baja, Mexico, with their children and grandchildren in the late afternoon. Their party of ten included the couple's son, Tony Rose, 28, and his wife, millionaire author Julia Rose, 26.

On the second day at sea, in the early morning hours of March 11, 2017, Tony Rose reported his wife missing to the captain of the ship. An extensive search was conducted to locate the missing passenger, Julia Rose, aboard the cruise liner, but she couldn't be found. According to her husband's statement, Mrs. Rose was drinking and acting out the night before her disappearance when the married couple attended the popular game show, The Newlywed Game. According to our sources, the couple had left the event early. In a statement to the police, Mr. Rose admitted that he argued with his wife on the way to their cabin and he returned to the couple's room alone. It's not clear what time the couple had separated.

Tony Rose's statement corresponds with the account of one of the bartenders that came forward as a witness who claimed to have seen Julia Rose arguing with an unidentified individual near the pool on Deck 5, used only by the crewmembers of the Princess Royal. The security camera captured Mrs. Rose walking alone on the deck, seemingly in distress.

Julia Rose has not been seen since.

The US Coast Guard and the Mexican Navy searched the waters along the coastline where the Princess Royal was cruising during the hours in question. She has not been found. A search and rescue attempt is still underway.

The Princess Royal is registered in the Bahamas and a detective with the Royal Bahamas Police Force was summoned to investigate the incident. No report has been released to the public about the progress of the investigation, but according to our sources, the disappearance of Julia Rose is being considered either an accident or a suicide. However, homicide has not yet been ruled out.

Julia Rose is a 26-year-old Montclair, New Jersey, resident. In 2014, her breakout novel about a young girl discovering a portal to a parallel universe became an instant #1 *New York Times* and *USA Today* bestseller. The four-book series is currently being adapted to the big screen by Lionsgate. The first movie, titled *The New Earth*, is set to release in 2021.

Fans of Julia Rose have demonstrated an outpouring of support for the author. Thousands of people posted on her social media sites praying for the author's safe return.

Mr. Rose couldn't be reached for comment.

The Royal Cruise Line and the FBI both issued statements declaring that the investigation is still ongoing and no further information is available at this time.

According to the accident lawyers at Madalon Law, who investigate cruise line crew and passenger disappearances, only a few people are reported falling overboard by the cruise lines each year, but the numbers are much higher.

The following statistics are quoted from their website.

- The longest a person was known to survive in the water after having fallen overboard is 18 hours.

- Falling overboard is most common during the night of a cruise.
- Those who fall overboard are most often residents of California and Florida.
- Most overboard falls are often alcohol or mischief-related, such as playing on railings or attempting to climb between cabins.
- Women are less likely than men to fall overboard.
- Only about 1 in 5 persons have survived falling overboard between the years 2000 and 2013.
- The average age of a person who falls overboard is 41 years old.

If you know someone who has disappeared while onboard a cruise ship, contact Madalon Law for consultation.

1

Revenge is a word I live by these days. The verb, not the noun. After years of fantasizing and planning, I'm finally in a position to act. So what I need is an action word to drive me.

The definition of revenge is to inflict hurt or harm on someone for an injury or wrongdoing done to oneself or another. Revenge takes you on a bittersweet, high-risk, and sacrificial mission. It's the collective noun of the old proverb: an eye for an eye. A motto our society no longer lives by or allows. According to Google, the use of this word has diminished since the eighteen hundreds. If this trend continues, people won't even think of this nostalgic word at all in the future. Perhaps our new motto will be: "Let fate decide," or "Turn the other cheek."

But not today. Or not for me, at least. Because I made a promise, and I tend to keep my promises.

I know I'm too cryptic, confusing even, but soon my story will make sense, and every bit and piece will fall into place. Soon, you will understand why I did what I did. And *then* you can judge me for my actions, as you see fit.

But I'm hoping you will take my side, because people who commit crimes must be punished, mustn't they?

On that, we both must agree.

*   *   *   *   *

As if the heavens were disapproving of my plans, it was a finger-numbingly cold and stormy afternoon as I entered the Manhattan sports bar on 7th Avenue. I held my cashmere coat over my head to keep my hair dry, even though ruining something so expensive made me feel dreadful and ungrateful.

Aware of every beat of my racing heart, I searched the vaguely lit and humid room for the familiar faces I came here to meet.

As I stood in the door, shaking the rain from my coat as drops of water ran down my nylons, a chill prickled the naked skin underneath. I shuddered, not simply from the cold but from the nerves that played at my insides.

"Annie!" someone called out.

It took me a second to react. Annie, yes, that's my new name.

I waved at Brooke, who was leaning out from a table, her arm in the air beckoning me.

Brooke Russell was Julia Rose's crusty and battle-worn attorney—she *used to be* her attorney before Julia was officially presumed dead nearly three years ago. From the day I showed up in Brooke's office with Julia's diary and a remarkable yet almost unbelievable story, she has been guiding me on my path of revenge at every step of the way. She has been my rock and moral compass, but nobody in the world knew that. It was our most kept secret.

On my way to the table, I folded the coat over my arm and adjusted my purse's strap over my shoulder, trying to look every bit a professional woman of law, which I was not—far from it. But I'd been preparing for this critical role for months, and practice had given me some confidence.

This moment was my final test.

I counted the heads of four individuals around the table. My anticipation, blended with surprise, accelerated my pulse and I needed to force myself to take the first step toward them.

As I waded across a tight pathway, my heels clicking on the painted concrete flooring, the program playing on the TV screens above the bar diverted my attention. An unofficial documentary about Julia Rose's life was playing.

"She jumped," said a woman sitting at the table I was passing.

"Probably the fame got to her and she couldn't handle it," added her companion. "Did you read her books? They aren't that good. More hype than substance if you ask me."

Hearing people talk ill of Julia infuriated me, especially when they didn't know her, never even met her. Though I wasn't at all surprised. Yesterday marked the third anniversary of Julia's disappearance from the cruise ship. Over the past three years, different theories had been debated online and reported in the news. Some going so far as to claim they'd untangled the mysteries surrounding her disappearance. As a result, the public's opinion has been misled, their opinions twisted, warped, and cheapened. Even the faith of Julia's most devoted fans wavered from the overwhelming amount of fake news in the papers.

The *facts* were made clear early on, and the path was set. Julia's husband wrote the narrative: she was drunk and irresponsible on the night in question, leaving a child without a mother and a loving husband without a wife.

Julia would be heartbroken to learn about the judgments people had passed on her so easily without knowing the truth.

The authorities weren't much help in uncovering the truth about what happened to Julia either. The Royal Cruise Line rushed to sweep the negative PR under the rug. The Royal Bahamas Police Force proved incompetent in running a high-profile investigation. The FBI was secretive about their findings, if they had any, releasing few official statements to the public, leaving the tabloids and readers' imaginations to run wild with theories.

Julia was a celebrated prodigy one minute and a lousy alcoholic mother and wife the next. She was never given a chance to defend herself, to clear her name. As it turned out, her family lacked the character to stand up for her as well. Of course, they didn't. They had their own names and millions of dollars in inheritance to protect. Only her brother spoke out against the Roses, while her mother cried on TV, begging the public for information.

On the other hand, the unfortunate widower, Tony Rose, had become the hero of the story. The public dubbed him a loving father and devoted husband to Julia, left to raise their child alone. People seemed to forget that Tony had the most to gain from Julia's death. He was inheriting her fortune. And while most families suffer from a sudden financial strain when the breadwinner of the house suddenly dies, Tony was blessed with a huge injection of income.

The immense media coverage on Julia's mysterious disappearance during a family trip rejuvenated reader interest in her published work. Discussions about her books dominated the book-lover world on Instagram, Goodreads, and Facebook, making Tony all the richer.

When I researched the case online in Brooke's house, I learned that the Bahamian detective held and questioned Tony as a person of interest in Julia's disappearance for a few days during the early days of the investigation. However, Tony paid for the best legal defense Julia's money could buy, and they soon released him due to insufficient evidence against him. Why the media didn't gnaw on that significant detail longer has always remained a mystery to me.

After spending years building up my hatred and plotting an act of revenge against Julia's husband, I was about to meet him for the first time, yet my emotions had to be locked up like a canary in a cage.

The conflicting feelings coiling in my chest pushed me to a brisker pace.

As I reached the table, out of breath and nervous, I witnessed one of the men seated there call out to the bartender in an ear-pleasing baritone, "Would you mind changing the channel, please?" I could only see the back of his head. Elongated in shape and covered in thick dark hair.

The stylish young man polishing a glass behind the bar reached for the remote at once. "Certainly, Mr. Rose."

No, this soft voice can't belong to a wife killer, I thought. When I first looked at his pictures online and saw his gentle eyes and charming smile, I kept telling myself that he must have the voice of the devil as a sign of his wickedness. But that's not what I got now. I felt cheated. Disappointed.

Brooke removed a white cloth napkin from her lap and set it next to her plate as she stood up to greet me. "I'm glad you could make it." She put a hand on my arm and turned me toward her companions. Her skin was dry and wrinkled like papyrus paper, and golden rings cut into her warm, blotchy sausage fingers.

"This is Annie Adams, my new assistant I was talking about," Brooke introduced me in a hoarse voice hardened by years of smoking and drinking hard liquor.

I nodded with a smile. Be charming, sexy even—I reminded myself.

"This is Tony Rose, his sister, Sylvia Rose, and his brother, Justin," my boss finished the introduction. Her name didn't suit her. I'd have imagined someone called Brooke as a tall, slender woman with a hint of elegance. Perhaps with long brown hair and a very feminine face. My new boss was short and stocky, with a waist-less barrel body. Underneath her close-cropped dark hair sat an array of distinct facial features framed with translucent-rimmed thick glasses on a wide-set face. She might have seemed intimidating to some, but I knew that the rough-around-the-edges appearance was only an act. Brooke's heart was in the right place, and she cared for Julia.

I offered my hand to Tony first.

He slipped his warm and moist fingers over mine, teasingly staring into my eyes.

I held his gaze.

Today marked my first day at my new job, and I needed to make a good impression. I'd dreamed about this opportunity for so long, planning my first encounter with Julia's in-laws, especially her widower. If I messed it up, my whole plan would collapse like a house of cards.

"Tony," I said, breathing the word with a purposefully sexy rasp. I leaned in enough to allow the neck of my blouse to separate from my chest, offering a discreet peek at my lace bra. Tony's eyes momentarily dropped down to my breasts before sliding away as he caught himself.

I moved on. "Sylvia. Justin."

Sylvia put her hands up as if offended. "Sorry, I don't like it when people touch me." She strained to smile, but the result turned out rather comical as her tight and rigid skin refused to budge.

I had read about Sylvia in Julia's diary. Tony's older sister was a hypochondriac and also addicted to plastic surgery. I recently started to follow her on Instagram. Selfies. Boobs. More selfies. She must have touched up her posted pictures intensively because even her thick layer of makeup couldn't disguise how unhealthy and aged she looked in person. But it was still an eye-catching package and a trendy one.

"Here, squeeze in." Brooke ushered me to sit across from Tony on her left-hand side.

Tony took a sip of his beer—dark and foamy. "So, Annie, is that short for Annabelle?"

"Just Annie. Plain and simple. Or you can call me Ms. Adams if you prefer formalities."

The server appeared, a tired-eyed young woman giving off the vibe of an overworked college student. "Are we all good here? Can I get you guys something else?"

I raised my finger. "I'll have a lemon ginger tea with honey, please." I'd managed to get my unquenchable hunger under control for a while now, after years of living in deprivation while I was in captivity, and I no longer felt the need to order every item off the menu. Since I'd been in New York, I'd developed a taste for tea, thanks to Brooke. She'd googled my symptoms and searched for healthy options to help me feel better. That was how I'd learned about herbal teas and their benefits. Brooke's interest in my health made me feel special—especially when she didn't seem to care about her own health.

The waitress smiled. "All right. Anything else?"

Tony put a finger up to draw attention. "It seems we are going to be here for a while, so would you mind bringing us another mixed appetizer plate?" Then he looked at me. "You must try their spinach puffs. The best in town." He teased, and I played along, acting excited about the food because that's what Julia would have done.

Brooke set down her fork and leaned against the backrest. "All right. As I mentioned earlier, Annie will be your primary contact with the office from now on. You can still reach me via email or phone anytime you need, but I will be passing down the dealings of the day-to-day operations to Annie."

Tony rubbed his hands together. "You'll hear no complaints from me."

Sylvia picked up her phone to extract herself from the conversation. It was only Justin who watched me with an intense, focused gaze as if trying to read me, peeling back the layers to see what was underneath, what I was hiding, if I was hiding anything at all.

Justin Rose was a self-made businessman who specialized in finance. He also benefited from Julia's wealth by overseeing her significant investments. According to Brooke, Justin had long developed a pathological need to upstage every man in the room, particularly Tony. He was a loud and obnoxious man who preached for socialism yet worked in the most capitalist business of all: investment and finance.

He didn't talk, only observed, like a predator on the Savanna, measuring up his prey and looking for weaknesses. I expected him to attack at any minute.

Bring it on, buddy; I'm ready for you.

When Justin refrained from commenting on Brooke's announcement, I decided to focus on Tony. "I'm familiar with the family's businesses and operations. I know Julia didn't leave a will, and you were the sole beneficiary of her assets."

Tony's eyes shrunk at my statement. No man liked to be reminded that his wife built his fortune. But if I doubted his worth, he would feel the need to prove himself to me. That was precisely why I was there: to strip this wife-killer naked, to force him to trip and fall, and with all that, hopefully, to expose himself.

"I've studied the contracts with Lionsgate and Celadon Books," I continued. "I understand that Julia didn't have any unfinished manuscripts we can work with, but she has a strong brand we can build on. I have a few ideas that I'd be more than happy to discuss with all of you at your convenience."

Tony pointed a finger at me and looked at Brooke. "She does her homework. I like her."

"Do I ever let you down, Tony?" Brooke reached for her whiskey and lifted the glass to her lips. She was a lawyer. Lying was as natural to her as breathing. What worried me was that the story about Julia and me rocked her to the core, and it showed. Considering all my options, I had no choice but to trust her. She wasn't going to fuck this up for me.

If somebody were going to fuck it up, it would be me. I was not a lawyer. I never went to college. At least not to a college where you learn from books. The school of hard knocks taught me everything I needed to know to survive. But I was a hard worker and committed. Brooke had been coaching me for this job for months, and I couldn't let her down. I couldn't let Julia down.

"So, how did you manage to snatch an assistant job with this shark of a lawyer at such a young age?" Justin asked calculatingly. "I don't mean to offend you, but how old are you?"

"I'm twenty-five," I lied. I turned twenty-two last month, but with makeup and the mature look of my face, people often believed I was older than I was. I could easily pass for twenty-five, if not older.

Justin played the superior intelligent businessman, yet he'd bought his college degree on the black market. I guess it takes one con artist to know another.

I remained confident and maintained eye contact, as Brooke had trained me.

"Let's just say the right connections and my extensive knowledge landed me this job." I winked at Justin. "I still have a lot to learn from Brooke, but I'm confident I will satisfy you all."

Tony tapped both of his hands on the table. "Well, I don't know about the rest of you, but I feel satisfied enough. So, let's get down to business."

The hook was set. Now I only had to reel them in slowly.

Box one checked.

2

My first meeting with Julia's widower, her lawyer, and the Rose siblings was three cups of hot tea and a bowl of chicken and wild rice soup with kale long. It was the kind of sophisticated cuisine I'd acquired a taste for since I moved to New York, unlike anything I'd ever dreamed of having the years prior when my life wasn't my own.

As the evening advanced, my lack of working experience in navigating the book publishing laws was overshadowed by my ideas of how to use Julia's brand to further increase the wealth of the Rose estate. The dollar signs flashing in front of their eyes subdued my clients' interest in questioning my background and refocused their attention to my ideas of how to revive Julia's name in readers' minds. It had been a while since the last wave of exorbitant income poured into the Roses' bank account, and it was apparent that they were desperate for a new plan.

After Julia's mysterious disappearance from the cruise ship, her book sales soared to new heights as if gossip-hungry readers hoped to find the answers to her tragedy between the lines of her formerly published works. Speculative theories had appeared online discussing the possibility that Tristan, the abusive male character in her *The New Earth* series, was based on her husband, Tony. Both names started with a "T." It made sense, and online trolls jumped at the opportunity to air their unsolicited opinions, having no consideration for who they hurt with their words.

The truth that I've learned from Brooke and heard from Julia was that Tony was never physically or verbally abusive toward his wife. If anything, he was the opposite of a dominant husband. When Julia became pregnant two months before her graduation from Brown University, Tony had become besotted with her and gave Julia a cheap but very tasteful zirconium promise ring. Before her belly gave away their secret, they married in a small but exquisite ceremony, inviting only close family and friends.

Tony would spend hours lying on Julia's lap and reading stories to her belly. His love for his expanding family could be measured by the quality time he spent with his pregnant wife. "I can't wait to have a mini-you in my arms," he would say to Julia, and from his flattering words, she was swollen with happiness, despite the difficult financial situation they suffered in those early years.

Ironically enough, it was Tony who aspired to be a writer. During his years at Brown, Tony penned stories about ancient heroes and worlds, following David Gemmell's footsteps, who was one of his favorite authors. But with a baby coming and a family to care for, he needed a more reliable job that would put food on the table every day.

Having only an academic education and lacking vocational skills, the soon-to-be father had difficulty finding employment. He thought about being a Realtor, but that required a long learning curve, which he couldn't afford without pay; nor was this highly personal job the right fit for his introvert-type personality.

His hands were too soft to work construction or landscaping. And he knew and cared little about manufacturing and sales.

With these limited options, he ended up landing a job as a floor manager at Home Depot. His position was far from what he imagined for himself at the age of twenty-three, far from the illustrious careers he craved while reading in the shades of oak trees on the university campus at Brown. Yet Tony did his duty to his family without complaining about his shattered dreams. He was thankful to be employed and able to support the ones he loved. And he adored Julia and the baby, and there was nothing he wouldn't do to keep them safe and happy. But it doesn't matter how beautiful a dream world we build in our heads for ourselves, sooner or later, we all have to wake up.

I marked the page in Julia's diary where I sensed Tony had reached an emotional turning point toward his family, especially his wife. It was the day Julia signed a five-hundred-thousand-dollar, four-book contract with Caledon Books. My favorite passage read:

Tony returned home with three dozen red roses tied together in one giant bouquet and a massive smile on his face· Yet his every word, every kind gesture, furthered my guilt for stealing his dream of becoming a published author· He had been working hard to earn a decent living for our family that consequentially allowed my writing career to bloom· I had become the thief of dreams· Guilt always overshadowed my joy of success in my work and my faith in the strength of our marriage·

Sometimes I would stay up at night, haunted by the question if I could hate my husband so profoundly as to find the will to push him to his death over the railing of a cruise ship? Would I be able to watch him fight for air as the turbulent black water swallowed his body, then return to my cabin, order another drink, and go to bed as if nothing had happened? Does evil sleep in us all, dormant until the moment it's awoken? Is it even right to blame the devil for our actions? Was Tony the one who killed his wife? Or was there someone else there that night who stole Julia's life? I wouldn't discover the truth until I'd made all the pawns on the chessboard transparent, starting with my number one suspect, Tony.

After the meeting at the pub concluded, Brooke drove us to her home on the east side of Montclair. It was a secluded private property with breathtaking views of New York City's skyscrapers beneath the endless sea of the blue sky.

The drive took us about forty minutes from the sports bar in Manhattan. This historical township was close enough to Brooke's law firm in New York City that she could commute to work and invite business partners and friends to visit, yet far enough away to keep her privacy if she wanted. Before my introduction as her assistant, I'd stayed with Brooke for nearly three months. I usually had her historical seven-thousand-square-foot Tudor-style home to myself while she was attending to her daily business in the city. The house was about fifty times bigger than the room I had to myself in captivity, or at least it felt that way. At first, the idea of not having the four walls protecting my back was frightening, but with time, I got used to the space.

Tony didn't know how far back my relationship with Brooke reached, nor did he suspect we were housemates, so when I turned down his offer to give me a lift home, he walked me to Brooke's car and watched me slip into the backseat.

As the Jaguar rolled into traffic, I looked through the back window at Tony standing on the curb, shoulders pulled in to fend against the cold. The dark sky was etched with silver lines of raindrops shooting toward the ground, like millions of needles falling onto the man's shoulders. I imagined them penetrating his skin one by one, causing him a protracted sequence of pain. That's how you will feel when I'm done with you, I thought, kicking off my shoes.

I spread myself out onto the backseat of Brooke's car, inhaling the mixture of earthy and organic scents, the wet leather of the seat, and the damp wool of my coat.

"Sit up and buckle up, please," Brooke instructed me. Our eyes met in the review mirror.

I pulled the seatbelt away from my neck with my thumb. "I'm buckled, see?"

"The improper use of a seatbelt does more harm than good. If we get into an accident, you'll get your head cut off." Brooke was always the bringer of gloom and doom, the foreboding mother figure. She had a story with a tragic ending for every situation I found myself in and a lesson to learn from it. At the beginning of our partnership, her never-ending warnings annoyed me, but over time, I grew accustomed to them. Brooke became the mother every girl needs but I never had.

I rolled onto my back and released the seatbelt. It recoiled and snapped back into place with a metallic clang. "See, I trust your driving abilities more than I trust technology."

My defiance brought on her disapproval, which she expressed with a drawn-out hissing sound, but at least it achieved her getting off my back.

"So, what was your first impression of Tony?"

"He's charming. I'm not surprised Julia fell for him." Talking about the romance between Julia and Tony made my skin crawl. I heard and read about Julia's most private thoughts and memories, making me feel as if I were the one experiencing them. I loved the stories as much as I hated them.

The itch refused to go away. Like a parasite, it crawled underneath my skin. I peeled back the silk sleeve on my arm and scratched the spot.

Nothing missed Brooke's attention. "Did you take your medication today?"

THIS LOVE KILLS ME

"I don't remember."

I licked the pink lines left by my nails on my arm and folded back my sleeve. Then I sat up and reached for my bag. My fingers prodded at the cluster of items, digging for the silver container where I kept my Methadone—the agent that kept me from relapsing. It didn't matter how many times I swore to Brooke that the detox and rehab had worked and I no longer craved the high, she insisted I stayed on the medication to keep me clean. Her lack of trust in my willpower was understandable. I told her that I was fourteen when my watchdogs put the needle in my arm at the brothel for the first time. Drug addicts like me are screwed for life, even if we manage to stay clean. And it didn't matter if I chose this life or if I was forced into it. The consequences were the same.

"Annie, you need to stay on top of this. You promised me."

"I know, I'm clean, am I not?" I held up a single pill and placed it on my tongue for her to see. "Down it goes."

Her concerned sigh filled the car.

"I know what I'm supposed to do. I won't fuck it up. I promise." I squeezed my shoulders between the two front seats and laid my head on her shoulder. She buried her short red nails into my hair and ruffled the strands.

"You know that I'm not only doing this because I respect Julia's wishes; I care about you too."

I kissed her warm cheek. "I know. I love you, too. You're the mother I never had."

That wasn't a lie. My birth mother was born Jessica Ohler—a know-it-all, platform-sandal-wearing goody-two-shoes with a long blond ponytail who was knocked up in high school by a third-string football player. Her parents couldn't imagine a newborn ruining their precious daughter's chances of getting into Penn State. I had become collateral damage—a mistake Jessica felt the need to fix many years later.

So I thought.

She showed up at my high school during my freshman year and introduced herself as the mother who gave birth to me. An unorthodox way of returning to a child's life that infuriated my adoptive parents. Yet I kept letting her into my life because she was filling the hole inside me with stories about my biological father and the love they once shared. I was no longer an unwanted byproduct of casual sex. I was the fruit of their love.

As enchanted as I had become, I didn't realize until it was too late that Jessica only needed me for my bone marrow. She preyed on my need to be validated to get what she wanted, and then she disappeared.

After that, I fell fast and hard.

A wave of dark memories of my old life washed over me, pulling me into the abyss. I swallowed some water, leaned back in my seat, and buckled up, trying to stop the flood. I was no longer a victim of my history. Thanks to Julia, I had a chance to be in charge of my narrative.

3

I spent the remaining hours of the evening in the library at Brooke's stylish home, where wood beams and panels creaked and passageways whistled from the draft passing through them as if the whole house were alive. It took me weeks to get used to the strange noises and stop imagining ghosts in every corner.

The library was a spacious, bright room with big windows and shelves laden with books to inspire envy. It was also my favorite place in the house because I could feel the walls around me.

The six years I spent in captivity was a life without natural light or beauty. Being held against our wills, we, the girls, only had our magazines and the stories we shared to bring a bit of light into our dark days.

My new free life was so precious to me, and I treated it like a fragile toy that could break any minute. Yet as the days went by, I slowly allowed myself to appreciate moments like curling up on the plush sofa by the window and staring at the backyard for hours.

Sometimes, after sunset, I turned off the light and watched the tall, lean trees, stripped of their leaves by the harsh winter, swaying in the moonlight. They looked like a forest of bony arms reaching up from hell—eerie dark silhouettes against the pale gray sky. I'd open the window to listen to the hooting of an owl sitting on a bare branch or the flapping wings of bats hunting over the brown grass.

But most of the time, I spent my time re-reading Julia's diary, memorizing her every word, soaking up her personality. Tony fell in love with Julia for the woman she was, with her thoughts, words, and style. If I was able to crawl into her skin and adapt her persona, Tony might find it hard to resist me. And I needed him to get close to me and trust me if I wanted to expose his crime.

Julia's diary wasn't the leather-bound book with thick pages and inspirational quotes one might expect a wealthy author to buy. It was a torn and worn composition book with missing pages and water stains that I found in the kitchen drawer one day as I was helping Kitana bake a cake.

Kitana was the oldest girl in the brothel at thirty-two. She had a long and wide scar across her face from an old knife cut inflicted by a client. The rumor was that the boss took pity on Kitana because she was damaged goods. Ornelas, the big boss, allowed her to live in the house as long as she paid for her food and board by providing services, like cleaning and cooking for the working girls. She was my best friend for a long time. The only person I could trust in that godforsaken place.

Then the members of the cartel brought in a new mystery woman one day.

Julia had washed up on the shore, unconscious and drenched in seawater, with a massive head wound. I immediately became fascinated by the mystery that surrounded her. She spent her first week with us in and out of consciousness, not remembering much. No doctor was ever called to tend to her injuries, so we never fully understood the reason for her amnesia, nor the extent of it. Ornelas gave Kitana a month to nurse the American woman back to health. If she had failed, Julia would have disappeared from the house one day without a trace.

It was no secret to us girls that if we didn't do what we were asked to do, or if we were no longer useful, we would end up as fertilizer in the greenhouses about a thirty-minute drive south from Ensenada, along Highway 23. When a girl disappeared overnight, we said, "Benito Juarez took her." It was the name of a long, lonely street snaking between the farms. There were nights when the thought of becoming a bell pepper sounded appealing to me; it sounded appealing to all of us.

In the next few months, I grew close to the American woman whose shoulders seemed to carry a heavy burden and whose eyes were dark with pain. Her increasing compassion for our predicament turned her into a bulldog of a protector for the girls in the house. She wouldn't hesitate to challenge Hector, who was one of the cruelest watchdogs, which was always a dangerous move. Julia endured endless beatings and abuse by our captors, but they could never break her spirit. Eventually, they did break her body.

Only then, when Kitana, who was the only one of us with access to the outside world whenever Hector took her grocery shopping in town, brought back a book with a picture of Julia Rose on the jacket, did we learn who our beloved American woman truly was. She was no longer a nameless sex slave. She was famous and rich, even though she remembered none of that.

The journal I gave Julia was supposed to help her revive her memories of the life she had. The ragged, dirty composition book would have been a piece of trash to most of us but became Julia's prized possession. She wrote down her thoughts every chance she had. I found entries from her going on for pages, but most of them contained only a sentence or two—short outbursts of thoughts. But the journaling was working, and slowly but surely, Julia's memories returned. And by reading her most inner thoughts, I had the opportunity to get to know the real Julia Rose and learn about her life outside the walls of the brothel.

Revisiting the dark places in my memory always evoked mixed feelings in me. On the one hand, all the hardship I endured made me stronger and empowered me. It also gave me Julia. On the other hand, it made me an outsider, always living in fear of never fitting into the picture-perfect world most people lived in.

I laid my hand on the cover of Julia's journal, envisioning the messy corner where she used to sit and write. Back then, nothing was our own, not even our bodies. We belonged to other people. Our only salvation was this little notebook and the thoughts we shared. Revenge was the only motivator that kept us alive and gave us a wisp of hope. It also helped me escape.

I slowly opened the diary because it had become fragile from use over the years. Pages had gotten loose, and the glue on the spine was deteriorating. I typed up a copy last month to preserve her memories. Brooke lent me her laptop to use. But I still liked to read the original because it brought Julia's spirit back to me. Whenever I spent time in Brooke's dark and ominous home library, I could almost feel Julia's presence.

As my mind lingered, the unpredictable early spring wind pushed the window open and whirled a few books off the shelves. With a gasp of terror, I looked outside at the dark, sentry-like trees swaying in the twilight. At the sound of the wind whispering eerily through the bare crowns of the trees, my skin prickled and a frisson of fear spiked through me.

"Julia?" I called out as the wind outside whipped against the house. "Is that you?"

The yard became a darker shade of gray as the moon disappeared behind a cluster of black clouds.

I pressed the journal to my heart with one hand and pushed myself off the sofa with the other. With a pounding heart, I stepped closer to the window.

The strong wind whistled and ruffled my hair. The siren of an ambulance echoed in the distance.

I pressed the diary more firmly to my chest when I saw a shining expanse of light by the patio.

Goosebumps broke out on my skin. I reeled back from the window and pressed against the reading chair, my warm, moist hand sticking to the cover of the journal.

"I don't believe in ghosts," I whispered to calm my nerves as I closed my eyes.

The wind chime hanging from the terrace roof on the far side of the house banged repeatedly against the pillar, echoing a disconcerting clank which only served to heighten my fear.

As I reached to close the window, I saw a shadow crossing over the cluster of trimmed hedges lining the patio.

I stood frozen, my body shaking. "I don't believe in ghosts," I murmured again as I extended my hand toward the handle on the window frame, peeking through squinting eyes.

I heard a jingling sound, like a tiny bell. A black cat leaped out of the shadows and landed on the windowsill. I screamed in terror as I staggered back against the wall and dropped the journal. The cat looked at me with her bright green eyes, a dead mouse hanging from her mouth. She hopped onto the sofa before dropping down to the hardwood floor and walking out of the library without another glance in my direction.

I grabbed my forehead as my fear began to disperse in waves of relief through my body. "You stupid cat!" I cried out as I bent down to pick up Julia's diary.

The composition book lay open to the first page.

Entry #1

I don't know today's date, but it is late spring and the year is 2019. I've been locked up in this underground hole for about two years now. That much I know. I've been keeping track of the days by carving lines onto the floor underneath my mattress.

Today was a special day for me. London pulled me into the bathroom, so excited she could barely speak. She found an old composition book, and she wanted me to have it.

"Here, start writing down everything you remember," she said, her childishly young face bright with excitement. "Maybe it will help you remember what happened to you." It was only a moment we had to ourselves before Perez ordered us to leave the bathroom and go back to our room.

Possessing my own diary is an opportunity that makes me equally happy and frightened. I'm delighted to have a chance to leave a legacy behind, to write down who I am (or at least what I remember of who I am and was) so I won't disappear completely. But this notebook is also the object of my fear because if Hector finds it and reads it, my own words could be used against me. It would also get Kitana and London in trouble.

Do I have the right to hold so much power in my hand?

Entry #2

A week has passed since my first entry. Trust me, I needed every bit of willpower not to write sooner, but I wasn't well enough to write.

The day after I started this diary, I found out that one of the girls in the house was having her fourteenth birthday. I thought I would try to convince our watchman, Hector, to give the young girl a pass for the special occasion. He wasn't as understanding as I had hoped he would be. He responded with a firm backhand across my face. I didn't reach for the spot where the pain flared up. I've learned that people do that for dramatic effect. An immediate caress doesn't possess the magical ability to heal the sudden pain or ease the rapid swelling.

I didn't look surprised either. I've been slapped in the face countless times in the past two years. It wasn't the first time and definitely won't be the last. To demonstrate my defiance, I held Hector's gaze, although my eye twitched from the uncontrollable tears welling up.

Hector's eyes glowed with rage. He was angry with me for undermining his authority in front of the girls. Once again.

"Did I ask your opinion, Blu?" he barked at me. His stubble-covered jaw tensed as he breathed hard into my face. I was called Blu because of the color of the sea that spat me out.

"It's her birthday, Hector," I pleaded from the mattress where he had tossed me, my back against the greasy beige wall. "Give the girl a break. Please!"

"The client requested her. Birthday or not. Trinity going." Hector gripped the young girl's arm and pulled her to him.

Trinity didn't resist. During my argument with Hector, she'd been leaning against the wall with her arms crossed, a blank expression on her face.

I remember the day when Guerrero and Perez brought her here eighteen months ago. She was a young girl whose birth name was Sophia. She was a frightened little bird, an *innocent child, not yet introduced to the cruelty of men. She had taken to me right away. Her face was always buried in my side. Her arms wrapped around my waist. I wish I could've found a way to protect her, to save her from this world of pain and suffering. But I couldn't save anybody, not even myself.*

Despite her young age, Trinity isn't a little girl anymore. She's grown mature and cold. I no longer wake up in the middle of the night to her crawling under my blanket, seeking shelter from her nightmares. Now she resists any approach of tenderness. I wonder if she dreams at all.

Ignoring the pulsing in my right cheek, I rolled onto my knees and pressed my palms together to plead with Hector. "Please, take me instead."

The watchdog's eyes shrunk. His lips stretched into a nasty grin. "You know you too old." Hector's English isn't perfect, but what he was saying was clear. My fate rested on his mercy. He allowed me to stay, and I owed him my loyalty for it.

Despite my desperate efforts, Hector dragged Trinity to meet a client. When he returned to the room, he took me into the bathroom, where he smashed my head against the mirror and made me rinse my mouth with bleach for talking back to him.

I feel better now. My head doesn't hurt anymore and my strength is returning. So here I am again, putting my thoughts to paper. It helps. It truly does. I feel less hopeless when I write.

If the events of my life are not in order and my entries seem incoherent, I apologize. Lately, I find it hard to focus and stay on point. From all these swirling thoughts about my past and messy dreams that visit me every night, my head is a mess. I'm hoping my friends here will help me untangle this big knot that sits in my brain.

London and Kitana translated the first three chapters of The New Earth Kitana found in a bookstore from Spanish to English for me. It's hard to grasp that I wrote those words, that once I was that woman in the picture on the book cover. She seems beautiful and content. I don't see that face now when I look in the mirror. I desperately want to remember what happened to me, how I arrived at this dirty Mexican brothel, but I can't remember. London says I must remain patient and stay consistent with my writing. I hope she's right and writing down my thoughts will help, because someone robbed me of my life and I don't want to die before I find out who is responsible.

4

The following morning found me tangled in my flannel sheets and lost in my dreams. Awoken by the stirring of the household, I pulled the warm blanket up to my nose. Overnight, cold air had seeped through the window I had cracked open before going to bed and chilled the room. Feeling cozy and well rested, I thought of my former roommates—the young girls I left behind in Mexico. We would have given a limb to sleep in a room filled with fresh air for just one night.

Memories of the girls fanning themselves with folded magazine pages to make that stuffy, humid air laced with the stench of urine and sweat somewhat bearable flooded my mind. We would drink water with ice and lemon juice to ease our thirst and subdue our hunger. We were always hungry, thirsty, and tired, and *always* on alert—a sequence of discomforting stressors on an eternal loop.

After my escape, guilt became a frequent visitor in my life. Like a parasite eating you slowly from the inside out, it consumed me. And no matter how much I tried to ignore it or bury it in the back of my mind, I often found myself facing my demons. I was free and lived in comfort, while the others were still suffering.

Driven by that very harassing feeling, I jumped out of bed and dropped to a plank position. "One, two, three…" I counted the pushups, fast and aggressive, while trying to quiet the voice in my head. I didn't travel across two countries and seek out Brooke's help for my benefit.

No matter how easily I allowed myself to fall asleep in the safety and comfort of Brooke's home, footsteps and voices still startled me and quickened my heartbeats. A few peaceful months couldn't erase the years of fearing human contact and the relentless fight for survival.

I recognized Brooke's approaching footsteps, and I rushed to the door to meet her.

"Jeez! You scared the shit out of me." Brooke staggered as she opened the door.

"You don't exactly walk like a ninja. I could hear you coming from a mile away." I smiled, jogging in place to keep my blood flowing.

"Tony called. You need to call him back."

A jolt of suspicion stilled my limbs. "That was quick. What did that bastard want?"

Brooke shrugged. "I meant to look at the video footage this morning, but I got caught up with some bills, so I haven't checked on him yet. I told him you'd call him back."

I snatched a pair of sweatpants from the back of a chair and slipped my legs into them as I headed out of the room. "Let's check on him now. I want to know what that clown is up to before I call him back."

Brooke leaned in and scanned the room, her eyes unmistakably falling on my little nest on the ground. "I thought you were okay with sleeping on the bed."

I bit down on my lip. "I need to have a wall against my back. Too much space here."

"I already told you we could push the bed into the corner."

I pulled my hair back and tied it up. "It's too high for me anyway. I like to sleep on the floor. Don't worry about it."

As I sashayed by Brooke, I tapped my shoulder against hers, softly, appreciatively, before starting down the corridor.

The surveillance room was the most secluded spare bedroom in the house and was located in the east wing, adjoining the laundry room and the garage. The old blower that heated the house didn't have the strength to push the warm air this far, leaving it one of the coldest spaces, so I grabbed a sweater and a cup of hot coffee on my way there to arm myself against the chill.

Brooke punched a six-digit code into the digital lock, opened the door, and switched on the light.

I took my place in one of the two rotating chairs and started scanning through the video images on the monitors on the wall. Brooke, already dressed for the day in her usual pantsuit, leaned against the desk and pushed her glasses higher on the bridge of her nose.

"Do you see him?" she asked, playing with the joystick of camera number one.

Squinting my eyes, I focused on the first monitor. "He's not in the hall. Not in the living room. Kitchen's empty. Bedroom empty. Study's—wait a second!" I leaned closer to the monitor. "Oh, that's just the new standing lamp Tony bought last week. It keeps messing me up. We need to move it to the right a little bit."

"Get yourself invited to his house, and you can do it," Brooke said flatly. She pulled a cigarette from her pocket and lit it, then coughed into her fist three times. I pushed the ashtray closer to her and handed her my coffee.

"Milk makes my throat feel weird. Toss me that water bottle from the corner."

As I reached for the bottle, I spied a shadow crossing on camera number four. "Wait! He's entering the bedroom. Turn on the voice!"

"Please. Turn on the voice, please," Brooke corrected me. "Don't roll your eyes at me, young lady. You need to get in the habit of talking politely, like a civilized woman. You're pretending to be a lawyer, for crying out loud. You can't lose control."

I gave her the eye. "You swear like a sailor."

She smacked my head. "Well, I'm not trying to charm Tony, am I. Julia was always so sweet and polite. That's the type Tony is attracted to when it comes to women. Do you think you're the only woman in Manhattan who has tried to get his attention? Women throw pussy at him from every direction. He's the most eligible bachelor in the neighborhood."

"Just turn on the microphone before he leaves, pleeeaaase!"

Brooke smacked my head again, shaking her head.

We watched Tony as he looked for something in the bedroom and then the master bath. He pulled out drawers and checked the medicine cabinet.

"Sammy, come in here for a second."

I turned the volume up on the microphone so his voice filled our small space.

Julia's son, who turned six last summer, trotted into the room wearing his pajamas, his head hanging low.

"I can't find the thermometer. Your mom was so much better at this than I am, but here, sit on my lap. Let me check your forehead."

The boy silently obeyed. Tony kissed his temple, then his cheeks. He placed the back of his hand on Sam's neck and forehead. "I don't think you have a fever, but you do feel warm. All right, go back to bed. I'll call the school."

"I'm not lying, Dad. My throat hurts when I swallow. I swear!"

"Open it big. Let me see."

I looked away from the monitor because I didn't particularly enjoy watching Julia's husband caring for their son so lovingly. These tender moments with his son humanized him and made him seem like a good person instead of a cold-blooded murderer.

I could still hear them talk. "Yeah, your throat looks a little red. Well, jump back into bed. I'll make you a cup of hot cocoa."

"Mom always made me tea when I was sick. And she gave me vitamins, and she would rub something on my chest."

"All right, buddy. I'll do that too."

Curiosity drew my eyes back to the screen, and I caught Tony embracing his son for what seemed to be an eternity, his face buried in the boy's mop of hair.

"I miss her, Dad."

"I miss her, too, buddy."

I turned off the microphone and pushed out of the chair. "Nothing incriminating to see here. Did you get his number? I'll call him back."

Brooke handed me her phone, already ringing.

"Mr. Rose! It's Annie Adams. Brooke Russell's new assistant. How may I help you?" I said, trying to make *my boss* proud of my ability to speak politely.

"I wasn't sure who to call because this recent arrangement is new to me, but I believe I'm supposed to call you with business-related questions, right?"

Brooke was making hand gestures to encourage me to speak up. "Yes. That's perfectly fine, Mr. Rose. What can I do for you?"

"I'm afraid I don't have good news. Lionsgate called. We hit another wall. It seems the documentary about Julia's rise to stardom didn't draw in the viewership we had expected. We need a new approach. Could you come over to the house this afternoon and discuss our options? Around four, perhaps?"

I muted the phone. "He wants me to meet him at his house," I told Brooke. "Should I agree or play it professional and ask him to meet me in the office?"

"No, no. You need to go. You can plant the speakers."

"Isn't it too fast?"

"Maybe ask him why he wants to see you at home, then see what he says."

I unmuted the phone. "Is it possible for us to meet in the office earlier in the day?"

Tony offered me a sigh, followed by a moment of silence. I watched him lean in closer to the wall mirror in the bedroom and scratch something on his face, a zit or an ingrown hair perhaps. "Sam didn't go to school today. He has a runny nose and a mild fever. I don't want to leave him here alone, but I also need to handle this problem. Sylvia and Justin are coming over at four, too."

"All right. I'll get your address from the office and meet you there."

"Thank you, Annie, for your understanding."

His pleasant voice and smooth manners pushed me further from my picture of a killer. Was this caring father truly capable of forcing the mother of his child over the railing of a cruise ship?

"We should go over the files one more time," Brooke suggested as I hung up the phone.

"All right," I agreed.

Brooke checked her watch. "But first things first. Let's eat some breakfast."

A couple of hours later, Brooke left for work.

I spent the rest of the day in her home office, going over the profiles of the ghostwriters Brooke had gathered. I also studied the plan to invest in real estate to create a safety net for Sam. Julia was afraid that Tony and his family would spend her fortune by the time Sam matured into adulthood and he would be left with nothing. The killer, or killers, deserved to be stripped of their comfort and wealth, but Julia was worried that if the Rose estate collapsed, Sam would suffer the most. So she'd made me promise that Brooke and I would do right by her son.

* * * * *

Brooke returned to the house a little before three o'clock.

She helped me pick out an outfit Julia would wear to a meeting. I felt more comfortable in a pair of ripped jeans and a cropped T-shirt, but we all had a part to play.

I slipped into a pair of beige dress pants and nude-colored heels and put on a light blue silk blouse. I let my hair down and rolled it into the same loose curls that Julia wore.

"Here," Brooke held out her hand to me with a golden ring in it.

"What is this?"

"It's a replica of Julia's favorite ring. I picked it up at the jeweler today. Here, put it on. It will freak Tony the hell out." Brooke smiled devilishly, letting out a series of short giggles that morphed into a pain-stricken coughing fit.

My smile dropped. "You should quit smoking."

"You should mind your own business." She pushed the ring onto my right index finger. "That's where Julia wore it." She reached for the glass of whiskey she had placed on the shelf in front of a pile of folded cashmere sweaters and drank it down in one breath.

Brooke's walk-in closet was like most of the private rooms of the house, professionally designed but in disarray. I once organized her clothes and shoes, but Brooke wasn't happy about it. "I operate in chaos," she had scolded me, rearranging her stuff with rushed, stiff movements. "I thrive in this environment. I knew exactly where everything was. Now look at this place! I won't find anything."

From that day on, I never touched her stuff again.

When it was time to leave for my appointment, I called for an Uber. I was fourteen when my *boyfriend* tricked me and kidnapped me, so I missed out on the whole high school experience, including driving school. It was Brooke who drove me around town. However, to avoid any suspicion about my relationship with my boss, she decided it would be wiser to hire a driver instead.

It was a short trip, crossing through bleak, post-winter landscapes darkened by the sun nearing its final glow. I leaned my head against the window, feeling its chill on my skin.

I arrived at Tony's house five minutes before four o'clock, chased by the same unpredictable wind that slammed open the window in the library last night. Rows of elegant evergreen bushes stood tall along the long driveway, like a welcoming committee, and led me to the front of the house.

Standing on the doormat, I gathered my windswept hair to the side and looked at the type of cars parked on the green: a Cadillac Escalade, a Bentley, a BMW i8. I couldn't help but think of the dirty old bedsheet Julia slept on for three years. Bile rose in my stomach.

Suddenly weakened, I knew I wasn't ready to enter the den of hyenas.

To calm my nerves, I looped around the side of the house and took out my JUUL. I inhaled the strawberry-flavored vape with my eyes closed. I focused on the pressure in my chest as the vape crept deep into the recesses of my lungs. Then I hit it again and again until I sensed the buzz coming from the nicotine. It wasn't the same numbness that had helped me slip away from reality when I was treated like merchandise and worked like livestock. Tobacco only gave me mild brain fog, but it still helped me relax and adopt the "I don't give a fuck" attitude I'd used to survive the years of torture and humiliation.

The cold made me shiver, and I folded my coat tighter over my chest. Despite my expectation, I wasn't calm. I was antsy. My nerves played sick games with me. Doubt about my ability to execute the plan coiled inside of me like poisonous snakes, weakening my knees.

I heard a rattling sound. I peeked around the corner to see the front door opening. I hid the JUUL behind me, wishing there was a pill I could take to make all these nagging feelings go away.

Tony stepped out to the front porch. "Are you coming in? You can vape in the house, you know."

My shock must have been visible because Tony pointed at the security camera by the awning. "Can't hide nowadays. Big brother is watching from everywhere." He gesticulated with his hands like an illusionist.

I returned the JUUL into my purse and approached the door. "I wasn't hiding. I arrived a little early and wanted to kill some time. I take punctuality very seriously." That was Julia's philosophy: always be on time. Not a minute late, not a minute early. Brooke had drilled that detail into my head during my training.

"All right. Come inside. I want you to meet Sam."

The gravel crunched under my feet, and I made a joke to break the ice. "No sneaking up on you either, it seems?"

Tony smiled and opened the door wide for me. "One can never be too careful. We had a few attempted break-ins after Julia's third book was released. A couple of fanatics managed to pass through the gate and get to our bedroom window. They were hoping to steal a part of her. Now I have cameras all around the property."

My chest tight from anxiety, I entered into a bright open entryway with elegant checkered tile flooring. I was aware of Sylvia and Justin being in the house with us, yet my mind kept sending signals of caution. Tony didn't know about my past. He was not a john but a business client. I knew that, but I had to keep repeating those facts in my head to appear sane and confident.

"How about the inside?" I asked. "Do you have cameras in here too?"

"Let's leave that to your imagination," Tony teased.

"Well, speaking as a lawyer, you do need to let people know if you're recording them." I knew little about the law, but my statement made sense to me. I also had to push him for answers because if I snuck around the house, then he'd know about it. That would pretty much blow my cover and kill my plans.

Tony remained calm, unsuspecting. "Don't worry. No cameras inside. But that doesn't mean you can go around stealing the silverware."

Brooke had trained me to remain composed and professional at all times, but I couldn't stop the grin from forming. "There goes my plan."

"Sorry, sweetheart." Tony feigned a sympathetic shrug. "Here, let me give a quick tour of the house, then let's get down to business before Sylvia loses it. And trust me, you don't want to witness one of her fits."

Three distinguished paths led from the entryway as if offering distinct life choices to the visitors. To my right, an elegant staircase covered with gray carpet curved to the second floor. Continuing straight would have taken me to the kitchen and dining room. On my left, an arched passageway offered access to the study. Faint voices filtering from that direction suggested that we were meeting in the study.

I was already familiar with the layout of the house. I had studied the architectural plans, the home's history, and Zillow. But Tony didn't know that, so I did my best to look impressed as he showed me around the first floor.

"Our street is one of the most prestigious in Upper Montclair. It wasn't easy to snatch a house here, I can tell you that. Without Brooke's connections and help, Julia and I would've never left our small apartment in Manhattan." I caught him looking away as if the memory of his wife still haunted him.

Tony led me into the spacious professional chef kitchen furnished with cream-colored cabinets and high-end appliances. The museum-like tidiness hinted that not much cooking was done there.

"It's beautiful. Very impressive," I offered, focusing on keeping a lid on my amazement. My adoptive parents had a decent middle-class home with basic wood cabinets. The brothel only had a stove and an ancient wood table full of grease stains to prepare food. Brooke's kitchen had about twenty cabinets, but they were old—stylish but outdated. Tony's kitchen was out of a designer magazine.

The tour continued toward the patio that ran along the entire length of the house. It was a private sanctuary enclosed by green bushes and trees that created barriers against any prying eyes or nosy neighbors. Bees buzzed around the colorful potted plants and crowded by the birdbath. The Roses' secret garden defied the season and stood proud against the chilly, rainy weather.

Tony swept away a few dry leaves from the paver stones with his feet. "Isn't this backyard to die for?"

Yep, Julia did die for it, I wanted to say. "Oh, yes, it's absolutely breathtaking. You have a charming home, Mr. Rose."

"Call me Tony. No need for formalities. Remember?" He closed his sport jacket tight, blocking out the wind.

"All right. Tony it is, then." I smiled and lifted my hand to brush my hair back, deliberately exposing the ring on my finger.

Tony's eyes focused on the fine jewelry, and his face dropped with seriousness. "Where did you get that ring?"

"What, this old thing?" I started turning the ring around my finger to let the stone catch the light that spilled from the kitchen. "My grandmother gave it to me before she died." I looked at it with nostalgia, just as I'd practiced. "She was a very petite woman. It only fits on my index finger, but I wouldn't take it off for the world."

Tony's face grew somber. "It's lovely," he said distantly as if his mind had flown away from the present.

"Is there something wrong?" I poked to get a rise out of him. If he simply decided to be a man and tell me the truth about Julia's *murder*, then he could save us both a whole lot of pain.

Tony took my hand into his and pressed on the ring for a closer examination. "I'm sorry if my behavior startles you, it's just...Julia had the exact same ring. She never took it off either. She had it on the night she disappeared."

I quickly withdrew my hand. "Oh, my goodness. I didn't know."

"I'm sorry. I feel strange right now." He was shaking by then, not violently, only subtle movements he tried to conceal.

It was a perfect and understandable opportunity for me to make physical contact with a man I just met, who was also my *client*, so I placed my hand on top of his. "It's all right. I understand. I've lost loved ones too. I know how painful it can be."

As if shocked by electricity, Tony stepped back from me and grabbed the back of his neck. "Uhm. I think it's better if we join the others. They must be wondering what's taking so long."

This was my cue. "Do you mind if I use your bathroom?" I asked innocently, slipping my ring hand into my pocket to evade his gaze.

"No, of course not," he stuttered.

I raised my brows. "I need you to point me in the right direction. I don't want to end up in a room where I'm not supposed to be."

My implication made his eyelids flutter as if the notion of having an illicit room was atrocious to him. "Oh, yeah, of course. There's a guest bathroom behind the staircase. I'll show you."

We walked toward the entrance, where he pointed me to a door. "There you go. I'll be in the study with the others."

I nodded slightly, pretending to open the door. I waited until Tony vanished from the hallway before rushing back to the kitchen. I took out the first mini-speaker from my bag and activated it. After a quick inspection of the room, I decided to hide it on the top of a cabinet.

I pulled out one of the barstools from the island nook and climbed on top of it. I attached the speaker to the inside of the trim, above the microwave, then pushed back the chair into its original place.

I hid another speaker under the piano strings in the family room.

One remained.

I checked my watch to see how much time had elapsed. One minute and five seconds. How much time does one spend in a bathroom?

Brooke was adamant about having a speaker in Tony's bedroom, so I rushed up the stairs, the thick carpeting muffling my footsteps.

Since I was familiar with the layout of the house, I went straight to the bedroom door.

My focus on planting the device stumped my desire to look around Julia's former sanctuary. Running out of time, I dropped to my knees by the dresser and attached the last speaker to the back of it.

Two minutes and one second had elapsed. I was pushing the limits of a simple bathroom break.

Leaving everything untouched, I rushed out of the room and gently pulled the door close. I turned toward the staircase, where I was confronted by a young boy in pajamas standing at the end of the hallway and staring at me.

As if scared by the child, I bolted down the stairs without acknowledging him, my pulse pounding in my ears.

I'd been caught. Busted! But he was just a child. I might be able to talk my way out of this situation if Tony questioned me.

Arriving downstairs, I slowed my movements and initiated a breathing exercise I'd learned from my shrink to slow down my heart. The kid was going to tell his father about me. What I needed was damage control.

"There you are." Sylvia showed herself in the passageway. "Bad food?"

Took me a second to refocus my attention. "Oh, was I away that long. I didn't realize, sorry."

"I wasn't timing you, but it seemed long, yes. You know, since I cut gluten from my diet, I no longer have diarrhea."

Her lewd comment took me by surprise. There was no privacy, nor decency, in the brothel in Mexico for us, but I always imagined rich, educated women to be a bit classier.

"I had to take Brooke's call. She wanted to make sure I found my way here okay. Then I heard a child's voice upstairs. I didn't mean to be nosy, but I couldn't ignore a child's calling. I saw a young boy upstairs. I believe he's your nephew, Sam. He looked like he needed something."

Sylvia strained to make a face, but her forehead was too rigid from Botox to make an impression.

"Okay, anyways, just follow me. I don't want to be here all night. I have a doctor's appointment at five. My thyroid is acting up again."

I ran my hand over my hair to make sure every piece was in place as I followed Julia's sister-in-law to the study.

The elongated room looked more like a drawing room than a study, with an array of elegant leather sofas arranged in a semi-circle. A carved wooden chest was used as a coffee table and had a spread upon it of meat, cheeses, and fruits for guests to enjoy. A surprisingly weak collection of books sat on the shelves by the wall in a haphazardly organized fashion. After closer examination, I noted they were mostly various translations of Julia's books. The gaping spaces on the immense bookshelves were taken up by framed photographs of the family. I refused to give in to the emotions conjured up by looking at them.

Sylvia picked up two pills and a glass of water from the round table by the door and swallowed them. "Tony, go check on Sam. Annie here says he's asking for you."

Feeling that my impromptu diversion was working, I let down my guard and, with confident strides, walked over to Justin Rose and shook his hand. Unbuttoning my jacket, I then took a seat in an armchair next to him, taking pleasure in the thought of how much Brooke and I were going to torture Tony that night.

5

Sitting stiffly in a leather armchair in the study that once belonged to Julia, I watched Justin Rose talking on his cell phone. He was loud and articulate, not attempting to keep his conversation private.

That was my second meeting with Tony's older brother, but I'd read enough about him in Julia's diary to look at him with a sense of familiarity.

Julia's relationship with her brother-in-law was wide-ranging. It started with a slow-burning need-to-know basis acquaintanceship, and then their friendship soared to extreme heights, just to later come crashing back down to earth.

The first time Julia and Justin met was on Thanksgiving in Tony and Julia's rented apartment near Brown University. The previous years, the Rose siblings would go home to their parents for the holidays, but that year was different. Barbara Rose's behavior had become so out of control that all three of her children decided not to subject themselves to their mother's craziness that year. Instead, they chose to have a peaceful Thanksgiving away from their parents.

According to Julia, Bill and Barbara's marriage was rocky from the beginning. Their love story was what some would call a cliché: high school sweethearts that became pregnant and then married because of it. Having a baby at such a young age, and without financial support, the teenaged couple found themselves going fast and hard down the rabbit hole.

Two years later, Sylvia joined the Rose family, adding further stress to the already worn-down couple's life.

Fast-forward another four years, Barbara and Bill found themselves in a relatively healthy and happy family environment, stepping up to the challenge of being parents and earning enough income to support it. They both worked blue-collar jobs, Barbara as a nurse-aid in a local hospital and Bill as a car mechanic. The young couple managed to maintain a decent little home in the suburbs, though not in the best neighborhood.

Life was good and comfortable for the Roses, and not all that unusual back in the mid-eighties. Maybe it was too comfortable and boring for Bill, who became tangled in a messy affair with one of his coworkers: Lisa, the bookkeeper.

Barbara plotted to have another child to save their marriage, and it worked.

For the time being.

That's how Julia's husband came into the world—an anchor baby conceived out of desperation, a fact the older siblings incessantly reminded Tony of when growing up. Maybe it was revenge, or perhaps the need to prove himself, that drove Tony to support his older siblings with Julia's fortune later on in life. It must have been his way of getting back at them where it would hurt the most—their pride.

Tony was only two years old when the tables turned in the Rose house. It was Barbara's turn to lose control. As if she were on a mission to make up for the time she missed out on in her twenties, she started partying hard. She got in with the wrong crowd, which introduced her to hard liquor and harder drugs. Barbara had become reckless and carefree in her affairs with doctors at the hospital. She earned herself an unflattering nickname. The other nurses called her "Easy Breezy" behind her back.

One afternoon, the then nine-year-old Justin came home early from school and found his mother in bed with a stranger. Not knowing what to do, he hid in the living room, listening to his mother's giggling and moaning. He'd never remembered his mother being so full of joy.

Julia heard the stories of what Justin had seen growing up whenever her brother-in-law had a few too many drinks. Alcohol always made him chatty, and his childhood stories ripped open old wounds.

By Justin's telling, he kept his mother's secret for years, but Bill eventually discovered his wife's double life, and all hell broke loose in the Rose house. Barbara accused her eldest of betrayal, and Justin could never convince his mother of his innocence. She began to hold a grudge against Justin, frequently subjecting him to passive-aggressive behavior that was noticeable to other family members. His mother's coldness toward him left Justin with a deep, emotional scar. Julia found it easy to sympathize with her brother-in-law. Her family was far from perfect too.

Justin was incapable of staying with a girlfriend for longer than a few months, and Julia blamed his lack of commitment on his broken relationship with his mother. Since that first Thanksgiving when the Rose siblings decided to celebrate without their parents at Julia and Tony's apartment, Justin seemed to rekindle his desire to spend time with family once again. Julia wrote about the frequent fishing trips, baseball games, and bar hops she went to with the two brothers. Wrapped in a bubble of fun and excitement, the trio forged a special relationship.

But every good thing seems to come to an end, and the trio's relationship was no exception. The bubble burst when Julia became pregnant.

Justin, though seven years older than Tony, was a young bachelor who loved to party and lived life on the edge. He struggled to find a way to adapt to his younger brother's new life as a family man. Their once tight bond began to unravel.

But the story didn't end there.

After a few wild years, Barbara Rose came back to her senses and asked her husband for forgiveness, though she never admitted her wrongdoings to her children. That same year, Bill started the tradition of celebrating their wedding anniversary on a cruise ship with their three children and their families.

One might wonder what would've happened to Julia if Bill and Barbara's marriage had failed and the anniversary cruises never happened.

Today, Justin was standing in front of me in the study of Julia's mansion, a reformed man and a seemingly successful financial adviser. He had everything to lose if Julia had pulled her money from his investment funds. And that was precisely what Julia had been planning to do. Only days before the Rose family boarded the Princess Royal, Julia had called together a family meeting, where she announced that she would no longer provide financial support to her extended family. She had given a six-month transition period to Justin and Sylvia to establish lives of their own.

Then Julia disappeared from the cruise ship.

So, yes, Justin, with his uncontrollable bursts of anger and short temper was a suspect in my book, but I still leaned toward Tony as the perpetrator of the crime because he was the husband and crime statistics don't lie.

Sylvia must have noticed my focused attention on her older brother because she called out to me.

"Don't bother with him!"

Stiffening up from being caught staring, I turned to Sylvia. "Excuse me?"

She gave me a wry smile. "My brother might seem like a perfect catch, but he's not husband material. Trust me on this one."

Justin must have overheard his sister's warning because he peeked up from his laptop, the phone still attached to his ear, and looked straight at me.

My face flared up.

Shifting in my seat, I leaned to Sylvia. "I wasn't looking at your brother. I was simply…I was mulling over some things, mindless thinking." I flicked my hand to emphasize how insignificant the moment was.

Sylvia looked away, grinning devilishly like a psychopath. It was difficult to picture her as a mother of two children. I barely knew her, but she'd already managed to crawl under my skin. I promised myself to torture her next—once I was done with Tony.

Hissing and sighing, Sylvia checked her phone. "Where the hell is Tony? He knows I have a doctor's appointment."

Justin, who finished his call and closed his laptop, shot a disapproving look at his sister. "Enough with your doctor's appointment. There's nothing wrong with your health. It's all in your head. You should find a good shrink instead of spending a fortune on charlatans."

Sylvia gasped, her eyes becoming glassy with tears. "Don't start with me again, Justin. Why don't you worry about your own mental health, huh? We both know there's plenty of dirt there to clean up."

Justin got a bottle of beer out of the mini-fridge and popped it open. "Whatever. I'm tired of trying to help you. If you want to destroy your health with all those prescription meds you're taking, that's on you, but I won't give you any more money to waste on doctors and procedures. Those days are over."

Red-faced, Sylvia straightened her spine on the sofa, ready to defend herself. "It's not your money, Justin."

"It's not yours either, *Sylvia*. Julia said as much before she died."

"Excuse me." I raised my hand, drawing both of my companions' attention to me. "What makes you say Julia is dead?"

Startled, Justin snapped his head toward me. "Oh, I forgot you were here. Sorry you got caught in the middle of this nonsense." He raised his hand and rolled his eyes.

"Oh, don't mind me. I usually don't get involved with the personal lives of clients, but I'd like to know…why did you say that Julia was dead with so much conviction?"

"Well, her body never turned up, that's true, but officially she was pronounced dead, wasn't she?" Justin said, looking at his sister for confirmation.

"Yeah, nobody could have survived a fall from that height. And even if she did, no one could have possibly lived long in that choppy, cold water at night," Sylvia added matter-of-factly.

Angered by their indifference, I had to force myself to speak calmly. "So, it was confirmed that someone pushed Julia over the railing?"

"Well, she did disappear from the cruise ship in the middle of the ocean," Justin concluded while helping himself to a second beer. "Everybody believes she jumped."

"Yes, but why? Why would a successful woman kill herself when she had so much to live for? She had a great marriage. A son she loved. A fabulous career. Money. Fame. She had plans for the future. So why would she jump?"

Sylvia gathered her hair in her hands and ran her fingers through it like a comb, her shaking legs tapping the floor. This would be the perfect time to give her a polygraph. "Who knows? She might have taken some downers. Most of those pills mess with your head. Suicidal thoughts are always one of the side effects."

"Do you know what she was taking?"

"I don't. Justin?"

He shrugged, sucking on his beer bottle.

"Did I miss anything?" Tony entered the study with Sam.

"No, absolutely nothing," Sylvia jumped to answer.

Tony nodded and placed a hand on his son's head. "Look, Annie, I'm sorry for dragging you here today for nothing, but we need to postpone the meeting. Sam isn't feeling well. I need to go to the pharmacy to get him some Tylenol."

"I also have a doctor's appointment in, like, what…twenty-seven minutes." Sylvia rolled her eyes as she picked up her purse and rose from her chair.

Tony looked annoyed as he disregarded his sister's statement with a flick of his hand. "Annie, could you squeeze me into your schedule tomorrow? I'll try to get a sitter for Sam. Let me know what time is good for you."

I draped my coat over my arm and stood up. "Do you want to come into the office or meet here again?"

He sighed. "There are too many distractions here. Let's meet for lunch."

"What time are we meeting?" asked Justin, setting the empty beer bottle on the table with a clunk.

"I'll see Annie myself tomorrow, then when you all can make yourselves available, we'll put together another meeting."

"I'm available for lunch tomorrow," Justin insisted.

Sylvia scooted closer to me as if trying to show a unified front. "Yeah, me too. I mean, I have a facial at three, but there's plenty of time to grab a bite before that."

Tony, giving up on getting his point across, placed his hand on his sister's back and started ushering her out of the room. "I'll call you all in the morning. How's that sound?"

His offer sounded lame, even to me, but it did buy me some alone time with him tomorrow, so I was pleased.

As I opened the Uber app on my phone, Justin stepped beside me. "Need a ride?"

"No, thank you. I already arranged a car," I said coldly. With stories of him fresh in my mind, I was starting to link him to the attempted murder too.

"Suit yourself," he grunted, swiping his keys from the table.

A few minutes later, Justin got into his Cadillac while Sylvia drove away in her Bentley.

There went Sam's college fund.

As I watched the dust settle on the driveway, Tony beckoned me to the door. "I asked you to see me alone tomorrow because we need to discuss some sensitive matters. Julia's final wish was to break up this family business and stop the needless hemorrhaging from her accounts. After her disappearance, I didn't manage the business well. I wasn't in the right state of mind. But the spending must stop; I can no longer support my brother and sister. And I need your help in executing a new plan."

So, you disposed of your wife. Now you're asking for my help flicking off your siblings so you can keep the entire fortune for yourself? I thought, but instead said, "Certainly, I'm all yours tomorrow."

My car arrived, and I got into the backseat, grinding my teeth. Tony jumped right back to the top of my suspect list. If he cared so much about his *late* wife's wishes, why wait three years to follow up on it? Oh, yeah, I almost forgot, because the money doesn't roll in like it used to, right, Tony?

My mind was so saturated with toxic thoughts that my plan of moving the standing lamp in the study that blocked the spy camera's view slipped my mind.

"Hold on a second," I instructed the driver as I pretended to look for something in my purse.

I stepped out of the car to face Tony, who was still standing on the sidewalk, waiting for me to leave. "I left my phone in the study. Let me just grab it quickly," I said, touching his arm.

Not waiting for the homeowner's permission, I raced back to the study to the spot where Brooke's brother had installed the camera in the wood panel above the window. Moving the lamp a foot or two was all I needed to clear the view to the entire room. Though the structure was massive, I'd still underestimated its weight and was only able to push it a few inches. I should have admitted failure and walked away to avoid getting caught, but if our spy camera in the study was blocked, what was the point of having it at all? What if Tony came here one day crumbling under the weight of his guilt to write his confession, and I missed it because there was an obstacle in front of the camera? What if he had a secret vault hidden among these books, and I couldn't see him opening it? Recording the movements in the study offered endless opportunities to spy on Tony and his family members, so I knew I had no choice but to give another try to move the lamp.

I peeked out of the room into the hallway to see if Tony had lost his patience waiting for me outside and was coming back to check on me.

He wasn't.

Breathing heavily, I dropped my coat and purse to the floor and rounded the lamp where I assumed a full, steadier stance and started pulling on the light fixture. It moved at a snail's pace, but at least it was no longer blocking the camera.

Hurry up! Tony might be coming! I kept repeating the words of caution in my head.

I wiped my forehead with the back of my fist and reached for my purse when I noticed the scratch marks on the hardwood floor. "Shit!"

I checked the entrance to the study again before I crouched down and spat on the carvings, the blood buzzing in my ears. I rubbed the saliva into the wood with a shaking hand. The lubrication seemed to do the job—for the time being, at least.

I heard footsteps.

From the panic, I could barely breathe.

I snatched my belongings and rushed out the doorway, slamming right into Tony outside of the study.

He gripped my arms with both hands to keep me at a distance. "Is everything all right?"

"Yep. Found it. It slipped between the cushions. These stupid phones are getting slimmer and tinier. As if the manufacturers want us to lose them and keep buying new ones."

Tony looked behind me, and I nervously followed his gaze. Was there even a space between the cushions? I couldn't recall. But when I looked back at the armchair, I realized there was not.

Too late to change my story, I licked my lips and freed myself from his hold.

"See you tomorrow," I concluded, strutting down the hallway with pretend confidence.

I got back into the car, only to be confronted by an irritated Uber driver, adding anxiety to my already rapidly beating heart. I wasn't sure if I wanted to cry or laugh at my incompetence. My body wasn't my own. Strange gurgling sounds erupted from my mouth, and I tried to cover them up with my hand so I didn't look like someone losing her mind.

"Tony, Tony," I whispered to myself. "You'll be the end of me too, dear."

6

Sitting in the immaculate backseat of a Honda Civic and listening to my Uber driver's stories about his children's college adventures, I welcomed the chime of my phone notifying me of a new message on Messenger.

I was part of a closed group on Facebook dedicated to Julia's mysterious disappearance and managed by a couple of her most devout fans and fanatic amateur crime investigators. I joined the other 123 members two months ago when I came across the group during my online research. It wasn't easy to get accepted into the obsessive and distrustful group that had been operating actively for three years. Gaining access to the inner circles was even harder because the moderators had experienced numerous gossip-seekers and tabloid writers in their first year of operation. After the big purge, the group's number dropped significantly, keeping only the most dedicated members that contributed valid information to the investigation.

A few stories from Julia's diary and private pictures of Julia from Brooke's phone helped me climb to the uppermost of the inner circle in a relatively short period.

Thanks to their detailed—borderline fanatical—data analysis, I'd been able to discover the exact timeline of Julia's final days aboard the cruise ship, down to her last minutes.

A new message from Helen Fray, the founder of the "What Happened to Julia Rose" group, always made my fingers tingle with anticipation. With a racing heart, I tapped open the message.

Annie, do I have a treat for you! You won't believe what just showed up in my mailbox. I was so excited I almost peed myself. One of the passengers recorded the newlywed show on her phone. THE WHOLE FREAKING THING!! And some! I just finished watching it. OMG! You must see this!! When can you come over?

For most people, watching someone else's home video equates to watching paint dry, but to me, this was the most exciting news I'd heard all week.

Tony had previously released to the media that Julia had been drinking heavily during the night of her disappearance, but nobody could ever prove that to be true. The FBI and the Bahamas Police had no comment on Tony's statement either.

This video may be our chance to discredit Tony, I thought, staring at the message with hopeful eyes.

I didn't have the patience to write back and wait for Helen's reply, so I called her instead.

She answered after the second ring.

"Did you get my message?" she gushed, not allowing me to greet her first.

"I did. That's why I'm calling. Are you home? Can I come over now?"

"I'm at work. But you can come to the store. I can slip out back for a minute."

The driver's eyes kept glancing up at the rearview mirror, expecting me to give him a new destination.

I checked the time on my watch. "What time do you get off?"

"Don't worry about it. I'm too antsy to wait that long. You got the address, right?"

"Yeah. Let me pull it up. I'm in an Uber in Montclair. I could go to you straight away."

"I can't wait."

"Hey, Helen!" I called out, trying to catch her before she hung up.

"What is it?"

"Was it Tony who pushed her over?"

"I don't know, but this video is a huge breakthrough for us. For Julia."

"All right," I concluded with slight disappointment. "I guess I'll see you soon, then."

After I disconnected the call, I leaned forward to speak to the driver. "I need to change our destination."

He looked over his shoulder and smiled. "Will it get me a five-star rating?"

I nodded, offering him a thumbs-up.

"You can change the destination in the app. Do you know how to do that?"

The change was already done. "Yep, expert rider here," I said, pointing at myself.

Thirty-five minutes later, the car dropped me off on Broadway, and I walked into Ross Dress for Less to meet Helen. I didn't have to look long. Her anticipation kept her by the window, her eyes scanning the street.

She grabbed my arm. "Come quickly. Let's go to the back."

"Your boss won't complain that I'm here?" I asked, looking over my shoulder to see if we had drawn any attention.

"I'd love to see him try. This won't take longer than taking a shit. I'm entitled to do that, am I not?"

I couldn't argue with her point, so I followed the foul-mouthed, overzealous woman—whom I'd grown to like over the past months—to the back of the store.

A laptop was waiting for us in a storage room filled with cellophane-wrapped shipping boxes on pallets. Helen took the MacBook, sat down on one of the containers, and put the device on her lap. I took my place next to her, trying to ignore the nauseating smell of cloth dyes and longstanding stale paper.

"So, this woman, Melanie, or whatever, found our group online, and she contacted me about this video," Helen started, rushing her words as she clicked away on the keyboard. "Which is absolutely insane, if you think about it, because I've spent years searching for the right insider video footage from the ship. You have no idea how many cabin boys and girls I've had to bribe to send me videos. Jeff and I dissected every frame of every video but never caught a break, none of them were worth the money and effort, and then *boom*, this woman finds me and sends me this!"

The footage was a bit shaky, and the focus was not always clear. The recorder was an amateur who was either intoxicated or had a spasm in her hand. I had to focus my eyes to find Julia and Tony in the crowd, but when I did, my stomach contracted to the size of a walnut.

"Oh, my gosh, that's Julia," I breathed the words, my hand over my mouth.

"I told you. This video is golden. Just watch…" Helen's puffy face was flushed a light pink, her eyes wide with excitement.

The person who recorded The Newlywed Game was sitting behind and to the left of the Roses' table. A female voice whispered into the recording. "That's Julia Rose. I can't believe it. I've read all of her books." A deeper, older-sounding male voice responded. "Who? I've never heard of her."

The video turned off, then came back a second later, focused on the same spot.

An enormous urge to climb into the frame and turn the angle around so I could look into Julia's face came over me. This video was like a tease, giving me only bits and pieces. I wanted more. Much more.

The movie's width wasn't wide enough to get a good look at the entire room, but I recognized it as the Princess Royal's piano room from the photos posted on the Facebook group. The walls, the furniture, and the carpet were busy and colorful and led my eyes away a few times from the couple I was most eager to see.

A distinct and pleasant male voice blurted through a microphone, introducing the rules of the game. People were clapping and laughing at his jokes.

Julia's cascade of blond hair came down in spiral waves over her back. It was heart-gripping to see the familiar floral dress on her, whole and unspoiled. When I first saw it on her in the whorehouse—as she lay unconscious on the table, drenched and dirty, men violating her one after the other—the dress was nothing more than shreds of dirty fabric.

I ran my hand over my face to wash away the heinous image that never stopped haunting me.

The camera zoomed out onto a little boy, who couldn't be more than two or three, fidgeting on Julia's lap.

Tony, wearing a white shirt and gray vest, sat on his wife's right, hunched over his drink. His face was clean-shaven, his hair styled into short, curvy spikes on the top of his head.

Next to Tony was his mother, Barbara. Her bulbous belly pushed against her breasts and bulged under a bright long-sleeve cotton shirt.

Justin was leaning over a plate of nachos on Julia's left.

I spotted a few more arms and shoulders, but the persons to whom those limbs belonged fell outside the camera frame.

"Do you see what I see?" asked Helen, looking into my face with a *duh!* expression.

"I'm not sure I follow."

"Just watch the drinks on the table."

I followed her instruction as the story unfolded in front of our eyes.

The MC asked for volunteers to play the game. The crowd nominated Julia and Tony. They seemed hesitant in accepting the challenge. Tony was smiling at the people around him, shaking his head no, while Julia used Sam to get out of the situation.

But the passengers wouldn't take no for an answer.

Julia gave in first. She handed Sam to Sylvia, who had just entered the frame, took a sip of her drink, and stood up, beckoning her husband to follow her.

They walked to the stage and joined the other group of couples.

Julia turned around and waved at the crowd. At last, I could see her face. She was so beautiful—rose-lipped and healthy-looking—like on the back cover of her book that Kitana had brought to the brothel from the market.

I closed my eyes to remember her face as I saw it last. Ashen. Sunken. Bruised.

"Did you see that she only sipped her drink? And what was that drink, anyway? It looked like apple juice or iced tea to me," Helen pointed out. "What do you think?"

"Did you manage to get a copy of their bar receipt from that night?"

"No, not yet, but Jeff's working on somebody. He used a facial recognition program to identify the servers from the piano bar. Ran the profile pictures of some of the crew and other party pictures he found in their chatroom against the video. He had one match: a twenty-one-year-old girl from Romania. He befriended her on Facebook and has been trying to convince her to help us with the investigation, but she's scared she'll lose her job. I don't think anything will come of it. But Jeff's still hopeful; I won't burst his bubble."

"Any lead is a good lead. Let me know if you hear something back."

"I always do."

Helen hit play on the screen. I focused on Julia. With her shoulders tensed and an irritated expression, I suspected she was either sad or mad. Tony reached for her hand, but she pushed it away in a most subtle way.

"Did you catch that?" I blurted out.

"Yep. Things don't seem to be so perfect between them like Tony stated."

The MC put the first question to the Roses. "When and where did you first kiss?"

All participants started to scribble on their personal whiteboards.

Julia and Tony's answers matched: four years ago, at a frat party.

"My spouse's first kiss made me think…?"

The answer to the second question made Julia hesitant. She started writing. Then stopped. Started again. Erased it. Wrote something again.

Tony read his note first. "Romantic," he said.

Julia turned her board toward the audience: "Wet," it read.

I caught Tony's eyebrows crease, his face change color.

As they waited for the other couples to share their answers, Julia avoided her husband's eyes.

At their table, Barbara kept leaning to Justin and murmuring.

The waiter appeared and set four drinks on the family's table. Barbara took Julia's glass and pulled it in front of her, which I thought was kind of odd. Why would she touch someone else's drink?

No time to dwell on that because the next question was announced, and the contestants were busy writing on their whiteboards.

"What was your worst date with your spouse?"

This question seemed to give more grief to my dear friend. I watched her standing in the spotlight with a grim expression on her face, not the one you'd expect from a happily married young woman on vacation.

Tony kept trying to get his wife's attention but to no avail. At the rejection, his anger was boiling. It was obvious.

When it was the Roses' turn, Julia urged her husband to answer first.

"Back in college, I took Julia to an Indian restaurant where we had some very, *very* bad curry."

The audience laughed and clapped.

Julia didn't find her husband's story amusing. And there it was. A slight staggering. A brief light-headedness. Julia touched her forehead, looking worried. The MC called out to her for the second time.

"Tonight. Our worst date is tonight."

Silence fell onto the piano room. People exchanged inquiring glances.

"Did she just say what I think she said?" shrilled the voice of the recorder.

The MC made a joke to lift the mood. I was too focused on Julia's face to pay attention, but it must have been funny because once again, the whole room roared with laughter.

"What is the first thing your spouse would buy if they won the lottery?"

Tony's hand was shaking as he wrote the next answer. I kept waiting for him to leave the stage, but he held on, bracing himself against the next tide.

When the MC got to the Roses, Tony insisted Julia go first. Once again, she wobbled, but this time it was so bad that she had to steady herself against a pillar.

A few people in the audience noticed it as well, their body language showing as much.

At the host's repeated request, Julia turned her whiteboard toward the audience, which, luckily for us, faced the camera. She'd drawn a coffin with a cross on top and a man standing beside it flanked by two figures with long hair and huge breasts.

The audience drew in a collective breath. Shock hung in the air that even I could sense from watching the video.

The board slipped out of Julia's hand. She tried to step down from the stage to retrieve it but landed on her butt instead. Tony appeared next to her in a flash and tucked his hand underneath Julia's arm. Justin joined him, and the two brothers helped my friend move away from the spotlight and out of the lens's view.

"There!" Helen pointed at the screen. "Look! Her drink is not on the table."

"Maybe the server took it," I said, my heart hammering in my chest.

As I stared at the frozen image, I heard blunt footsteps approaching. A ginger man with narrow shoulders and extra-wide hips stopped at the door and checked his watch. "What are you doing here, Helen? It's not break time yet."

"Why? You need me for something?" Helen snapped back in a tone some people might consider rude.

"Don't be smart, Helen. I'm not paying you to have a date in the storage room."

"All right, Dennis. You got me. Very funny."

"It wasn't a joke."

"Look, I finished the inventory. The paperwork is on your desk. I have something important to discuss with my friend here. You can take it out of my break time. How's that sound?"

Dennis straightened his tie. "Make it quick. I need you on the floor. The new girl is running around aimlessly again."

"I'll be right out, boss!" Helen saluted.

Once Dennis left the room, I turned to Helen. "Aren't you scared you'll get fired?"

She waved me away. "Nah. I'm the only one here who knows her math and isn't glued to a damn cell phone."

She used her fingers to enlarge the last frame of the video. "Where is Julia's drink? I think I know. I think she was drugged, and her in-laws took her drink to hide the evidence."

"You think they're all in on it?"

She rubbed her eyes and pinched the bridge of her nose. "Look, I've been drunk many times. You don't go from normal one minute to falling down the stairs the next. Alcohol doesn't work that fast. Drugs do. The server didn't come back to their table. We both saw Barbara pull Julia's drink to her. But, you're right, let's not jump to conclusions. Tonight, I'll take apart this video frame by frame, and I'll send the pictures to Jeff. I won't stop until I find out where that glass of amber liquid went."

I tapped at my thighs. "Let me know if I can be of any help."

"Oh, it's not over yet. There's more footage," Helen teased.

The next few shaky clips betrayed the actions of the videographer. She seemed to rush after Julia and Tony, following them down the carpeted hallway and out to the deck. By the angle of the footage, I could tell that the passenger didn't let herself be seen.

This is it, I thought. I'll see who pushed Julia over the railing!

"What the hell is the matter with you, Juls?" Tony scolded his wife as he and Justin dragged her out of sight. "How much did you drink?"

Julia pushed her husband away. "Why, only you can embarrass me?"

"What are you talking about?"

"Don't play coy with me!" Julia roared, raising her open hands in the air at her husband.

Justin got a hold of his sister-in-law again. "Not here. You guys made enough of a scene tonight. You want to end up in the papers tomorrow?"

"What do you care, Justin?" Julia sneered. "Are you scared the rising empire will collapse, leaving you without a job?"

"Don't be ridiculous, Julia. You need to go to your room and sleep it off."

Tony put a hand on his brother's shoulder. "Go back to your room. I'll take care of Julia."

Justin hesitated, nervously playing with his hair.

"Just go check on Sam, please. I'll stay with my wife," Tony said to his brother.

"Aren't you the responsible father," Julia mocked before buckling over and falling on her face.

"Go!" Tony shouted at his brother as he squatted down to pull his wife back to her feet.

The camera followed Justin for a second, then snapped back to Julia and zoomed in on her face. She was drooling. Her mascara smudged over her eyes and cheeks. She looked desperate and in pain.

"I know about your affairs, *my beloved husband!*" she cried, pulling on Tony's collar.

He pried her fingers off, and she fell back to the ground. "I'm not discussing this with you here. You're drunk."

"I'm not drunk—I'm tired. You all put so much pressure on me. I can't do this anymore."

Tony stood up and looked out to the dark sea. "Oh, your life is so hard writing stories, going to parties. You stole *my* dream!" He pounded on his chest. "*I* was the writer. Not *you!*"

Julia leaned against the side of the cabin and folded her hands in her lap. She looked like a beggar on the street. "You're as much a part of this as I am."

"No. I'm not. I'm your sidekick. I'm the magnificent Julia Rose's husband. I'm the support team. A shadow."

Enraged now, Julia attempted to stand up on her own. "You enjoy the benefits of my work as much as I do!"

"Enough! I'm not gonna have this conversation with you now. You will never understand how I feel."

"But your lover does?"

Tony smoothed his hair back in frustration. "What lover? What are you talking about?"

Julia steadied her head as if she were trying to stop it from spinning. "How can you look into my eyes and lie? I hired someone to follow you. I saw the pictures, dammit!"

Tony froze, his eyes burning into his wife's face.

"I can't deal with you right now," he said in a low voice and walked away, leaving Julia on the floor. The video went black.

"What happened?" I blurted out, feeling robbed, unfinished.

Helen shrugged. "Melanie told me she offered Julia her help, but she said Julia wanted to be left alone, so she walked away. She said she felt bad about recording Julia's private conversation with her husband and decided to leave her in peace."

"Un-freaking-real," I said, shaking my head in disbelief. "Can you imagine if she'd followed Julia?"

"I'm sorry, but that's all I got."

"Are you kidding me? This is a ton. I could kiss you right now." I pinched Helen's face and puckered my lips.

Helen pulled away and closed her laptop. "Did you make contact with Tony?"

"Yes, I did."

"Well, maybe you can find out more about this, then? Let me walk you out."

Standing by the cashiers, Dennis was eyeing us, tapping the face of his watch.

"Call me if you guys find something else."

"Always do."

"We're gonna nail these sons of bitches, don't worry," I promised.

"Oh, I know. And trust me, sister, that's all I've been thinking about the past three years. I can't stand by this injustice, and I hate failing. Nobody fucks with a beautiful person like Julia. And Jeff is a pro at busting people who post about them abusing animals and doing horrible things. He can find the smallest clues on a photo most people would miss. We've been very successful at bringing justice to the innocent. We won't stop until we clear Julia's name too."

After I said my goodbye, I stepped out into the gloomy night, cutting through the sea of people passing in front of me on both sides. The right thing to do would be to call for a car or see if Brooke was in the city.

Instead, I googled for the closest bar and chose to slam three shots of tequila. I then had a stranger bang me hard enough in the bathroom stall to take my mind off it all.

7

Brooke never set a curfew for me, but she did worry like a mother, so when the clock chimed one in the morning and I was still not home, I feared her wrath.

My adoptive parents were very strict about how late I could stay out at night. In the brothel, Hector regulated every minute of my life. So finally having freedom was liberating. Still, causing Brooke grief always made me feel guilty. I should have been more considerate of my host, but the tequila shots did little to help me stay on course.

Nestled against the Uber's backseat door with my head swimming in oblivion, I was too tired and intoxicated to think clearly. But as the steeply pitched gable roofs and the embellished entryway came into view, gray and mysterious under the spell of coach lights and thick fog, I sobered to my predicament.

I pulled out my cell phone to check for missed calls and messages. Sure enough, Brooke had tried to reach me a dozen times in the past few hours.

Driven by shame, I asked the driver to drop me off at the gate by the foot of the hill. I would make the rest of the trip on foot, sneak into my room, and pretend that this night had never happened.

As I stepped out onto a carpet of wet leaves in heels, my ankle went out of balance, and I slammed back against the door. The driver rolled the window down. "Are you okay, sweetheart?"

She was a pretty, middle-aged woman who drove for Uber at night to pay for her son's college tuition. I remembered that much from our conversation on my way home from the bar in Manhattan.

Her situation evoked both admiration and fear in me. I envied her for having people in her life she loved so much that she would drive drunk people around in the middle of the night to support them. Her willingness to do so much for others also scared the life out of me. Julia did everything she could to make the people she loved happy and comfortable, yet they betrayed her. Unconditional love has the power to destroy us and isn't always rainbows and comfort. It can be pain, heartache, and forgiveness.

I was never going to expose my heart to anyone, ever. I was never going to let myself be vulnerable ever again.

After I assured my driver that I was fine and didn't need more assistance, she drove off into the night.

Standing at the end of the long driveway, I felt a slight drizzle on my face. It was cold, but a welcome relief on my overheated face. The night was quiet and peaceful. If the world hadn't been spinning around me, I'd have enjoyed it more.

The windows on the house were black. Brooke must have gone to sleep.

I didn't walk far up the road before a dark shadow moving between the fat limbs of the oak trees caught my attention. Stunned immobile by fear, I focused my eyes through the veil of fog obscuring the night landscape.

The first thing that popped into my mind was that Ornelas's men had found me. I was careful not to leave a trail tracing my journey back to America. I even lied about where I was heading to the coyote who helped me sneak across the border. I created an entire cover story for myself, and I made sure to tell it to everybody who cared to listen. I was mindful of my situation. Without any detours, I'd traveled straight to New York City to meet Brooke. And even if my former captors had my adoptive parents' address, they couldn't find me there. I hadn't contacted them since I'd arrived back in the States. I never even called them to keep them safe.

I did stalk my adoptive mother on Facebook to see pictures of my old family and how they were doing without me. Her account wasn't private, so it was easy to access her page. But I never commented or liked her posts. Even if I did, she wouldn't know it was me. I used a fake name on my account: Kate Potter—a yoga instructor's name I found on a DVD in Brooke's house.

Panic touched me when I realized that my thoughts were too mangled by fear and alcohol to think clearly. I couldn't retrace my steps in my head to see if I'd somehow made a mistake along the way. But if Guerrero or Perez was here for me, it meant only one thing. I must have given away my location, made a mistake.

Fear gripped me in the same way it did under Hector's rule. I knew the watchmen would not take me back. I was too *old* for the brothel. They were here to execute me for running away.

The dark figure moved again. Warm urine trickled down my inner thigh, and I collapsed to the ground in an attempt to hide in the shrubs. As the cold and fear sobered me, I groped the forest floor for a branch or a rock, anything I could use as a weapon. I wasn't going down without a fight. Not after what I went through to get here. Not until my job here was done. Not until I avenged Julia.

My fingers landed on something hard. It was a piece of asphalt broken off from the edge of the road. Not what I was hoping for, but better than nothing.

Clenching my jaws, I gripped the weapon, anticipating an attack. Who did Ornelas send to kill me? Guerrero? Perez? Delgado?

A branch broke in the distance as if someone had stepped on it. The sound echoed through the dark.

By then, my heart was pulsating in my ears and hammering inside my throat. I should have listened to Brooke and packed a knife or pepper spray in my bag. I told her if I survived Mexico, then nothing here could scare me. But I was scared right here alone in the night, hunkered down in my soiled pants, nobody having my back.

More moving shadows broke the streams of light that speared through the trees in front of the house.

All hope was lost.

With a bit of luck, I might have been able to fight off one attacker. But four or five of them would overpower me for certain.

My fingers relaxed, and the piece of asphalt fell to the ground. Nobody is that unlucky, I thought. After seven years of struggle and pain, I was supposed to have my seven years of plenty and happiness. I felt robbed and cheated by fate.

What were they waiting for? Why didn't they ambush and kill me already? I wanted to scream at them. Tell them to come and get me because I didn't have all night.

I looked down at myself, clothed in darkness. Maybe my old watchmen didn't see me because there was no light behind me to illuminate my figure.

I stole a peek at the main gate behind me. I could make a run for it. Make it out to the main road and bang on the neighbor's door for help. It seemed doable.

The hoot of an owl drew my eyes back toward the house. That was when I saw the first. Then came a second and a third. In full view, a group of seven deer crossed the driveway ahead of me like they owned the place.

Fucking deer! I grunted to myself as my fear morphed into frustration. Then anger. I felt an urgent need to throw something at them. To shoot them dead. Not having a better option, I started running toward the four-legged intruders with my arms in the air and growling like a wild animal. Startled, the herd galloped away and disappeared behind the house.

Panting heavily, I made it to the main steps by the house entrance where I sat down on the cold, wet stones and dropped my head into my hands, promising myself not to touch another drop of alcohol ever again.

My skin was prickling inside my coat. I needed something to take the edge off. "I can't," I whispered. "I promised Brooke I'd stay clean."

I dunked my hand into my purse and groped for my prescription instead. I popped one in my mouth.

Fuck. Fuck. Fuck. What a night!

My hair was soaked. My coat was damp—what a fucked-up way to end a successful day.

After a few minutes of self-pity, I gathered myself and made my way inside the house, but I was too agitated to go to sleep.

On my way to the surveillance room, I saw Hector in every plant, every painting, and every piece of furniture that lurked in the shadows.

I'd been paranoid before, especially during my walk across the border, but not since then, not like this.

I grabbed Brooke's half-finished water from the desk and drank thirstily. Then I turned on all the monitors, looking for Tony.

He was in his bed, watching TV. The time on the screen showed 11:59 p.m. He'd been suffering from insomnia, I knew, though I never caught him staying up this late.

"Where the hell have *you* been?" Brooke's voice thundered from the doorway, nearly making me fall out of my chair.

"Shit! You scared me," I said, rubbing my knee, which had hit the edge of the desk. "I was out."

Brooke lit a cigarette. "No shit. But where were you?"

Suddenly exhausted, I smoothed my hair back. "I went to see Helen after I met with Tony."

My statement made Brooke's face change, and she nearly choked on the smoke.

"She showed me a video a passenger recorded in the piano room. Julia and Tony were playing The Newlywed Game."

"Wow! Why didn't you call me? I would have wanted to see that too."

"It all happened so fast. I'll ask Helen to email me the file tomorrow."

"How was it?"

"How was what?"

"To see Julia?"

I rubbed my eyes and took a deep breath, trying to pluck the right words from my tired, dizzy brain. "She wasn't happy. Something went terribly wrong that night. She accused Tony of cheating."

"What? That's new."

Smoke slithered from Brooke's nose and mouth as she talked, and I fanned it away from my face. "Yep. Julia didn't mention who the woman was, but she seemed absolutely certain that Tony was cheating on her. She said she hired a private investigator who took pictures of Tony with another woman. Do you have any clue who that may have been?"

"No, she didn't mention anything about it to me, but I can look through the paperwork in my office. If she hired a PI, there must be an invoice somewhere."

"Fucking asshole!" I grunted.

"Watch your language, Annie. It doesn't suit you."

I pulled the cigarette from her mouth and took a drag. "It suits the real me."

Brooke lit a new cigarette for herself. The room started to smell like a cheap Tijuana bar.

"Did you manage to hide the speakers?"

"I did. I put one in the master bedroom too." I cracked a smug smile.

Brooke bobbed her head. "The bastard is still awake. You wanna see how it works?"

I raised my brows. "Oh, yes, I do."

The cigarette hanging from her mouth, Brooke took out an iPad from the drawer on the desk, moved the microphone in place, and clicked start.

The ten-minute recording contained Julia's altered voice. Brooke's brother—the one who installed the surveillance system for us and the spy cameras in Tony's home—put together a clip by cutting and pasting different words of Julia from her TV interviews into a sequence. Then he edited the whole thing and altered her voice to make her sound like a ghost. The guy was a genius. The whole damn thing was perfect and creepy as hell.

I checked the Post-it notes on one of the monitors for the list of speakers and the places where I hid them. Speaker number two was in the bedroom. Brooke pressed play on the app and gave me the silent nod to flip on the switch for the right speaker.

"Tony, I'm cold." Julia's voice was so eerie and mysterious that I felt cold running down my spine. I had to look behind me in the dim room because her presence seemed real.

I muted the microphone.

"Oh, my gosh. I got goosebumps!" I showed my lower arm to Brooke.

"I feel like this room is haunted. Too bad Tony didn't notice it. I think the TV is too loud."

Julia's husband was unfazed by the voice of his deceased wife. Brooke was right.

"I'll make us some coffee," Brooke announced with a tap at her thighs before pushing out of her chair. She stopped on her way out of the room and turned. "Or you just want to go to bed and try it again tomorrow? Maybe he won't stay up so late tomorrow night."

I turned my head around in circles, the bones in my neck cracking. I felt the need to rest, but my mind was too agitated. It was either stay here and wait or go to bed with a racing mind.

"I'll stay up a little bit. You go to bed. If he turns the TV off, I'll wake you."

Brooke flapped her hand at me. "I'll stay for a little bit too."

Once Brooke returned from the kitchen, she sat down in her chair and rotated it to face me. "So, what happened at the meeting? What's Tony's new plan?"

"I don't know. We never got to talk. Sammy is sick."

"Is he all right?"

"Just a common cold, I think." I looked away, recalling Julia's son's face in my mind. "Cute little fellow. He looks so much like her."

"All these years, and I still can't get past her tragedy. She was so young and full of life. So talented. The world is a darker place without her."

When Julia and I were together in the brothel, I tried to imagine how her life must have been before she ended up with us. I pictured her swimming in the sparkling blue water of her infinity pool at her white marble stone mansion, surrounded by tons of friends and family. I thought her life was a constant party filled with earthly goods and laughter. I never thought of her as a victim of adultery. The stories in Julia's diary suggested that they'd had a perfect marriage. So, she either refused to pen her bad memories, or she only remembered the good times of her former life as she slowly recovered from her amnesia.

I smiled at Brooke. "You know her life wasn't always about pain and suffering in the pit," I began. Brooke refused to say, or even hear, the words "brothel" or "whorehouse." "There was no sunlight in the basement where we lived. We had a few windows, but they were all boarded with plywood. Julia was concerned about the kids not getting any vitamin D. She said that being locked up inside was bad for our health. Kids needed fresh air, sunshine, and daily exercise. I helped her pull out the nails from one of the pieces of plywood that covered the only window in the kitchen. On those rare days when Hector took Kitana to the market, we would remove the piece and look outside.

"Julia would line up the kids and have them close their eyes and soak up the sunlight." The memory warmed my heart, and I smiled, letting out a sigh of relief. I should revisit the few sweet moments we had in that hellhole more often.

"I don't remember that story. Was it in the diary?"

"No. I ripped those pages out and left them with Kitana. She said she would read them to the kids as a bedtime story."

Tears gathered in Brooke's eyes. It was strange to see that tough, crusty woman get emotional. She touched my hand, and I continued with the story.

"One day, this shaggy dog showed up outside of the brothel. It looked like an old shepherd dog with a white-and-black coat. He had a super-cute face. There was a long picket fence separating the sidewalk from the road. This dog would sit behind the fence for hours on end, staring at a big bouncy ball on the other side. A few passersby would stop and throw the ball back to the dog. He'd fetch it, wait for the person to leave, and push the ball over the fence again. Then he would lie there until the next gullible victim showed up. The kids would get a kick out of it. We'd bet on who would stop and throw back the ball. For a few moments, we forgot about our lives and simply laughed and enjoyed the moment."

"It's a very cute story, Annie," Brooke said, choking on her emotions.

I didn't mean to make her tear up. I just wanted her to see that our lives weren't all bad. We did have a few moments of joy. Even at that moment, as I recalled the memory, I sensed a smile curving my lips.

"The funniest thing about that dog was that the fence didn't enclose the property," I said, laughing. "It was only a long straight fence along the sidewalk. So, when the dog was tired of the game, he walked around it and left. That clever dog fooled dozens of people every day into playing fetch with him."

"I'm glad to hear that, despite the pain and suffering, you did have some happy moments," Brooke said.

There was only one problem with all my happy stories: they all had terrible endings. "Not for long. Hector found out about the window. Maybe someone snitched, or he noticed that we were getting a healthy glow on our faces. I don't know. But he blamed Julia. She paid a heavy price for doing something nice for the kids. Again." My joy was gone; my heart sunk into my stomach. "She endured the most brutal treatments I'd ever seen, but she'd rather carry everyone's cross than let those kids get hurt."

A moment of silence stilled us.

"I need a drink," said Brooke at last, getting up from the table.

"I'm sorry. I shouldn't have told you the story."

She bobbed her head with a thin smile. "No, I'm glad you did. Helps me keep Julia's memory alive."

I folded my arms on the desk and laid my right cheek on top. "I miss her so badly."

Brooke stared at me for a long moment. Then she wiped her glasses on her shirt. "I'll bring you a drink too."

8

My face was lying in a pool of saliva when Brooke shook me awake. The skin on my forehead ached where my watch had left an indentation, and I rubbed it to ease the discomfort. I didn't remember how we fell asleep or when, but one look at the row of empty beer bottles and the ashtray full of cigarette butts in front of us gave me a pretty good idea.

"What time is it?" I groaned, lifting my head and moistening my cracked lips with my tongue.

Brooke's creased face focused into view. "Four in the morning." She took her glasses off and rubbed her eyes. "The bastard is finally sleeping. If you want to do this today, then now's the time. If not, let's go to bed."

I grabbed the bottled water on the desk and rinsed the sour taste from my mouth. "I'm already up. Let's do this."

Brooke tossed back the last sip of brandy from her glass, pulled her short, curly hair back into a tiny ponytail, and signaled me to go ahead.

"Tony, I'm cold," Julia's recorded ghost voice oozed.

I put on the headphones to make sure the speaker hidden behind the dresser was working. "Play it."

"Tony, I'm scared."

From the creepy, echoing voice that slithered through my headphones and seeped into my ears, I shuddered. "Fuck, that sounds spooky."

I handed the headphones to Brooke, and she put them on.

"Tony, my husband."

Brooke's eyes widened. She must have experienced the same sensation I did.

There was movement on the screen. Tony was stirring in his bed.

"Should we crank up the volume?

Brooke put her nicotine-stained fingers on the button and turned it up slightly.

"Tony. Tony. Where are you?" Julia's digitally altered voice breathed the words softly, stretching out the syllables.

The night vision feature on the spy camera was top quality. Although the image was only shades of gray, when Tony's eyes popped open, they were like white marbles. The image was insanely creepy, and I almost fell out of my chair.

I pointed at Brooke, and she once again pressed play on the iPad.

"Tony, I'm cold."

I tried to put myself in Tony's shoes and imagine what I'd do if I heard my long-lost lover's voice in the middle of the night calling out to me. I'd freak out for sure.

Tony turned on the nightlight, climbed out of bed, and left the room. I followed his movements through the spy cameras.

First, he went into Sam's bedroom, where we lost sight of him. Anticipation nearly ripped me apart as I waited for him to reappear in view of the camera. When Brooke gripped my hand on the table, her touch startled me.

A couple of minutes later, Tony stepped out of his son's room and looked downstairs over the railing. I pictured myself pushing him over the barrier. Wouldn't that have been ironic?

Soon he was on the move again. Once he left the hallway, he was out of sight for a while until he showed up on the kitchen camera. He filled up a glass with water from the refrigerator dispenser, drank a few sips, then climbed the stairs and slipped back into his bed.

Brooke and I exchanged silent glances. There was no need for words. We both knew that the possibility of his wife's spirit haunting him had rattled Tony.

We waited for about ten minutes, then Brooke played the recording again. "Tony, I'm scared."

This time, his body snapped forward, and he flicked on the light without hesitation.

"Tony, my husband."

He jumped out of bed and leaped across the room, turning on all the lights.

Brooke was about to start the recording again, but I stopped her. "Let's not overplay it. We should let him believe he was dreaming it all. If we come on too hard, he'll know something's off."

Brooke stared at the screen, moving her face as close to it as it could get. "He looks scared. Let's record him. Maybe he'll feel so guilty that he'll go down on his knees and beg Julia for forgiveness."

Leaning back in my chair, I cracked my spine. "I don't think it will be that easy to get a confession out of him." I looked at my tired friend. "Your doctor friend still on board?"

"Yep. I talked to her yesterday. She's ready whenever we are."

I covered a yawn. "I'm going to bed. If I stay up any longer, I'll look like shit tomorrow at my meeting with Tony. I don't think he feels close enough to me yet to open up about the haunting, but hopefully soon. Then we're golden."

Brooke turned off the monitors. The sudden darkness that fell upon the room made me uneasy, and I looked behind me at the shadows.

"He will. I've known him for years. He always comes to me with his problems. That's why I was shocked to hear about an alleged lover."

I made a face. The biggest life lesson I'd learned in the whorehouse was that, sooner or later, all men cheat.

On my way out of the surveillance room, I put my hand on Brooke's shoulder. "Your brother is a freaking genius."

Brooke rolled her eyes. "Just don't tell him that. He's already in love with you. Stupid fool."

My boss's comment caught me by surprise. "He's old enough to be my dad."

"I know. Tell *him* that." Brooke picked up a few empty beer bottles from the table. "Help me clean this mess up, then get your ass in bed. I don't remember the last time I stayed up this late. I'm too old for this shit."

*   *   *   *   *

One would assume that after a night of booze, sex in a bathroom stall, and devilish excitement, I'd be ready to hit the sack and get some shut-eye, but the rest of my night was anything but restful.

I dreamed about the dog that tricked people into playing fetch.

I dreamed about Julia sitting crossed-legged on the stained mattress, hunched over her notebook, writing down her memories.

But the worst nightmare I had that night was when I pictured myself sitting on the sofa in Tony's living room, reading a book, and it was me instead of Tony to whom Julia's apparition appeared. She looked like a walking floater—a pale woman with white, cloudy irises and yellow teeth. Water dripped from her hair and dirty dress, pooling on the hardwood floor around her. She was holding the red heels she'd worn at The Newlywed Game. She came closer to

A . B . W H E L A N

me and leaned over my book, water droplets soaking the pages. "Don't forget about me," she said, her breath steaming the air. The book slipped out of my hand and landed on the floor with a thud.

Then I woke up, drenched in sweat, my hair sticking to my forehead.

I lit a cigarette and stood by the window, guilt descending on me. What if we were emotionally and psychologically torturing Tony but he wasn't the one who tried to kill Julia? What if he was genuinely suffering from the loss of his beloved wife? But he was cheating on her. He was unhappy and angry and, most of all, envious of Julia's success. He had the most to gain. But where was the alleged lover now?

If he turns out to be innocent, I thought, I'll go straight to hell. But as I put out my cigarette and climbed onto my mattrass, I decided that it was a risk I was willing to take.

9

Julia Rose's Diary

Entry #17

Hank came to visit me today. I don't think Hank is his real name because when he first selected me from the lineup, he introduced himself as Frank, but if he wants to be called Hank from now on, it makes no difference to me.

We are not supposed to ask personal questions of the clients and complain about our predicament. Asking them for help warrants a brutal beating. Everyone told me that opening my mouth would have dire consequences, but I didn't understand what they meant until I learned my lesson the hard way. But to truly believe in something, the information has to come through personal experiences. We need to see things with our own eyes to believe them. This point of view contradicts people's belief in God, but let's not get into that right now because I get riled up about the topic. Free will or not, if there is a God,

then why would he or she let innocent children
suffer?

Please forgive me for deviating· My mind tends to
wander these days· If once upon a time I had the
discipline and concentration to write a book, I'm
surely not that person anymore·

Back to today's story·

Hank is one of my favorite clients out of all the
American men who come to see me and pay for my
company instead of a child's—men I vehemently
despise· He always says I remind him of his daughter
who died from an overdose when she was twenty-two
years old· For the hour he spends with me, he only
wants me to listen to his stories and look at family
pictures with him·

His wife looks like a bitter old hag· She doesn't smile
in any of the pictures· When I pointed that out to
him, Hank said he was responsible for his wife and
daughter's unhappy life· As a busy dentist, he gave
money instead of his time and attention· He thought
money was what they wanted· It wasn't long before
his wife was hooked on prescription drugs, numbing
her brain to get through her days of existence with
no purpose· Then his daughter started stealing pills
from the medicine cabinet for herself and her friends·
Hank didn't notice what was going on in the house
until it was too late—until his daughter was already
addicted to crack and heroin· He blamed his wife for
being weak and worthless, failing at the only job she

had to do. Now they go on cruises a few times a year
to get out of the house, to forget their failures.
I know the story well. I've heard it a million times.
Today, Hank cried when he showed me pictures of his
daughter's sweet-sixteen birthday bash, twenty years
ago today. The girl looked happy to me, living the life
of what most teen girls must have dreamed of,
driving her brand-new white convertible, surrounded by
family and friends, not knowing the real pain that life
can dish out.
I, too, have a child out there somewhere in the big
world. I don't remember giving birth or even being
pregnant, but I have a Cesarean scar to prove it. I
often run my fingers along the thin line, trying to
remember, but I fail every time. What kind of mother
forgets the face of her child? Maybe I too was a bad
mother. Maybe my career as a writer was more
important to me than spending time with my child.
Perhaps I will die in this hole and my family will be
better for it. That's why nobody has found me yet.
No one is looking.

Entry #18
Hello there again. I'm sorry for not writing lately. My
last entry turned out so dark that I couldn't bring
myself to come back to it again. Kitana said that
there is no way on earth I was a bad mother. And
it's highly likely that my family is looking for me, but

there is no possible way for them to know where I
am. She said I shouldn't give up hope.
London managed to steal some heroin from Gonzales,
and we shared it against my better judgment. I've
been under the effects of it the past few days, so I
don't remember much, but I feel better now. London
is one of my favorite people here in this shameful
place. She has an unbreakable spirit.
I shouldn't be a bad example and shoot up with her,
but sometimes the weight of responsibility here can
be too heavy for me to carry. There is a monster
inside of me that comes out of its cave at such times
to control me. No matter how hard I try to silence
it, it doesn't go away. It roars inside my head until I
give it what it wants.
This morning London and I made a pact. We promised
to help each other find the strength to defeat our
monsters. We will not bow to its will anymore. I'm
trying to be strong for her and play my part.
Fortunately, London doesn't know that many nights
when everybody is asleep, Hector brings me the needle
and takes me away to ride the magic carpet with
him. Hector gets off on his control over me. He
prefers me compliant. He is my real monster.
All right. I promised myself not to let my mind
paddle into dark waters again. So today, I will share a
bit of good news.
I've been listening to Kitana's translation of my book
I supposedly wrote in a life that's no longer my own.

I do it for the same reason I always do, to help me recall the memories of my forgotten life· But every page, and every chapter, is a new surprise without a hint of familiarity· It's hard to fathom that I wrote this book· But I won't give up, not even when the headache comes in the wee hours of the night· I know that eventually, I'll reach the point where I can exclaim, "I know what's happening· I wrote these lines·"

We are halfway through the book, and it hasn't happened yet, but I remain optimistic· We still have the other half to read·

Hector caught me with the book today· I was staring at the Spanish words that described the part when Tristan helped Julieta escape from prison and he proclaimed his love to her under the three moons on the balcony of his treehouse· I remembered the beautifully written romantic part that was so captivating that I didn't hear Hector's footsteps until it was too late· I tried to hide the book, but he'd already seen me with it·

With a stern face, he ripped off my blanket and exposed the book· He didn't seem mad, but I still shrunk away from him·

He took the book· Then he grabbed my hand· He dragged me to his room and ordered me to sit·

"I know who you are, Julia Rose·"

His statement, like a sucker punch, hit me in the chest·

"I gave the money to Kitana to buy your book, but I knew who you were all along. I wasn't sure if you were pretending to have amnesia or if it was real. I know now it is real."

He leaned against his desk and folded his arms and legs. I gathered myself on the bed; the anticipation of the unknown kept me on edge. Hector showed no emotion, and I never knew what would come next, a beating, sex, lecturing, or nothing at all.

But today, at that moment, I felt the power to ask questions.

"If you knew who I was, why didn't you tell me?"

He scratched his head and rubbed his eyes as if he were tired—not physically but tired of life.

"After I found you on the beach and brought you here, the internet was full of the news of a famous American author's disappearance at sea. I knew it was you. But you didn't know who you were."

For two years, I've been living in oblivion, and Hector had information about who I was all along. Seething with a wave of boiling anger, I scooted to the edge of the bed. "You let me sink into the abyss when you had a life vest for me?"

Hector's dark, unyielding eyes bore into mine. The silence in the room stretched out longer than I could endure.

Driven by blind madness, I jumped up from the bed and leaped at him. I started banging my fists against

his chest, crying from frustration. He seized my
wrists and held them firmly.

"Sit down!" he growled at me. "Don't make me hurt
you."

I wiped away my tears as I stepped to the side, but I
refused to follow his orders, instead choosing to
remain standing an arm's length away.

"If I had told you, or anybody, who you were, then
Ornelas would have asked for ransom from your
husband." He said this so calmly, as if he hadn't
announced his responsibility for my doom.

I clasped my face with my hands, staring at him in
disbelief.

"I have a husband, and you didn't contact him about
me? He would have paid you. I'm sure. Then why?
Why did you do this to me? Isn't it money that you
care about?" I felt my insides crush—my whole world
collapsing, my faith in humanity evaporating in a wisp
of smoke.

Hector started scratching his stubble, staring at me
intently.

"I read every article, every bit of news I found about
you and your disappearance. Do you know that the
police were investigating your husband for it?"

My neck collapsed; my face drooped. "What do you
mean?" I had no memory of a husband or a child. I
was too young to be married. But even if I had a
family, I couldn't be that horrible of a person that
the man who wanted to spend the rest of his life

with me, who wanted me to be the mother of his
child, could hate me enough to kill me·
I felt my entire body wither away, my hopes for a
better future slipping between my fingers·
"Who is my husband?"
"Some dude called Tony Rose·"
"Can I see him?"
Hector chuckled· "I don't carry a picture of him in
my wallet·"
"Can I see him on your laptop or phone?"
Hector bit down on his lip, then after a short
consideration, he pulled out his cell phone, typed on
the screen, and turned the device toward me·
It was a picture of me—when my hair was still
voluminous and my face smooth—with a dark-haired
man with a chiseled jaw· We sat behind a table,
signing books in a place that looked to be a bookstore·
With my fingers, I enlarged his face· His teeth were
unnaturally white· His smile seemed fake· His eyes
didn't sparkle with love for me· We were like two
strangers sitting next to each other· Like a writer
and editor duo· Or master and apprentice· Seeing this
strange man who was supposed to be my husband
gripped my soul·
I'm still in shock as I'm writing these words· My
entire image of me being happily married to the love
of my life and raising our child together was
shattered· I considered the possibility that the
photographer caught us at an unfortunate moment·

But Hector showed me a few more pictures, and our smiles always looked forced· Was it a mask we wore in public or was it indeed the actual declaration of my married life?

"Look at this lot·" Hector swiped picture after picture on his phone· "Your in-laws look like clowns· Check out your sister-in-law· She got some issues·" Analyzing the online pictures, I had a flashback—the first one since I started to keep a diary· I was with my sister-in-law in a doctor's office· She sat next to me while I filled out her medical record questionnaire· She tried to answer every question with a yes, proclaiming to have had every listed illness at some point in her life· I remembered arguing with her to take the answers more seriously and to stop making up lies about her health· That was my first solid memory· It felt real, not a dream or a figment of my imagination·

"Can you tell me what happened to me? How I ended up on the shore of Mexico?"

Hector set his phone on the desk, teasing me to pick it up and run away with it·

"The papers said you were drunk, and you jumped or fell, but I never believed it· I think somebody in your family pushed you over and left you for dead·"

"What gives you that idea? Why would they do that?"

"I dunno· Just a feeling I have·"

I let silence consume the space between us. I used it to gather my thoughts.

"Do I have children?"

"You have a son. Sam. He is around four or five, I think."

I touched my stomach as warm teardrops welled up in my eyes. I didn't know his face. I couldn't remember his voice. But I missed him with all my heart.

"Can I see him?"

"There are no pictures of him online."

"How is that possible?"

"I dunno. Maybe you tried to keep him out of the public's eye."

"Why are you telling me all this now, after all this time? Did you change your mind about the ransom money?"

Hector clicked his tongue and slapped his hand across my face. "Stupid woman!"

His reaction took me by surprise. "What did I say?"

"I need no money from no stupid husband!"

"Then what do you want?" I asked, the trails of salty tears stinging my face more than his strike.

"I want you to stop moping around about a life that only exists in your head. Your family wanted you dead. They won't pay money for you. No one is looking for you. Your husband is probably happy you're gone. Your life is here. You could be my woman."

Hector's attraction toward me was always noticeable. His intentions not so much. But this was the first time he'd said what was in his heart out loud. He was a man who expressed his feelings using his fist or a backhand. I was a prisoner; he held the key. What kind of utopia did he live in to believe that we could ever be lovers?

"I want to go back to my son!" I screamed at him, driven by basic instincts rather than the manipulation tactics that had served me so well with him. But during that moment of pain, I exposed myself to him. I stripped my soul naked. I stood in front of him, vulnerable.

I fell to my knees and wrapped my arms around his ankles. "Please, Hector, let me go back to my family."

I don't know what happened to me, but that wretched, weak person wasn't me. I completely lost control.

"They tried to kill you, you stupid bitch!"

"Please," I begged, kissing his shoes. "Please. I'm begging you. My son needs his mother."

Hector kicked me off him and abruptly left the room, slamming the door behind him so hard that pieces of plaster fell to the floor. I dropped to my side, my whole body shaking from my violent crying. I missed my son, my life as a mother, so painfully, even though I couldn't remember him, or any of it. It was instinct, the most basic and original instinct of all. The door slammed open against the wall, and Hector barged his way through the room to me like an angry bull· He grabbed my shoulders, tossed me onto the bed on my stomach, and climbed onto my back·

"You are mine now," he kept murmuring in my ear while I cried, wanting to die·

I'm sorry, but I can't do this anymore· Writing in this beat-up notebook doesn't help me remember my past· It only keeps the wounds of the present open and raw· I'm going to sleep now, and by the grace of God, oh, I hope I never wake up·

Entry #19

It's morning, and I don't have much time to write, but I wanted to let you know that I'm all better now· I had a dream, a beautiful dream, about my baby boy· I know he had blue eyes like the azure of the sea· I know he had a mop of dirty blond hair· I know he liked to ride his little motorcycle as fast as the wind· I know his favorite ice cream flavor was banana and that he loves mango smoothies· But I will tell you all about my dream when I can sneak away for a moment· And don't worry about me· I don't want to die anymore· I will get back to my son· Whatever it takes·

10

"Shit! We slept in!" Brooke's cracked and panicky voice dragged me out of my sleep as she barged into my room with a pillow-creased face and tousled hair. I propped myself up onto my elbow just in time to see her rush back out and vanish. Julia's open diary slid down my chest and onto my tummy from my movement. I left my messy nest on the floor and crawled onto the bed to reach the nightstand for my phone. The time 11:15 a.m. popped up on the screen.

"Shit!"

I pressed the home button to see if there were any messages or missed calls from Tony. An array of notifications flooded my screen.

A Messenger message from Helen:

Jeff found something on the video. You need to see it. Call me. Don't tell Brooke.

An odd message, I thought, considering Brooke was the wheels of the operation, while I was the engine and Helen was the headlight. Brooke was as much a part of this investigation as Helen, or Jeff, or even me. So why the secrecy?

A text from the guy I met in the bar last night:

I had fun. We should do this again. Call me.

My headache told me to delete his text and number, but I wasn't in the state of mind to carry out such a definitive action, so I ignored it for the time being.

Three text messages from Tony.

At 8:46 a.m.: I made reservations for us at Takashi on Hudson St. for 12:30 p.m. See you there!

At 10:02 a.m.: Hi Annie, did you get my message about our lunch date for today? Please confirm.

At 11:08 a.m.: If you don't get back to me in twenty minutes, I'll have to cancel our reservation. I hope you are okay. I tried to call Brooke. She didn't answer her phone either. I'm starting to worry. Call me!!

Call me! Call me! Call me! Why was everybody so needy this morning?

Phone in my hand, I leaped off the bed and rushed out of the room to catch up with Brooke. She was standing in the hallway in front of a long mirror, a lit cigarette hanging from her mouth, putting on mascara as she balanced on one foot and tried to squeeze the other in a narrow shoe.

"What happened? The alarm didn't go off?"

She shrugged and emitted a throaty gurgling sound.

"Did you talk to Tony this morning? He said he was calling you?"

She stepped down on both feet, took the cigarette out of her mouth, ashes dropping everywhere, and looked at me in the mirror as she checked out her impromptu makeup. "You need to handle Tony alone today. I'm already late as hell. My phone has been blowing up all morning. I gotta go." She spat into a potted flower and hurried down the corridor toward the main door, picking up her briefcase and purse on the way. "There's coffee in the pot. I'll call you later." Her voice lingered, even as she was already out the door.

Out of all three, Helen's text message was the most intriguing. However, Tony's was the most urgent. He answered after the second ring. "Are you okay?"

"Yes, I'm good. Look, sorry for not answering the phone. Busy morning. I didn't even have time to check my messages."

"Oh," Tony said, sounding disappointed. "And here I thought I was your only client."

I caught the time on the wall clock, and realizing how little time I had to get ready, I pulled my legs out of my boxer shorts. Tripping over my feet, I started to rip off my tank top as I made my way to the kitchen for a cup of coffee. "No, but you are my favorite," I said, holding the phone to my ear with my shoulder.

After grabbing a mug from the dishwasher, I filled it up with coffee.

Tony laughed on the other end of the line. "Is that what you tell all your clients?"

"Busted," I admitted, filling the rest of the mug with milk until it spilled all over the counter. "Okay, Tony, I'm sorry, but I gotta go. See you at 12:30, all right?"

"Oh, yeah, see you at Takashi."

Having no time to do a Google search on the restaurant, or even call Helen about her message, I dropped my phone onto the dresser, jumped in the shower, and dressed in record time.

I never was one to pamper myself in the bathtub for hours, sitting in bubbly water while rose petals floated around and burning exotic scented candles while listening to relaxing music. I was more of a jump in the shower, wash up, shave with a dull razor, and rinse off type of girl.

Back in Mexico, our monthly supply was a dozen razors that we had to share between twenty-five of us. It was better not to think about whose hair was stuck between the rusty blades. I used to tell myself that people had it far worse during the two world wars.

Yet, even with my expert skills in making myself presentable using a minimal amount of time, I was still eighteen minutes late for my appointment with Tony.

The drive from Montclair to Greenwich Village, north of SoHo, would have been forty minutes on a good night, but during the midday rush, it was excruciatingly long and would have tested the patience of the most seasoned commuter.

I was not a New Yorker. I was a Palmdale, California, girl from a blue-collar family. I was fooled by a boy, kidnapped, and trafficked to Mexico as a sex slave when I was fourteen.

But for Tony, I was a local law school graduate who had snatched a highly coveted assistant position at the Russell & Associates Law Firm in Manhattan.

When I walked the streets of New York City, I had to force myself not to look like a tourist. West Village, with its long streets guarded by giant green-crowned trees and historical buildings with their brick facades and fire escapes I'd only seen on TV, was especially challenging to ignore.

The first thing Brooke nailed into my head was that tourists always wander around aimlessly in the city, looking up and around as if they are lost. New Yorkers move with a purpose, and they move fast. They don't twist their heads around looking up at buildings and landmarks.

Her other advice on traveling through the city was not to look people in the eye on the subway because it was rude and there was a time when it was an invitation for a confrontation. I had yet to test my subway-riding skills because I'd been relying on yellow cabs, Uber, and Lyft to get me around the city.

At the curb in front of Takashi, I shot out of the car with haste, wearing a brown knee-length leather skirt and a cashmere long-sleeved top with a matching coat. My hair hung to one side in a slick, silky cascade. My lips were red. The inspiration for the attire came from Blake Lively. Julia wrote about her adoration for the young actress's fashion style. After the successful ring incident, I decided to keep looking like Julia—not a replica of her that would have been recognizable to her husband, but to mimic her style.

The neon lettering of the liquor store across the street reflected off of the black glass of the Japanese restaurant's facade. A group of Buddhists with conga drums hanging from their necks passed behind me. Their music added a nice rhythm to the already boisterous traffic. "Don't gawk," I reminded myself before entering the establishment with confidence.

I told the kind-faced woman at the front that I was here to meet someone. When I noticed Tony waving at me from the back, I pointed him out to her.

"I'm so sorry I'm late," I said, relieving myself of my coat. "The traffic was insane."

"Don't worry about it." He smiled, leaning back in his seat, hands resting on his thighs. "At least you texted me to let me know. That's more than I could ever expect from Brooke." He laughed.

"I heard the stories."

"Have you been here before?"

Tony's question was an invitation for me to check out the place. I looked around to take it all in, but not so long as to give away my amazement. "No, I don't think I have."

Tony leaned in. "Oh, you'd remember if you had! They serve the best authentic Japanese food. Since I had so much free time on my hands, I took the liberty of ordering for us. I hope you don't mind?"

"That's fine. I trust your taste."

He winked at me, not in a teasing, flirting way but more as a positive acknowledgment.

The server arrived with an array of thinly sliced marinated meat, fish, noodles, and sauces she set on the table. She fired up the infrared grill installed inside the middle of the table and left.

"Sake?" Tony lifted his little clay cup.

"I usually don't drink on the job, but I guess I can make an exception today."

We clinked glasses. "To a successful partnership."

"To us," I said, to add a bit of a personal touch to our toast.

I might have been an expert drinker when it came to tequila, beer, or Bacardi, but it was my first time trying this Japanese fire drink. I think it showed on my face.

"So, how long have you been in New York?"

I licked my lips, the taste of sake strong in my mouth. "What gave me away?"

"I sense a hint of an accent." He tilted his head like a listening dog. "West Coast, somewhere. L.A., perhaps?"

Weeks of training with Brooke couldn't take the California girl out of me. I felt my face flare up. "Busted. Again."

Using chopsticks, Tony put a slice of meat on the grill. It sizzled, sending up a veil of steam between us. The sound was so sexy, so intimate.

"So, what brought you here?"

"If I said I'd had enough of the sunshine, would you believe me?"

"Nah, I don't think so." He pinched his chin and looked at me with intense eyes, trying to read me. "You're here for the excitement. You've seen countless movies set in New York City. Crowded streets. Dark alleys. Yellow cabs. Opera. Broadway?"

"Money. Fame. The truth."

He dabbed his chopsticks in the air at me, deliberating. "I don't believe that. There is something in you that must have grabbed Brooke's attention. That's not easy to achieve."

I dunked my head. "My charm?"

He smacked his lips and smiled.

My eyes dropped to the grill. "I think your meat's done."

"Almost. See, when the edges curl up like this, then it's time to flip it. Go ahead, give it a try."

Never in my whole life had I held a pair of chopsticks. Properly eating in a Japanese restaurant wasn't a skill we'd thought to practice. So I picked up a bowl of soup from the selection, which came, crucially, with a spoon. I held the bowl out to Tony for the meat.

"You know, West Village used to be a run-down neighborhood. Passing through here was like being in a post-apocalyptic movie." Tony mused, looking out of the window at a red fire truck driving by with blaring sirens. "The mayor cleaned this place up, but it still managed to keep some of its original charm."

"I should get out more," I said as an invitation. "Get lost in the city."

"If you need a tour guide, I'm available." He placed additional pieces of meat and fish on the grill, flipped a few, and removed a narrow strip of beef. "Here, try this. It's to die for." He held a piece of dangling meat in front of my mouth as if we were on a date. Brooke would have scolded me if she knew I'd allowed Tony to feed me, but the moment took me away, and I complied.

"This place is quite romantic," I said, cherishing the sweet and spicy flavor lingering on my tongue. "We're talking face-to-face while grilling nibbles of meat and fish on hot plates. A wall of fragrant steam between us. The music."

"I know, right?" Tony agreed, dipping his meat in a bowl of sauce and noodles. "I like to come here, not only because the food is fantastic, but because I enjoy the fragrances of the hot steam hovering in front of me. It's a unique dining experience. Very exotic. I'm impressed you feel the same way."

"I have to admit, I'm pleasantly surprised. This place is not what I thought a traditional Japanese restaurant would be like," I said.

"I believe the owner is Korean, but he grew up in Japan. He does a great job combining the two cultures into one unique cuisine. It's like going on a journey of tastes and textures. It's not dining; it's an experience."

"Do you come here often?"

His smile faded. "Julia introduced me to this restaurant. Her dad was a huge food enthusiast. He would go on vacation for the sole purpose of trying new gastronomies and restaurants. He read volumes of books about food preparation and dining cultures. He was a pretty good chef himself; the most incredible meals I ever had were at his house."

"It must have been hard to lose your wife in such a mysterious way."

I noted a slight surprise in his expression. "It was a terrible accident. I only hope it was quick and she didn't suffer."

My toes curled up in my shoes. My fingers gripped the napkin. If only you knew, I thought. Oh, your wife felt pain, all right. Pain and humiliation for three long years while you were revisiting your favorite exotic Japanese restaurant on her dime.

I pretended to check the time on my watch because my appetite had disappeared. "Let's get down to business. I have to be back in the office soon."

"Oh, okay. I didn't mean to waste your time with my blabbering. I thought you were all mine for the afternoon."

"Trust me, I'd rather enjoy a long meal here with you and maybe grab a bowl of banana ice cream or a mango smoothie somewhere else than do depositions all afternoon, but a girl's gotta make a living, right?"

Tony put his hands together in front of his face. "Sammy loves banana ice cream and mango smoothies. Those are his favorites."

I touched my heart. "Oh, I guess your son has some West Coast blood in him after all," I said, playing into his surprise. I knew what his son liked. I'd read it in Julia's diary.

His eyes dropped to my hand. "You're not wearing the ring?"

I touched my finger. "Oh, that silly thing. No. After our last encounter, I felt it was inappropriate. I didn't want you to think of your wife and be sad every time you meet me because of a piece of jewelry."

"It's not only the ring. Your whole being and personality remind me of her. You two would've been great friends, I'm certain of it."

"I'll take that as a compliment." I spooned some soup into my mouth and set the bowl aside on the table. "So, what is this great plan of yours for the future of the Rose estate? It must be big if you wanted to discuss it with me first, without your brother and sister?"

Tony's shoulders stiffened. All of a sudden, he was all business. "Well…" he cleared his throat, "you already know that Julia wanted to break up our party of five. Her family is well off, always has been, so, in the beginning, it seemed natural to help out my side of the family with our fortune. See, the money came fast and in unfathomable amounts, and we didn't take the time or have the opportunity to wrap our minds around what to do with it all. Then Justin suggested we invest some of the money in the stock market. We had no time for that or the knowledge of how to do it, so when he offered to manage Julia's accounts, we said yes.

"Then Sylvia would show up asking for money. Once, she was behind on her taxes and needed help. Then she had trouble paying their mortgage. Julia decided to give my sister a title in name only, PR manager, to justify the money she was giving her. But then the plastic surgeries began and the special diets, and money began flying out the window."

The server interrupted Tony when she reappeared to take our empty plates and inquire about our desire to order something else.

Tony tried to pressure me into having dessert, but my stomach was in a knot, so I politely refused. I caught the waitress making a blasé face when Tony said we'd be okay for now.

"So, where was I?" Tony asked once we were alone again. "Oh, yeah. Then my mother started pressuring Julia into paying for the family's annual cruise ship vacation because she thought the cost was a drop in the bucket for us." He rolled his eyes, clearly disagreeing with his mother's assumption.

"At first, Julia was generous and happily shared her wealth. But back then, we didn't look at the bank statements. How much money was coming in? How much was going out? We had no clue. Following Brooke's advice, Julia met with our accountant, and after that, she was determined to put an end to the hemorrhaging of cash."

"What did the cash flow look like?"

"It was still positive." Tony shook his head, convincingly. "The problem was that Julia had a top-rated popular series that brought in all the money and fame, but she never stopped worrying about what would happen if she were a one-book—or in her case—a one-series wonder. What then? We needed to invest in real estate or start some kind of brand—a clothing line or something—to cash in on her fame, but we didn't do any of it. We simply spent the money hand over fist."

"I assume your brother and sister didn't take the news well."

"Not at all." Tony's phone buzzed on the table. "It's Sylvia. She's upset about not being invited to lunch. She'll come down with a new illness today, I'm sure, trying to get my sympathy." He rolled his eyes. "She's a hypochondriac, if you haven't noticed. Every day is a new sickness with her."

"I don't judge people, especially my clients."

Tony tilted his head. "Come on. We all do. You may not want to admit it out of professional courtesy."

I closed my eyes for a prolonged moment and opened them with a sigh. "Okay. I guess I can say that yes, I did notice your sister *may* have issues with plastic surgery. Also, I *may* have heard some rumors in the office too."

"See. Julia would roll over in her grave if she found out that three years after her death, I was still spending money on meaningless things. She always wanted to start a non-profit organization. She had plans to help a local animal shelter whose owner we knew. The place is in desperate need of a renovation. She also wanted to start a local scholarship fund for kids. I should have focused on those ideas after she passed, but I failed her."

Listening to Tony's larger-than-life speech riled me up. He should have used Julia's money to keep looking for her, but that option didn't seem to cross his mind.

I should have brought a bottle of laxative with me to pour into his drink. I could have used the time he was on the toilet to scroll through his phone and discover his secrets. He killed his wife for money, yet he was pulling this theater for me about his interest in animal shelters and scholarships? If he'd wanted to spend his money on helping those in need, why didn't he? Who stopped him?

"So, what do you want from me?" I asked with a blank face because that was better than the alternative going through my mind.

He looked to his right, then left, as if assessing the possibility of other restaurant guests eavesdropping on our confidential conversation. "We need another source of income, but Julia is no longer with us. She did start to write a new book—a spinoff from her *The New Earth* series, but she only finished the first few chapters. We need a ghostwriter who could write more books—

finish a whole new series, perhaps. Publicly, we would announce that Julia wrote the books. We would stick to that statement."

"Oh, I didn't know it was a whole series. I thought we only needed someone to finish Julia's last book as a tribute to her."

"Yeah, but one book won't bring in the money we need. There's the house and Sam. He's young." He dropped his head into his hands. Then he ran his fingers through his hair and clamped his neck. "I'm sorry. I must sound desperate, but we need the money, and we need it fast."

"What about the upcoming movies?"

"They've been pushed back a few times. It's the unusual circumstances surrounding Julia's death that scare the producers. And you know, a teen blockbuster movie is always risky. *Twilight* was a hit. *The Hunger Games* was a hit. The *Divergent* series was a flop. If we had a tell-all on Julia's life and death, it would be a different story, but people are beginning to forget about her. We need more books and more stories to revive the interest."

"Well, Brooke told me that hiring a ghostwriter had been the plan for some time. I've seen the list. There are some promising candidates, but this is no secret. Why did you want to meet me alone, without your brother and sister?"

The server refilled our water glasses. Her constant reappearance suggested she wanted us to pay our bill and leave so another tipping customer could take our place.

"Brooke has already taken care of the paperwork identifying the roles of the people in the company, Justin and Sylvia are out, but Julia never had the chance to sign it. During these past three years, I haven't been in the right state of mind to handle business. But it has to happen now. I need to withdraw the money from the investment accounts, but Justin won't make it easy. I also need to fire my sister as PR manager. You have to make this all look like these decisions are beyond my control. We need to come up with a plan to cut financial ties with my family without them blaming me for it. After all, they're my family, but I simply can't foot their ridiculous expenses anymore."

I leaned back on my chair, thinking. My birth mother told me all about her scams to keep the money coming in. How to stage a work-related accident and file a claim for benefits with workers' comp; sue Costco for negligence, file for bankruptcy. She was a master at manipulating the system.

"How about you tell Justin and Sylvia that the estate is going under? They need to leave the company before the IRS goes after their assets too. If they're truly in it only for the money, I bet they'll run the other way."

"Bankruptcy, huh?"

"You could play the hero. You'll take the financial hit. Once they're out of the company, you come forth with the manuscripts a few months later. You say you were cleaning out Julia's office, or the attic or whatever, and you found the finished books. Julia had kept it a secret because it was her next big surprise."

"The books get published. We get rich again," Tony finished my chain of thought.

"Well, success is never a guarantee, but we could hope for the best."

"You're a freaking genius. I could kiss you right now!"

"I'll take a pay raise instead." I smiled.

"How about a drink later tonight?"

A drink sounded pretty good at the moment, but it was too early in our relationship to let my guard down, and I was well aware that drugs would follow the booze for me. I couldn't trust myself. My slip last night was proof.

"Maybe some other time. Look, Tony, thank you for lunch. It was an experience, but I need to go. I'll get back to the office and discuss the details with Brooke. I'll call you once we draw up the paperwork."

"Sounds fantastic." He waved at the server for the check.

"Make sure you start complaining about the financial situation and the IRS to your family. They'll digest it more easily if the news doesn't come suddenly."

"All right. I'm on it. And hey," Tony called after me. "Thank you for joining me for lunch. I had a great time."

I nodded, refusing to admit that I had a lovely time as well. There was something about Tony Rose...As much as I despised the man, I found myself attracted to him. Could it be the pheromones? Julia married the guy—she must have seen something in him.

As I stood on the curb, waiting for my car, I reminded myself that Tony was most likely a cold-blooded killer who pushed the mother of his child to her death. If there was any doubt in my mind that Tony could do something unethical for money, it disappeared after our business lunch.

Being so rattled on my way home, I forgot to call Helen. But she rang me.

"I left you a message. You didn't get it?"

"Yeah, I got it, but I haven't had a chance to call you yet."

"Whatever. Check this out! Jeff finished breaking down the video frame by frame. We would have missed it if he wasn't so enamored with the job. You will not believe who was there at The Newlywed Game..."

"Why do you always have to be so mysterious, Helen? Just tell me."

"No, I won't ruin your surprise. I'm texting you the picture right now. Enjoy. I won't post it on Facebook till tomorrow morning, so call me back with an explanation! At nine a.m. sharp, it goes up."

I heard the beep from the incoming message on my phone as we talked. The envelope icon on the top of the screen taunted me. I hung up the phone and opened it. The image that loaded on the screen made me choke on my saliva.

11

For over two hours after sunset, I sat in the living room on a leather armchair, flicking the light switch on and off and waiting for Brooke to come home from work so I could confront her about my recent discovery.

My mind kept racing back to the first few nights I spent in this big old mansion where the hundred-year-old floorboards creaked even when nobody was walking on them and the air smelled of stained leather, aged wood, and dust regardless of how many times the rooms were aired out.

When Brooke was in the city, I was left alone with my demons. Every time I passed through the musty dim halls, chills would touch my neck and run down my spine, forcing me to turn around to see if someone was behind me. It would get to the point where I would become scared of my own shadows. For weeks, uncertainty and anxiety were my companions whenever I read in the library or watched TV in the living room because Julia's ghost was haunting me, especially on stormy nights. I sensed her presence in every raindrop and gust of wind.

No woman in her right mind would choose to live alone in such a ghostly, cold, and lonely place. So what was Brooke hiding?

Brooke never talked about her life. I may have been too self-centered or focused on my revenge to ask her why she wasn't married or had children, but she never brought personal topics up either.

Not until I saw Helen's photo did I realize that Brooke's home lacked any kind of personal element. There were no framed photos of her family hanging on the walls or displayed on the mantels above the fireplaces. This house had no identity—it could have belonged to anybody. If I thought about it, apart from a few bits and pieces I'd picked up by living with Brooke—such as that she smoked and drank like a broken, bitter old sailor, watched real-life crime reenactments on *Investigation Discovery*, gorged on cheese and crackers, and had no hobbies—I didn't know Brooke at all.

Had she been leading me like a horse to water? What if the reason Brooke had no men in her life was that she was in love with Julia? What if her feelings went unrequited and she killed Julia out of blind anger and passion? I never liked what-ifs. They made me feel antsy, restless, and obsessed. But the content of the photo message created a doubt in my mind and left room for little else.

The German butcher knife that I tucked between the cushions of the armchair pressed against my thigh. I wasn't keen on using it, but if Brooke didn't come up with a reasonable explanation and perhaps became aggressive once I told her I knew her secret, I might have to use the knife to defend myself.

I'd come to like Brooke during these past few months. She cared about me and accepted who I was. She mothered over me, and I appreciated her for taking me in on a promise of a simple letter that could have been easily a forgery.

My suspicious mind, full of conspiracy theories, made me feel guilty, yet the distinct possibility that I misread Brooke nagged at me. I prided myself on being a darn good judge of character, and the possibility that I misjudged Brooke made me question that ability.

As I flicked the reading lamp on and off, I revisited my times spent with Brooke, looking at them from a new angle. Had she ever approached me intimately or touched me in any other way than a mother would caress her daughter?

No, that never happened. Brooke was a decent woman and a great friend. So why was I having second thoughts about her character?

As doubt wriggled its way into my mind, I turned over the print I made from the photo Helen texted me and looked at it again. There was no doubt in my mind that the woman sitting at Julia's table in the picture was Brooke Russell: my boss, my accomplice, my friend. Her being at the crime scene hours before Julia disappeared made absolutely no sense; her not telling me about it made even less sense.

Unless she was hiding something.

The grandfather clock chimed nine when the bright beams from a set of headlights wiped across the living room ceiling. I heard a car engine shut off, a car door slam, and Brooke's footsteps on the gravel as she approached the house. The front door opened and closed with a familiar soft thud.

I spotted the weak glow of her phone screen casting a blue shine onto the walls as she moved along the unlit hallways toward me.

I flipped the switch, illuminating myself sitting in the armchair.

As if suffering from a bad conscience, Brooke jumped and dropped her phone. "What in the name...Annie?" she grunted at me.

I tossed the print to her feet. It landed by her toes, image up.

She picked it up along with her cell phone.

I remained seated, watching her turning on more lights to brighten the room.

"Where did you get this?"

"What were you doing on the cruise ship on the night Julia was pushed into the ocean?"

She placed her purse, keys, and phone on the table by the door and turned to face me. "I brought her the contracts. She had the whole Rose family together in one place, and on the last night of their vacation, she was going to execute her plan to sever ties legally with Tony's family. She needed me there. I boarded the ship two days after them in Mexico. We didn't tell the Roses why I was there. But I guess it was rather obvious because I experienced a fair amount of hostility from them. They knew about Julia's plan; it wasn't a secret. I guess my presence made it real."

"Why didn't you tell me about this?"

"You didn't ask."

I grabbed my forehead in disbelief. "Why would I ask about something I had no idea about? Does that make sense to you?"

"It's irrelevant if I was there or not. Julia never had an opportunity to sign the papers. She disappeared before we could have the family meeting."

I jumped out of the chair to confront her. "Of course it's relevant that you were there! It makes you a suspect like everybody else who was there."

Brooke tossed her hands in the air and returned to her purse, from which she removed a pack of Marlboro Lights.

"If you think I'm a suspect, then so are the other two thousand passengers on that ship."

I pierced her with my eyes. "Did you kill her?"

The lighter fell from her hand before she could light her cigarette. "You can't *possibly* be serious. What reason would I have to kill her?"

"It doesn't matter if you had a reason or not. You were there, and you didn't tell me."

Shaking her head vehemently, she picked up the lighter and lit her cigarette with trembling hands. "I'm fifty-two years old. There are a million things I haven't told you."

I scoffed. "This is a little bit different, don't ya think?"

She exhaled the cloud of smoke right into my face. "No, I do not think it's different. I know I didn't try to kill Julia, and you should know it too. I took you in on your word, and on what, a beat-up diary you told me was Julia's? If we start questioning each other, then *I* should be the one asking the questions."

Watching her puffing away made me ache for a smoke, but I was too proud to ask her for one, so I marched off to the kitchen for a beer. I yanked the refrigerator door open, glass jars clinking against each other on the racks, and took out a bottle of IPA.

I held the door open for a moment.

Then I grabbed a second one.

Back in the living room, I offered one bottle to Brooke. "Here."

She hesitated to accept my peace offering, and after leaving me hanging for a moment to make her point, she ripped the bottle out of my hand. Her gesture empowered me to bum a cigarette off her.

I sipped at the beer and lit the cigarette, watching Brooke remove her jacket and scarf. She seemed calm—annoyed, but calm.

"I don't know what to think. I'm so fucking confused. I don't know what's up or what's down anymore."

Brooke opened her arms. "Welcome to real life, kid."

"Don't do that."

"Do what?"

"Treat me like I'm a child."

She threw her hands into the air, giving up, and started toward the kitchen.

I followed her like an embarrassed puppy that had just pooped inside the house.

"How did the meeting go with Tony?" she asked over her shoulder. She took out two frozen dinners from the freezer and placed one of them in the microwave.

I opened the drawer to get us forks. "You know, I don't think Tony is our killer. He truly seems to care about Julia and her son. I don't get a killer's vibe off of him."

"Bundy was a charming man. The Unabomber was known as a caring, kind man—strange and antisocial perhaps, but nice, nonetheless. Don't let him fool you. Most domestic murders are committed by the spouses and driven by greed or jealousy."

I rubbed my face. "I don't know. Maybe I'm just too tired to think straight."

The microwave hummed on, and we looked at each other with a strange hostility between us. "Did you see anything suspicious on the cruise?"

Brooke took off her glasses, shaking her head, and rubbed the bridge of her nose. "Don't you think I've asked myself the same question a million times? No, I didn't see anything unusual. I mean, the mood was definitely heated during the game night, but after Julia and Tony left the piano bar, Barbara suggested we all go back to our cabins and call it a night. I went back to my lonely little hole and got shitfaced. Is that what you wanted to hear?"

"You got drunk, so what?"

Three beeps marked the end of the heating process for the food. Brooke took out one dinner in a plastic tray and placed the second one in the microwave.

"She called me because she needed my help ... and I ... I let her down."

Her voice was breaking. I thought she was going to cry. Out of instinct, I wrapped my arms around her like I used to hug the little girls and boys in the brothel when they were crying.

Brooke signed. "Before you showed up here, I kept telling myself that she must have died on her way down, or on impact. From that height, dropping onto the water is like hitting concrete. But since I know that she survived the fall and most likely swam for a while or tread water until she passed out, I can't get the picture out of my head. I feel ... *responsible*."

I loosened my grip on her. "You know, Julia believed a school of dolphins saved her life. She kept having these dreams about riding on the back of something rubbery and slippery. She wasn't alone in the dark waters."

"Thanks, Annie, for saying that, even if it is highly unlikely. But the idea of Julia riding on dolphins to the safety of the shore is a much nicer picture in my head than imagining her drowning in cold, black water."

With trays of microwave dinner in our hands, we returned to the living room.

Brooke kicked off her shoes and plopped onto the sofa. She pulled the ashtray closer to her on the table and put out her half-finished cigarette.

"Do you want to stop? Forget our plan?"

Covering the bite of mushy chicken and broccoli in my mouth with my hand, I said, "No, that's not it. I think we have a good plan. I was wondering if I should start going after Sylvia, though. Women can be downright evil when it comes to protecting the things they love, and Sylvia *loves* money."

Brooke set her tray on the carved, polished wooden table and washed down her dinner with a big gulp of beer. "What's your plan with her?"

"She thinks her health is fragile. I should make her sick—truly sick. Most people confess their sins when they believe they're dying."

"How will we get her confession? Hire a fake priest?"

"Or we send her to your therapist friend."

Brooke pushed the beer bottle closer to me on the table and went to pour herself something stronger. "It might work. Any ideas about how to make her sick?"

"I've been thinking about it: a regular dose of laxative in her food would work, a little arsenic perhaps—not enough to kill the bitch, only enough to give her excruciating stomach pain. Slipping a few drops of acid in her facial creams. Liquid nicotine in her drinks, or pulverized glass."

"Geez, I can't believe I let you live with me. Maybe I should update my will with a footnote naming you as my killer if I were to die under suspicious circumstances." She laughed, and I laughed with her.

"Maybe you should," I said, sinisterly. "But, in all seriousness, when you work in the kind of place I worked as a young girl, you come up with all kinds of ideas on how to hurt the people who hurt you."

"Well, try not to let revenge overpower your life. Grief and revenge can consume you, trust me, I know."

Brooke's face had darkened, making me wonder what else she was hiding from me. Whatever it was, I had to accept that I wouldn't find out about it today. I needed her support, financially and emotionally. And even if it was hard to admit, I cared about her. But caring makes you vulnerable, and I didn't come here to get hurt again. No human would ever have that kind of power over me ever again.

"Let's grab more drinks and see what the bastard is up to tonight," offered Brooke.

As determination and suspicion turned my thoughts sinister, I walked behind her down the hallway and toward the surveillance room, making a plan to ransack her office tomorrow when she was out of the house.

If Brooke was being honest, then no harm, no foul.

12

The last few days had taught me that if Brooke had any dirty secrets hidden from me, she was smart enough to keep them outside of the house. I couldn't find any discerning or remotely suspicious material about Brooke, and not for my lack of trying. It wasn't only the interior design of Brooke's house that lacked a personal touch. Her cabinet drawers and closet contents gave away little about the person who lived in the house. Did she always clean up her trail of breadcrumbs, or did she feel the need to safeguard her life from me? I didn't know. I only had the glimpses of Brooke's life she was willing to reveal to me. And even if I felt I could trust her and considered her to be my closest friend and ally, I realized that I didn't know Brooke at all.

Since the night I accused Brooke of lying to me and being a possible suspect in Julia's murder, I'd spoken little to her. I made a habit of not leaving my room until I heard her drive off to work. In the evenings, I stayed away, roaming the city or having a few drinks in dingy bars to pass the time until she'd gone to bed so I could save myself a confrontation.

I knew I would have to look her in the eyes eventually. I was only delaying the inevitable.

When I lay in bed alone, I became more conscious of the murmurs of nature outside of my window. Somehow, I'd become more aware of my surroundings than before when my mind was synched with Brooke's. I missed the connection we'd developed over the last few months, the times we spent spying on Tony or cooking up evil plans over a few drinks. My disconnection from Brooke was sudden, as if someone had cut the string linking us, leaving behind a hollow feeling of loneliness.

I still spied on Tony, but I did it mostly alone.

Did Brooke withhold information from me? Yes, but I shouldn't have attacked her so vehemently. Julia trusted her. I should've at least given her the benefit of the doubt before accusing her of such horrible things. I'd been burned so many times, and it was quite possible that I could no longer trust a human being. Without overcoming my shortcomings, I was only cutting the tree underneath me.

Brooke didn't need me. She was a financially established woman with powerful friends and complete control over her life. My life story was one that any self-respecting woman would do anything to hide. Compared to Brooke, I was a useless, worthless, lost little girl who tried to play dress-up and pretend to be someone else— someone better. From the first day I crossed the threshold of Brooke's house with my single plastic bag of belongings in hand, I anticipated the moment she would tire of me and kick me out. I might have just given her a reason to make that happen.

I curled up in a ball on my bed, contemplating my options. Who could I turn to if I needed someone to talk to?

My mind conjured up the image of my adoptive mother. I could pick up the phone and call her or send her a message on Facebook. I imagined how she would react. Would she cry? Would she say she has missed me?

She was at a ballet recital with my sister only two days ago. Their life functioned fine without me as if I'd never been part of their family. Did they even think about me after so many years of being gone? Did they blame me for not listening to their words of caution and believing a stranger instead?

My mind went to the last memory I had of my mother. She was twisting a kitchen towel in her hand, the smell of burnt butter filling the air. "You are not going to end up like your mother!" she screamed at me. "Now go to your room and forget about that man. He isn't good for you. He is nothing but trouble!"

At fourteen, I was already a willful little thing. I hated to be compared to my mother, especially after I'd given up bone marrow to save her life, and once she had what she wanted, she disappeared.

Again.

She had a new family with two children a decade younger than me. She never was accepted to Penn State and probably didn't even finish community college, yet she was allowed to have children. My grandparents forced her to give me up because I was in the way of her bright future. Then why did she never come back for me when her future prospects dimmed down?

My adoptive mother knew how deep her words cut me whenever she suggested I'd follow in my mother's footsteps. She should have known me better. I could never have been as callous as Jessica.

The more I considered calling my adoptive mother, the more I realized she wouldn't offer me any comfort. She'd blame me for what happened. She would say she told me that man was trouble. I knew I'd made a mistake. I paid dearly for my childish naïveté and lack of discipline. I didn't need her to remind me of the consequences.

Besides, by making contact with my family, I'd be putting them in harm's way. The cartel likely had surveillance on my childhood home in case I showed up there. They'd be eager to snatch me, execute me, or drag me back to their whorehouse. I'd kill myself before going back to Mexico.

The blood buzzed in my ears from overthinking my life. Restlessness was taking hold of me. I couldn't breathe.

Before Brooke returned home from work, I left the house and walked down the street to get some fresh air. I was walking faster than usual. Random self-degrading words swirled inside of my head: Idiot. Failure. Disappointment. I tried to steer my mind to the pleasant moments I'd shared with Brooke in the past three months: our times cooking breakfast, our failed attempt at making homemade doughnuts, the laughs we shared sitting on the patio.

I started to walk faster.

What should I do? Apologize to Brooke? What if saying sorry wasn't enough anymore? What if she accepted my apology but asked me to leave anyway? She would be fine without me, but where would I go? What purpose would I have without the pursuit of Julia's killer? Without money and friends, I'd end up back in Palmdale with my family or on the street. Both options meant the end of me.

I should apologize to Brooke.

But what if Brooke did have something to do with Julia's disappearance? What if I was looking the other way because I was scared of losing everything Brooke offered me?

A car zipped by me on the dark street, startling me from my musing. I stopped to get my bearing. Without realizing it, I'd walked to the house of Brooke's therapist friend.

Giving in to Brooke's nagging, I had agreed to take a few sessions with her to help me heal the wounds of my past. We came here to Valerie's private residence for an introduction a while ago, but the therapy sessions were at her office in New York City.

I wasted an hour on three different occasions sitting on her sofa in silence.

Therapy wasn't for me. My anger and resentment for the world were what motivated me to find Julia's killer. My desire for revenge was what I needed to find the person who pushed Julia off the cruise ship. Healing my wounds would have robbed me of that drive. I had to keep my wounds open and raw. I needed that pain to drive me.

Besides, what would talking about my shameful past and mistakes accomplish anyway? Even Brooke looked visibly uncomfortable when the topic of child prostitution arose. It's a dark stain on our society, a boogeyman, that ordinary people can't digest and officials won't do much to eliminate. It's like a dirty secret nobody wants to know about in their own backyards. Whenever a kid went missing in our neighborhood, my parents hugged us a little tighter. They talked about empathy and pity, but mostly they were relieved it wasn't their child. So, what was the point of talking about my kidnapping? I didn't need anybody's pity or empathy.

"Annie!" I heard my name ringing in the gloomy evening.

I turned to see Valerie standing on her front porch, her arms folded and holding the front of her beige cardigan together. She was a petite, fragile-looking woman in her late sixties and she looked even smaller now in the orange glow of her coach light. She always had an aura of emptiness around her, a look of pain I could sympathize with. This woman knew pain and grief, as I did.

"Hi." I waved.

She stepped down from the stairs and approached me on the sidewalk. "Out for a walk?"

I cracked my knuckles, looking for an escape. "Yeah, I needed some fresh air."

"Would you care to come in for a cup of tea?"

I licked my parched lips and looked behind me to see if someone was out in the neighborhood to see me. The street was deserted and quiet. "I don't want to intrude."

"Don't be silly." She lifted an inviting arm toward me. "Come inside. I'll get the kettle going."

I looked down at the long curving street one more time, taking in its gaping loneliness. Then I stepped inside Brooke's friend's house.

13

Valerie's house was dimly lit and had a musty odor as if it hadn't been dusted for years. She walked in front of me with the slight shuffle of a weary traveler toward the living room, passing cream-colored walls covered with framed family photos. The atmosphere of her home was a clear contrast to her bright and cheerful office. I wondered if this place had seen happier days before the tragedy.

Valerie showed me to a dusty armchair by a window covered with heavy drapes and turned on the lamp on a small round coffee table next to me. The warm glow that spilled over the elegant furniture gave a funeral-home-like feel to the room.

Valerie didn't head toward the kitchen to put on water for the tea. Instead, she opened a door on a cabinet, exposing a hidden bar. She poured two glasses of chocolate liquor from a golden orb-shaped bottle.

"This liquor is better when it's chilled, but I don't mind it either way. Do you want me to get you some ice?"

"It's fine," I said timidly and took a glass from her.

The drink was warm and sweet. I sipped at it, puzzled. Valerie drank down the whole thing and poured herself another one.

"Are you sure I'm not imposing?"

She waved her hand at me. "Not at all. Most of these days I try to avoid the company. I only meet people when I'm at work, but

I'm glad you're here. I wasn't having a good day." She glanced at a teen boy's picture on the table then back at me. Her face looked more shrunken and paler as if she had aged a decade in a moment.

"Do you want to talk about your day?"

"Do you want to see an old woman cry?" She gave me a sad smile.

"You aren't old."

She scoffed. "Our age isn't measured in years but how heavy our heart is."

"Then I'm at least forty."

We shared a cynical laugh—a momentary relief from the tragic life we've shared. She had lost her son. I had lost my innocence and youth. Our story wasn't the same, but our pain bonded us. This woman needed a friend tonight more than I did. My stories wouldn't cheer her up, but maybe if I opened up to her—after three failed attempts—she'd feel some professional satisfaction.

I wedged my hands between my thighs. I noticed an open sore inside my lower arm and started scratching at it. "How much do you know about me? What did Brooke tell you?"

Valerie set her half-empty glass on the table and crossed her legs. "Brooke told me that you were helping her unravel the mysteries surrounding Julia Rose's disappearance. I know you are going after Tony Rose. You look a lot like Julia. It's easy to see why Brooke chose you for this role."

I licked my finger and rubbed the saliva onto the bleeding sore. "Brooke didn't choose me. I had information about Julia. I came to her."

I saw Valerie's shoulders droop. "I'm sorry. I didn't mean to imply that Brooke hired you for a role or something."

I looked up at her to see her reaction to my next statement. "When Brooke hired you for my therapy, did she tell you why I needed counseling?"

"She told me that you had trouble with drugs and that you were keeping some very dark secrets that are eating you alive. She thought you needed professional guidance to find your way back to the light."

I pursed my lips to hide my smile. Nobody in my life had ever cared how I felt. I was punished if I stepped out of line, but no one was ever interested in finding out why I made those choices.

"I was kidnapped at age fourteen and sold to a Mexican cartel in Baja where I worked for seven years as a sex slave before I managed to escape."

Years of practice must have helped Valerie absorb my words without showing shock or pity. I was grateful for that.

"Would you like to tell me more about it?"

I looked down at my hands. "Actually, I wasn't kidnapped. Not really. I tell that to people because I'm ashamed of how naïve and stupid I was."

"You don't have to feel ashamed with me. We all make mistakes and regret them later. Life isn't about what you've done in the past but how you overcome your failures and move forward from them."

Our eyes met for a second. I felt the heat rising to my face and looked away with haste.

"I can tell you about failures because that's all I have."

"Why don't you start at the beginning. Tell me about your family."

"I was adopted as a newborn by a family that was very strict. My adoptive mother controlled every aspect of my life. She would always check my cell phone, my computer. If I got a text during dinner, I had to show it to her. While I was at school she would go into my room and look through my drawers, open my boxes, check my pockets, hoping to find my secrets. She thought she was clever about it, but I always knew she was snooping through my stuff. It hurt me that she didn't trust me, especially as I didn't have anything to hide. I went to school. I had good grades. I did my homework. I was a good kid."

"Did you have any friends your mother didn't like?"

"I only had a few friends. I used to invite them to hang out at our house after school, but my mother would eavesdrop on our conversations and scold us if we said a bad word. Once she even sent a girl home because she thought what we had talked about was inappropriate. After that, I stopped inviting friends over. They didn't want to come over anyway."

Valerie followed my story with gentle nods. I stopped to see if she had any questions, but she motioned to me to continue.

"One day I didn't go home directly after school but went to the mall with friends. I'd turned fourteen and I wanted to taste a little bit of independence. By then, I was an angry teenager because I couldn't get over my birth mother ditching me. I had friends whose parents adored them. They weren't any different from me. I couldn't understand why my mother didn't love me. What made me so unworthy of her love to give me up?"

"It's common for adopted children to blame themselves for their birth parents' actions. They search for reasons as to why their own mother would abandon them. Some kids try to be their best all the time to prove their worth. Others will do anything in their power to fit the stigma they've given themselves of being unworthy. The truth is, it's never the baby's fault. Mothers don't give up their babies because they were crying too much or didn't have a cute face. The reason for adoption is always personal and reflects the mother's current situation, not the child's."

"I wish somebody would have told me that back then, but I couldn't talk about my feelings to my adoptive mother. She hated hearing about Jessica—my real mother's name. And my friends didn't know I was adopted, so I couldn't tell them about my problems either. I was stuck with the secret inside me, making me sick."

I stopped to finish my chocolate liquor and asked for a refill as a deterrent. I no longer wanted to talk about Jessica or my feelings. I supposed if Valerie was going to help us nail Tony, hearing about my journey may help her understand my motivations, but I was not a puzzle she needed to solve.

When Valerie returned from the bar with the refills and sat down, I continued in the direction I wanted to go. "So, I was at the mall with my friends, looking at earrings, acting silly, when this guy walked up to me. He said I was beautiful and that I should be a model. He kept telling me that I could make a fortune with the look I had." I shook my head and closed my eyes. It had been a while since I allowed my mind to revisit those shameful memories.

"It seems to me that you are blaming yourself for believing this guy."

"I knew there were guys who were trouble. My friends warned me not to give out my address or phone number to anybody. But Alejandro was different. He didn't try to invite me somewhere or offer me a job as a photo model. We only talked. That was it. But after that first time meeting him, I thought of him often."

"It's normal for a young girl to be flattered by praise. Did you see him again?"

I'd been chewing on the inside of my mouth and now tasted blood. Talking about Alejandro always made me anxious and uneasy. Falling for him was a horrible mistake. The memories remained an open sore on my heart. He was unfinished business that would haunt me for the rest of my days.

"A few days later, I ran into him again at the mall. We talked again. He bought me ice cream and a pair of earrings. I didn't want to accept them, but he insisted." I made these statements as fast as I could, using short sentences to show Valerie the memory no longer affected me. "Then we started meeting regularly. He'd come to my house, and I'd climb out of the window to spend time with him. We watched the stars from the hood of his car. Ate more ice cream. He seemed to pay attention to everything I said. He asked me about my favorite music. The next time I saw him, he brought me a mixed CD he thought I'd like. When I needed some supplies for art class, he took me shopping. He kept saying how beautiful I was, and I guess for an insecure fourteen-year-old girl who never heard she was beautiful at home, it was music to the ears. My parents didn't want me to dress sexy or cause unwanted attention. They valued obedient behavior over appearances. Sports for girls was only another way to flaunt their bodies, so I wasn't allowed to play. So, hearing from a stranger that I was beautiful was mesmerizing." *Here we go again. I'm trying to explain my decision by passing the blame.*

"It's common for teenagers, boys and girls, to seek approval outside their circle of family and friends."

"I guess I was a statistic, then, because I had become obsessed with Alejandro. He seemed to understand me. He listened to my problems. He cared about me. And I opened up for him like a book." I hesitated to finish my chain of thought because humiliation began to bubble up in me. But I was already stripping naked in front of Valerie, so what the hell? "I loved him," I admitted, then waited for the therapist to tell me that the situation I found myself in was my fault.

"Most teenage loves are infatuation-based. That's why girls at this age are so vulnerable. You're not the first, or the last, to fall for a sly fox in sheep's clothing."

"I should have known better." I insisted on proving to her that it was my fault.

"Did your parents ever warn you about those types of men?"

I scoffed. "No way. Emotions. Boys. Sex. These topics were taboo in my house."

"A mistake many parents make. We don't treat our kids as equals to us. We try to control them and force our wills on them without listening to what they need or want." Valerie's eyes glossed over as if she weren't only talking about other parents but herself.

I refused to cry, so I hurried along. "Well, my secret didn't last long. A neighbor told my mom that she saw me getting out of a man's car, and she flipped out. She was going to cut me off from my boyfriend and my personal life. She threatened me with total surveillance. I couldn't bear the thought of not seeing my boyfriend again. I called him and asked him to come and get me. I snuck out of the window in the middle of the night, and we went for a drive. He said he couldn't live without me. I told him I couldn't either. I cried. He suggested we do something to stop my mother from separating us. He said we could go to Mexico and spend a few days at his uncle's tropical resort until my mother calmed down. Make her miss me. I didn't have a passport, but he said it was okay because I could hide in the trunk of his car while we crossed the border. I believed him, and when he popped his trunk ten minutes away from the Mexican border, I climbed inside willingly." I buried my face in my hands, trying to hide my shame. That moment of stupidity still gave me chest pain.

I avoided looking at Valerie as I continued. "The next time the trunk opened, two men dragged me out of the car and down a flight of stairs into a basement." I shook my head and let out a nervous chuckle because my story sounded insane, even to me. Maybe if I had heard more stories about strangers and wicked men who kidnapped women and kept them in basements, I'd have been more cautious. I'll never know.

Valerie handed me a box of tissues. I took a couple and blew my nose.

"I know what you must think of me. I think the same."

"You were entrapped by an experienced con man. You were innocent. None of this is your fault."

"It was my fault. I should have never trusted a stranger over my parents who loved me."

"If we knew the consequences of all of our actions, then nobody would ever make a mistake."

I wiped my nose.

"What went through your head while you were locked inside the trunk? I assume you suspected that something was wrong when you spent more time inside of the trunk than expected."

"First, I was lying there, thinking of warm sand and blue water. I was nervous because we only kissed before and Alejandro never pushed me to do more. I wanted to give him something to repay his kindness. But I was a virgin then, and I didn't know how to…you know. Then when the car kept driving for a long time, I began to worry. I thought maybe he had to get far away from the border to open the trunk safely. But then I started to get thirsty and had to pee. I banged on the trunk, but the car didn't stop. Then I screamed, but he kept going. I started to panic. When we finally stopped, my face was numb from crying."

"Have you looked him up since you escaped your captors?"

I expected Valerie to lay another line of wisdom on me or try to explain away my bad decisions, but not a straight question like that. "I did. He's dead. OD-ed four or five years ago in some dingy motel room."

"I assume you held resentment against him for tricking and betraying you. Did you think about confronting him while you were in captivity?"

"Oh, yeah. All I could think about for years was to have a chance to see him again and ask him how he could do that to me."

"Do you see Tony Rose in the same light as Alejandro?"

I clenched my jaw as shock took me aback. Sometime during the evening, Valerie had transformed from a grief-stricken old lady in need of company to a professional headshrinker, and I didn't notice.

She moved to sit beside me. "Do you feel short-changed for never having a chance to confront your kidnapper?"

I held her gaze. "No...I mean, I don't know." She made me feel confused.

"Is it possible that you decided to pursue justice for Julia because you couldn't get it for yourself?"

"What Brooke and I are doing has nothing to do with me."

She took my hand. "I believe you, but I'm also worried about you. I spoke to Brooke about this when she asked me for my help. You know I am willing to do anything I can to get justice for Julia, but I don't want you two to get ground up in the process."

I jolted up from the sofa. "You don't need to worry about me."

Valerie joined me. "You two are good?"

"Yeah, we're fine. Why wouldn't we be?"

She sighed deeply. "We can't always fix the mistakes from our past. Sometimes living one day at a time means we've already turned over a new leaf."

Like you're doing? I wanted to ask but nodded instead. Valerie was a therapist who didn't follow her own advice. It was like Brooke preaching to me about a healthy lifestyle. Why do people who are full of advice never live by their own principles?

I checked my phone and pretended to be shocked at how late it was. "I think it's better if I head home. Brooke must be worrying about me."

Valerie escorted me to the door and stayed on the porch as I walked away, her figure fading into the evening mist. I half walked, half ran home, chased by the demons of my past. It was a mistake talking about my past because it made me feel weak and vulnerable.

I stopped for a moment to text Valerie and asked her not to mention our little meeting to Brooke.

The one good thing that came out of recalling my past was that it made me remember that just because people are nice to me, it doesn't mean they have good intentions.

14

It had been one hundred and eight days since I first arrived in New York City, and exactly fourteen days since Brooke and I declared psychological warfare on Tony.

A lot had happened in the past two weeks, but to my dismay, it resulted in little progress for my investigation.

The identity of the person who attempted to kill Julia remained a mystery, and the failure and frustration were starting to get to me.

At least Brooke and I were on good terms, or I should say we were on better terms. I never had the chance to apologize to her because she beat me to it. She said she regretted not telling me that she was on the cruise ship the night Julia disappeared. After her apology, mine seemed irrelevant.

I played Julia's ghostly voice to Tony every night, driving him to the edge of insanity. But Brooke seldom joined me. I felt more alone than ever.

My mood had darkened to the point where my attitude had become blatantly nippy. Every little sound and movement irritated me. I'd sit in the kitchen with a cup of coffee, cursing out the landscapers for using their lawnmower and leaf blower somewhere in the neighborhood every damn morning. I was angry at the pilots flying helicopters over our property and at the firemen for using their sirens as they raced along the main street.

I stooped so low as to yearn for the quiet of the whorehouse in Mexico. I may have sounded ungrateful, but I needed a moment to gather my thoughts. I needed peace. But I wasn't getting either of them.

I knew I had hit an all-time low when the singing of birds in the woods started to irritate me. Every day and every night, the land around Brooke's mansion turned into a freaking National Geographic nature episode. The crows and ravens croaked, the owls hooted, dogs barked, mourning doves cooed, and raccoons lurked and rustled under my window. But the most annoying of them all was the family of nightingales. Every goddammed night they sang an array of disparate melodies in rapidly changing tunes that kept me up all night.

When I complained to Brooke about the noise around the house, she said that staying up half the night in the surveillance room and spying on Tony every waking moment wasn't good for my mental health. She warned me that the mind needed rest, and if I kept up with this obsessive behavior, then it wouldn't end well for either of us.

She was right, of course, but how could I sleep when that rich bastard still hadn't admitted to his crime or proved his innocence. I should have followed my plan and gone after Sylvia, but I had become obsessed with watching Tony's daily life. I couldn't move on to another suspect until we'd ruled out Tony one hundred percent. And Brooke wasn't much of a help.

According to my adoptive mother, I always had a self-destructive side. She may have been right because I decided to take another look at Brooke. By snooping around Brooke's house to find her skeletons, I dug myself an even deeper emotional hole.

Brooke's story of bringing the contract to the cruise ship, per Julia's request, sounded convincing, but like Julia used to tell me, "Trust but verify."

Fortunately, ransacking Brooke's office didn't confirm the results I feared. Brooke wasn't in love with Julia. So my theory of love-gone-bad revenge flew out of the window. She had a man she loved. I found on her bookshelf a photo album of pictures of her life when she was happily married to a guy named Robert Flynn. He must have been sick and spent some time in a hospital—that much I learned from the photographs. And then he passed away. When or how, I didn't know. But based on Brooke's youthful appearance in the pictures, it had to have happened decades ago.

Bluntly bringing forth the information I found in Brooke's office was out of the question. With my recent attack on her about the screenshot from The Newlywed Game recording, I was already walking on thin ice. Admitting my disregard for her privacy would have been the final straw. If she kicked me out, I'd have nowhere to go.

On days when we sat together in front of the monitors, surveilling the daily lives of the Rose family, I attempted to direct the conversation to get Brooke to open up and share about her married life. She never walked into my trap. As irritating as it was, I had to be content with the information I had discovered. And for the time being, that had to be enough.

Despite the chilled atmosphere, we were a good team. We played the recording of Julia's altered voice for Tony every night. He started to crack. I could tell by the increasing amount of alcohol he consumed each night. By the end of the second week, he refused to sleep altogether. Leaving the lights on in the bedroom, Tony would sit on the bed, pressing against the headboard and hugging a pillow. He looked like a scared little boy waiting for a monster to step out of his closet.

Some nights, I would find him sitting on a barstool in the kitchen in a pair of boxers and a wrinkled white T-shirt, his fingers wrapped around a bottle of vodka, with no glass. He began looking like a man at the end of his rope. As the days went by, his five o'clock shadow turned into a spotty beard and his hair grew into an uncombed mess.

Watching a once confident man start to weaken began to get to me. I told myself that no man would ever evoke any compassion from me again, but I was breaking my own rule, and Brooke was watching me like a hawk.

My only consolation was that Tony had support. Barbara, his mother, had become a frequent visitor to the house. She arrived in the morning to take Sam to school and brought him home in the afternoon. She fixed snacks for her boys: hot dogs, PB&Js, grilled cheese sandwiches, or she brought pies from Costco and coffee from Starbucks, leaving no cliché untouched.

The jury was still out on my feelings for Barbara. She seemed to enjoy gulping down big glasses of red wine or a few mixed drinks in her son's company on the patio. She certainly had a sweet tooth. I frequently caught her attacking the pies with a fork in the kitchen.

One day, she might arrive dressed nicely and cook a decent meal or tidy up the house. The next, she'd show up at the house tousled, appearing disoriented as she bumbled around the house, accomplishing little except for making me wonder if she had a split personality.

None of my notes about Barbara were alarming or even noteworthy. The only thing I considered odd was that Bill never accompanied his wife to Tony's house.

Then, after two weeks of sleepless nights and anticipation, we finally had a breakthrough one morning.

Tony called Brooke and complained about his insomnia. Though he didn't mention his hallucinations, he asked for the number of the therapist that Brooke used to see years ago, which Brooke had been hinting at for days.

I thought Tony's comment presented me with an unmissable opportunity to pry Brooke for the truth about her past, but she shot me down, saying her counseling sessions weren't any of my business.

Brooke was a tough woman. A survivor. A warrior in a man's world. Admitting weakness was not an option for her. I'd learned that much living with that strong, lonely woman.

I was trimming the rose bushes at the back of the veranda to take my mind off of things when Brooke opened the sliding door, holding her cell phone high. "We got a date!" she exclaimed, her face glowing with excitement. "Tony called Valerie. He made an appointment for tomorrow at three."

Swept away by the good news, I pressed down too hard on the stem of a red rose, and it pricked my finger. Blood oozed from the tiny wound, soaking through my glove.

"Is she ready? She knows what to do, right?"

Brooke made a face. "You can trust her. She won't let us down."

"This is the best news I've heard all week." I dropped the clipper into the basket on top of the cut roses.

"Are you done?" Brooke asked, holding the door. "If yes, then come in quickly—I have a surprise for you."

I didn't like surprises. Maybe when I was a little kid I enjoyed them—a secret party, a big bag of presents—but not anymore. Not since I learned how painful surprises could be.

My stomach was tight as I approached Brooke.

She ushered me back into the kitchen, where an eccentric-looking woman was standing with a big, boxy suitcase dangling from her hand.

"Where can I set this down? It's heavy," the woman said in a thick accent that I didn't recognize but guessed to be Eastern European.

"Here, let me help you," offered Brooke, relieving the woman of her luggage.

My uneasiness heightened as I took in the woman's appearance. She was pale-skinned and skinny, her collarbones showing in the V-shaped opening of the neck of her floral top. Three oval stone pendants were hanging, connected, and increasing in size on a leather strip necklace. A collection of thin bangles jingled on her wrist as she passed the suitcase to Brooke. Once relieved of the weight, she grabbed her lower back, moaning as she stretched her spine. She wore a headband, pushing back her brittle, washed-out red hair with exposed gray roots. Her face was round. Her facial features were small and insignificant.

"This is Lena. She's a psychic, a medium, from Poland. We will be conducting a séance tonight," Brooke announced breezily as if simply stating our dinner plans for the evening.

I set the basket and my gloves on the kitchen counter. "A séance for what?"

"We will attempt to invite Julia's spirit here tonight," said the woman.

I thought of the day when I was reading in the library and the window slammed open, scaring me half to death. It was only the stupid house cat that had jumped at me and not a ghost, but still, my heart had leaped out of its cage. I didn't want to feel that again.

Ignoring the witch, I looked inquisitively at Brooke. "You know that Julia won't have the answers to our questions," I said without actually saying what I meant: murder, killer.

"I know, but I thought it would be fun to try summoning her. I thought you'd be up for it." She opened the top cabinet and lifted out a bottle of red wine. She poured it into three glasses and topped them off with Sprite.

I took the spritzer from her. "What do we need for this séance?" I grimaced.

The woman called Lena unlocked her case and lifted out a round tabletop folded into quarters. "Where can I put this?"

Brooke led the woman to the family room, where she removed the chess set from a small square table.

"Would you mind grabbing the candles from my suitcase?" Lena looked at me as she pointed to her luggage.

Fuming, I strode to the kitchen and crouched by her stuff. It was full of junk; I refused to look at it. The whole idea of talking to someone in the afterlife was nonsense. But I couldn't help seeing the picture of Julia that Brooke must have given to the witch. Staring at her photo, I decided to give this foolishness a try. Maybe if I expected an otherworldly visitor, and it wasn't a surprise, it might not be so scary.

I returned with the three candles and followed the woman's instructions, setting them in a circle in the middle of the round tabletop.

"To increase our chances of making contact with Julia, do you have something of hers? Hair. Tooth. A piece of skin or nail."

That was a bizarre request. "No, we don't keep pieces of nails or the skin of dead people around. What do you think this is? *The Silence of the Lambs*?" I grunted, convinced once again this was utter nonsense.

"Tony never threw out Julia's personal items from their bathroom. Her hairbrush should still be there with her hair tucked inside," Brooke said as if the witch's request wasn't awkward.

"That would work," said the witch, like she knew what she was talking about.

"How is that gonna help us?" I complained.

Brooke bobbed her head with a sinister smile. "Sam's with his grandparents' and Tony's checked in at the Four Seasons. He told me he needed to get out of the house for a while. He asked me to call my concierge friend there to get him a suite."

Brooke's eyes bore into me in a mischievous way I'd never seen before.

"Why are you looking at me like that?" I asked.

"Are you up for a little breaking and entering?" she said, then gulped down her wine spritzer. Without allowing me to reply, she turned to the witch. "Give us an hour. We'll get you what you need."

15

After leaving the witch (whose real name was Lena Gorski, and she wasn't a witch but a Polish immigrant) alone in the house, I jumped in the car with Brooke to drive to Tony's house.

Beautiful lush trees and oversized luxurious homes raced by the windows as we drove on the darkening streets dimmed by the setting sun. I looked over at Brooke, driving with determination, noting her childish excitement.

When I first arrived in New York, I'd followed Brooke around for five days before making contact.

My first impression of her was that she was an angry, bitter woman, hardened by what I assumed was a tough life and the monotony of her days.

Like clockwork, she showed up at her office at the same time every morning. She wore dull-colored pantsuits, indistinguishable and boring. I imagined her going into a department store and buying the same-style outfits from the rack.

She bought lunch every day at the same deli. Sitting alone, she would eat her soup and sandwich, and either a cookie or a brownie, and wash it all down with Diet Coke.

She made it easy for me, or anybody else, to observe her. Her attention was so focused on the screen of her cell phone that the whole world could have come crashing down around her and she would have missed it. Once, I even managed to steal her handbag off the backrest of her chair. In the deli's restroom, I shuffled through the contents of her bag—just to get a better feel of who she was. After all, I was supposed to trust this strange woman with the biggest secret of my life.

I'm not sure what I expected to find, but I remembered returning her purse with a sense of disappointment. She didn't even notice it missing.

When she finished her lunch and left the deli, I felt a strange connection to her. She had prescription medication for anxiety in her handbag—hydroxyzine (25 mg), little green pills. I wasn't the only one hooked on drugs. Here was this privileged woman with all the money and success on earth, yet she was scared and stressed, just like the rest of us.

Brooke seemed to be driven by duty and devotion, not allowing herself ever to be spontaneous or even silly. I hadn't planned on doing such a lengthy reconnaissance of her daily routine, but the woman intimidated me, and I kept pushing back the date to approach her. Of all the horrible people I'd encountered in my life, I hadn't expected to be scared of a crusty old attorney.

But I was running out of money. My motel room bill was sucking me dry financially. Driven by dire need, I entered the tall office building in downtown Manhattan and took the elevator to the Russell & Associates office located on the twenty-eighth floor.

Without an appointment, I couldn't get past the front desk attendant. I had to plead with the snobby, anorexic woman to call Brooke and tell her I was here regarding Julia Rose.

In hindsight, I know I was wrong to blame the receptionist for not taking me seriously. I looked like a runaway from a halfway house dressed in tacky clothes and bleached hair with my dark roots exposed. Even my hygiene was questionable. I owed my transformation from ugly duckling to beautiful swan to Brooke.

But there is power in love and friendship, no matter where you come from or who you are, and the mention of Julia's diary granted me access to Brooke's office.

I marched toward the double wooden doors, the worn notebook pressed to my chest and a grin painted on my face, like a hero who carried an invaluable artifact.

Two hours later, I was still in Brooke's office, where I watched her reading through the stained and torn pages from the opposite side of her desk. Other than canceling all her calls and appointments for the day, the grimacing hag never looked up from Julia's diary. Not once.

Her eyes lingered longest on the final page. Julia never had a chance to finish the diary and give it a conclusion. It abruptly cuts off mid-thought, so there wasn't much to read on the last page, yet Brooke stared at the half-blank page for long minutes as I sat there watching her.

At last, she closed the notebook and set it carefully on her desk as if it were a fragile glass ornament. "How much money do you want for this?" she asked, coldly indifferent.

Without a word, I handed her the letter Julia had written at the brothel for me to give to Brooke if I ever got out, explaining her wishes and instructions regarding her money. Julia had asked her loyal attorney's help to support me on my mission to find out who had pushed her over the railing and to her *death*. She asked her trusted old friend to handle me with care because few women in Manhattan had seen the horrors I had experienced.

Brooke unbuttoned her jacket, took off her glasses, and wiped the tears from her eyes. Without a word, she rose from her chair and walked around her desk, where she bent down and embraced me. She cried as I'd never seen an adult woman cry. "I'm so sorry," she kept saying, and somehow during this unexpected display of emotion, I found myself comforting her.

That very day, I moved into Brooke's mansion.

There was no transition to Brooke's transformation. No baby steps. No learning to walk before we ran. One day she was an unapproachable woman, deterring every friendly contact and living her days in utter loneliness. She seemed to find a new purpose in life with me in the house, and she took me under her wings as if I were her long-lost child.

And now here we were, wearing black from head-to-toe, armed with a determination to break into her client's home. Boy, we'd gone far in a short amount of time.

Brooke noticed my stare but didn't question me about it.

She punched my thigh. "Look at us! Two vigilantes on a mission."

"You do know if we get caught, we're screwed, right?" She had sacrificed too much already by helping me.

She gave me a lingering stare with squinting eyes. "There is no situation I can't talk myself out of, darling. But don't worry, we won't get caught."

"All right," I said, swallowing hard and wondering why a foolish séance was so important to her. I didn't believe any of that nonsense, and as a woman of law and order, she shouldn't either. But restoring our friendship was important to me. Maybe this mission was the one that brought us back closer again.

The trip was a short twelve-minute drive. We parked along the curb between two streetlights and planned to cover the rest of the distance on foot.

Before we left Brooke's house, we double-checked the monitors in the surveillance room to make sure nobody was home, but we still had to beat the security system which Tony had hired Kevin, Brooke's brother, to install after the break-ins. When Brooke called her brother from the car, he explained that these wireless systems were safer because nobody could cut the wires, but they did have a weakness. A stronger signal on the same frequency could overpower the system and jam the cameras. Kevin owned such devices and agreed to bring us one.

He didn't park, only pulled up next to us and rolled down his window. Holding a small black box, he extended his hand toward his sister. "I don't want to know. Just leave my name out of it," he said, winking at me before driving off.

Armed with the activated jamming device, Brooke and I scaled the driveway and ran around to the back of the house. Brooke had a spare key to the house that Julia had given her many years ago as a precautionary measure when the entire Rose family had left for a cruise, and we used it to gain access to the house without breaking a window.

The alarm started beeping the moment we set foot inside the kitchen. Brooke raced to the home security panel to punch in the code. Although Kevin told us that Tony had never changed the original passcode, the possibility that he had changed it in the past few days could have determined our fate. As strange as it might sound, the anticipation made me feel alive.

The code worked, and the beeping stopped.

Brooke beckoned me further into the home, and she met me at the staircase, looking both proud and relieved for disabling the alarm.

"People are too trusting nowadays," she remarked, pulling on her collar to signal her pride in gaining us such easy access into her client's home.

"Like you were when you believed every word of some white-trash girl who showed up in your office?"

She snapped her fingers and pointed at me. "Touché."

With the sun nearly set, I urged Brooke to get on with our search before the night swallowed us.

We made our way up the staircase. It was a cautious, slow climb that got my heart racing. The house was supposed to be vacant, but I felt the jitters of a burglar. I was thankful that the floor didn't squeak like in Brooke's house. If it did, it would have sent me over the edge.

Once we reached the second floor, we went straight to the master bedroom to access Julia's bathroom. When I was there to hide the speaker, I didn't have enough time to stop and ponder the significance of this very room. But I felt the importance of me being here now. This room was where Julia had slept for years, where she made love to her husband, where she dreamed.

"Tony's kept everything the same as if Julia still lived here," said Brooke in a low voice. It seemed the same thoughts were haunting her too.

"I wonder why? Is it guilt, or because he truly loves and misses her?"

Brooke looked back from the arched entrance to the bathroom. "Hopefully, we'll find out tomorrow."

I stayed behind by the bed. It was messy—tangled sheets and mounds of blankets suggested that the last person who slept here had a restless night. I took a pillow and pushed it to my face. It smelled like Tony. Disappointed, I set it back in its place.

"I found Julia's hairbrush." Brooke's whisper made me shiver. The room already had an eerie feeling to it. With the curtains drawn, not much street light could seep into the room. There was also a sour odor lingering in the air, and stuff was everywhere.

I tripped over a pair of slippers on my way to the bathroom, where Brooke was pulling out long strands of golden hair from Julia's hairbrush. There was a small bottle of perfume on a tray by the mirror—CK One Shock. I sprayed myself with it. In the second drawer, I found various items of makeup. I ran her red lipstick over my lips.

Brooke looked up from the envelope where she was placing Julia's hair, and her forehead creased. "I don't think the FBI will be investigating a few pieces of missing hair, but it would be wise not to leave too much of our DNA around, don't you think?"

I know she loved Julia like a daughter, but she would never be able to understand the depth of my relationship with her. We were sisters, survivors, and each other's emotional support. We shared our food, our bed, every aspect of our lives. We weren't two people. We were one. And when Julia was gone, it was as if someone had ripped my arm off and left me to bleed to death. It took me a long time to gather myself and pick up the pieces. If Ornelas hadn't sent me to Tijuana, I'd still be licking my wounds in the brothel. But he did send me away, and using the open streets to my advantage, and with a little bit of help, I managed to escape the pimp who bought me.

Touching Julia's things was like a drug to me, like medicine, that would help me grow my arm back. But Brooke was right. I needed to be smarter and more mature.

I nodded at Brooke to acknowledge her point. But when she wasn't looking, I slipped the lipstick into my pocket and closed the bathroom cabinet drawer.

As we headed back downstairs, I found myself dragging my feet. There was so much I wanted to see in the house, so much of Julia's life here to discover.

"Can we stay a little longer?"

Brooke gave me a quizzical look. "Why would we do that?"

I shrugged. I didn't know how to explain to her how I felt.

"The witch is waiting. We need to get going," Brooke said, pulling me with her down the stairs.

She sent me to the patio door and asked me to wait there while she reset the alarm. She was halfway there when the porch light turned on and the silhouette of a figure appeared in the milky glass of the front door.

Brooke came to a sudden halt, then started dashing toward the alarm panel. After just a few steps, she paused, spun around, and ran back to me before freezing again, as if deliberating if she should hide somewhere instead.

"Run to me!" I growled at her under my breath, trying to keep my voice down. I vehemently waved at her to hurry.

The door should have been open by now, but it sounded as if someone were trying several different keys in the lock.

"Run to me!" I called out to her again, and this time she listened to me.

My racing heart almost ripped open my chest from the anticipation.

When Brooke was only a few feet from me, I pressed the single key into the keyhole. Holding the door, I waited for Brooke to pass behind me. When she was clear, I looked up to see the main entrance swinging open as I closed the patio door and locked it.

Breathing heavily, I slipped the key into my pocket and leaped down from the patio. Brooke grabbed hold of my shirt and jerked me back against the wall of the house.

"After all this, you wanna get caught?" she scolded me, waving the jamming device in my face.

"Do you think the camera caught me?"

"I guess we'll find out soon enough."

We stayed low as we made our way back to the front of the house. We spotted a gray minivan parked in the driveway.

"Whose car is that?" I whispered.

Brooke shrugged. "I don't know. A repairman? We can check the monitors when we get home."

She used the jamming device again to override the signals of the front cameras. When it was safe, we ran back to the car as fast as we could.

We both ripped the doors open and jumped inside, panting like runners after a race. I craned my neck to see past the barrier vegetation to the house. The light was on downstairs in the living room, but I couldn't see anybody.

Brooke pulled the envelope from her pocket and checked the hairs inside. Sighing, she leaned back against the headrest. She turned her head to me, a large grin spreading on her face. Despite the severe consequences we might have to face later, we both burst into a fit of laughter.

"Now, that was a rush," Brooke said as she started the engine.

16

After we returned home from the burglary, Brooke marched toward her house, holding the envelope with the strands of Julia's blond hair like a huntress holding her trophy. I followed close behind her, thinking about the mystery person who had shown up at Tony's house as we were fleeing. The intruder's repeated attempts to open the front door and the strange car in the driveway suggested that it wasn't Tony.

My desire to see the person's face on the spy cameras sped me along the stone entryway, disregarding the witch, Lena, who'd sent us to obtain Julia's hair for the séance in the first place.

"Mrs. Gorski, we're back, and we delivered!" called out Brooke, hooting into the stale air of the arched entryway. "Brooke Russell always delivers!"

"When you're done congratulating yourself, meet me in the surveillance room," I told her as I passed her from behind in a hurry. With one misstep, my right foot slipped on something, and I kicked up in the air, falling hard onto my butt. Groaning in pain, I reached for my tailbone.

Brooke crouched beside me. "Are you okay?" she asked, offering me her help to get up.

My hand landed in a wet puddle as I put it down to support myself. "What the...?" I brought my hand to my face and sniffed at the liquid. It was smelly water. "Why is the floor wet?"

Before Brooke could answer, I noticed that her right shoe was muddy and the bottom of her pant leg was soaked.

"Did you step in the pond at Tony's house?" I asked as if I were talking to a naughty five-year-old.

Looking down to examine her shoe, Brooke said, "I must have, but I don't remember. We were in such a hurry to get out of there."

I sighed with a prolonged blink. So far, the day had been a disaster. For starters, I was too tired and grumpy to begin with, and now my tailbone hurt. I wanted to take a long hot bath, go to bed, and welcome tomorrow with a fresh start. I'd had enough trouble for one day. The tomorrow that promised a chance at a bit of success with Tony's therapist couldn't come fast enough.

"I'm going to check the monitors to see who was at Tony's. Why don't you go upstairs and change?" I said to Brooke as I got back to my feet. My butt was throbbing, but the humiliation hurt more. "What do you think about postponing this whole séance nonsense for another day?"

"No, we have what we need, and Lena's already here!" Brooke snapped at me. I could hear the irritation in her voice. "Mrs. Gorski, where are you?" she yelled up the stairs. "Great! She probably robbed us and left."

The witch appeared in the hallway, exiting the study, just as Brooke put her hand on the railing, preparing to go upstairs. Mrs. Gorski dangled a linked chain with a trinket at us.

"There's great spiritual activity in this house. I predict our séance will be a success," she said with her Polish accent.

I threw my hands in the air and walked away from these two crazy women.

I used the passcode on the door to gain access to the surveillance room. The monitors were still active, so it took me only a few seconds to find the intruder who disrupted us at Tony's house. It was Bill Rose, Tony's father. He was sitting on a kitchen barstool, eating ice cream out of the container with a spoon, his cell phone held up to his ear by his shoulder. I increased the volume on the device to hear him talk.

"Nothing so far...I'm in the kitchen...No. No. I'm eating carrots and hummus...I didn't touch the pie...I know about my blood sugar. You and your mother don't have to remind me about it every day...No, I'm not a child...Okay, Tony, I know. I'll call if I experience something unusual...No, I'm not scared. Should I be?...I didn't forget to take my heart medication...Can an old man have some peace?...You asked me to do this. Now let me do it...I'll call you...Okay. See you in the morning."

"Annie," Brooke's panic-stricken voice echoed through the air. "Come up here quickly!"

There was an edge to her voice that suggested she was in trouble, so I jumped out of the chair, slammed the door shut behind me, and raced to the staircase, passing the witch as I bolted up the stairs.

Brooke was sitting on her bed barelegged, no shoes but still wearing her wet socks.

"What the hell is that?" I yelled as my stomach sunk in disgust.

"It's a leech," she said, holding her forehead. "Oh, my gosh, I'm going to pass out. Hand me a cigarette." She pointed to her dresser. Sure enough, there was a pack of Marlboro Lights resting on top, along with a lighter.

Unable to move my gaze from the black slimy creature attached to the back of her lower calf, I pulled out cigarettes for Brooke and me. I lit them simultaneously and handed her one.

"Do you need me to call 911?" I asked, feeling the bile twisting in my stomach.

"Do you have your phone? Google how to remove a leech."

As I was typing the words in the search bar, the witch poked her head through the doorframe. "What is all this ruckus about?" she asked, a can of Sprite in her hand. She must have helped herself from the refrigerator. When her eyes landed on the parasite, her face flushed with excitement. "Oh, look at this cutie! Leeches are extraordinary animals, you know? We've been using them for medicinal purposes for centuries."

"That's great, but do you know how to take it off?" Brooke whimpered, puffing smoke as she talked.

The witch extended her hand toward me. "Give me your credit card."

I looked at her in disbelief. "Nothing is free nowadays, I guess, huh? I shook my head. "I don't have one. Where is your wallet, Brooke?"

"On the dresser," she said hurriedly through pale lips, pointing with her shaking finger. "Give her what she wants. I don't care how much it costs; just get this thing off me."

I pulled out a Visa card from Brooke's leather wallet and handed it to the witch. She ignored my grimace of disapproval. I waited for her to pull out an iPhone with a card reader attached from her pocket, but instead, she knelt by Brooke and pressed the edge of the card against the creature's mouth.

"Once you break the vacuum, they pop off rather easily," the witch explained. I watched her technique, feeling embarrassed by my narrow-minded comment. I'd trained myself not to trust people for years, and my approach impaired my ability to see the good in others. Moments like these told me that I had a long way to go to become an emotionally healthy person, if ever.

"Here she comes," the witch announced with a proud, coy smile. She grabbed the other end of the slimy, worm-looking animal and held it up for us to see. There was smudged blood on Brooke's calf, and I gagged from the thought of the creature sucking her blood.

The witch flushed the parasite down the toilet. Brooke finished two cigarettes and a two-finger brandy I brought up from the family room before she found the strength to get off the bed and put her pants on.

"Look, it's late. It's been a hell of a day. What do you say we cancel this stupid séance?" When I realized that the witch could hear me, I looked at her. "No offense."

"None taken."

Brooke splashed her face with cold water. "You think, after all we've been through tonight, I'm giving up now? This close to the goal?" She grabbed a towel to dry her face. "You heard Mrs. Gorski. This place has great spiritual energy. We have the hair. I'm going through with this tonight if it costs me my life."

There was no point in arguing. Brooke was like a dog with a bone. She wouldn't stop until she'd finished what she started. That's what made her an excellent attorney. She never gave up.

Ten minutes later, the three of us sat around the round tabletop the witch had laid on the chess table as if we were having a casual evening—as if Brooke and I hadn't gone through hell and back to reach this peaceful moment. We were holding hands like a family during a Thanksgiving blessing. The flames of three candles in the middle of the table flickered in the dark, although I didn't feel any breeze in the room. By then, the world outside was dark, as was the inside of the house.

My hands were hot and sweaty. I wasn't sure if it was because I was holding a stranger's hand or because my body reacted that way to my rapid pulse.

I never liked the dark. I feared it when I was a kid, and I feared it now as I listened to a Polish hag chanting and murmuring under her breath. She told us to keep our eyes closed, but I peeked a few times. The glare of the flames highlighted each tiny hair on Lena's pale face. The pores on her skin were unusually big and gaping, though it looked otherwise smooth and healthy.

Suddenly she let go of my hand, grabbed the strands of Julia's hair, and tossed them into the flames. The old brittle pieces immediately ignited, and the smell of burnt hair filled my nostrils. It was nauseating. Not because the smell was horrendous but because it was a part of Julia that entered my lungs. It was like inhaling someone's ashes. Disgraceful and disgusting at the same time.

"Julia Rose, show yourself!" the witch yelled, grabbing ahold of my hand and Brooke's. "I know you are here. Give us a sign!"

I sat unmoving without breath, looking through the slits of my eyes because I was too terrified to close them completely.

From the atmosphere in the room, all the hair on my body was standing on end. Brooke's grip on my hand grew tighter, her nails digging into my flesh. I wanted to scream at her or free my hand, but anticipation immobilized me.

"Julia Rose, give us a sign!" the witch shouted again.

At her commanding voice, the table moved and scraped over my thigh.

I jumped up from my chair like a popup toy, tipping the tabletop over in the process. The candles rolled to the ground with a loud rumbling sound. The hot wax spilled onto Brooke's foot, and she cried out in pain.

As the flames extinguished on the floor, darkness swallowed us.

My heart had never beaten so fast. I felt I had to flee for my life.

Driven by madness, I threw myself toward the wall, tripping over furniture. My hands tapped the wall, fumbling for the switch.

"Turn the damned light on!" Brooke shouted.

"I'm trying," I whimpered.

When my fingers touched a switch, I flipped it on. The brightness illuminated Brooke blowing air onto her toes and the witch sitting in her chair with an expression of utter disappointment about the total mess I'd made. I turned on all the lights in the living room before I approached them.

"Now look at what you've done, Annie. There's wax all over the hardwood floor," groaned Brooke.

Trembling with fear, I said, "I'm so sorry. I told you I couldn't do this." I felt the walls closing in on me, the demons coming for me.

"This floor must be a hundred years old," the witch observed, and Brooke nodded in agreement.

Not able to face the disaster I'd caused, I backed away from the table and ran to my room. I closed the window, shut the blinds, and threw myself onto the mattress on the floor in the corner. Covering my ears with both hands, I started to hum a nursery song I knew—my only comfort when I was scared.

17

Wrapped in my blanket like a cocoon, I watched a spider weaving a beautiful web underneath the windowsill. It was depressing to think about how this corner meant the entire world to this creature and that my room was her universe. If only she had crawled over the ledge and made her way to the other side of the window, she would have found herself in the vast garden. But this little insect paid no heed to the possibilities of a different life. She was too focused on her own little world and her need for survival to consider any other options.

Felt a lot like my miserable life.

Comparing my life to a spider was disheartening. It made me feel primitive. Yet my need for a lifestyle change was screaming at me to take action.

But how could I shed my urge to find the truth about Julia's disappearance? How was I to shake my need to seek justice for someone I loved? How could I walk away from it all? The mere thought was confusing and maddening. And I was losing control.

The only way I knew how to numb the pain and clear my mind was the very thing that was killing me. My adoptive father used to tell me that the world can take everything from you—your name, your wealth, your reputation—but the thing it can't take away from you is what's inside of your head. And you must never stop learning and experiencing life because, in the end, your wits are all you have.

He'd be disappointed to find me ignoring his advice and poisoning my brain.

Maybe I wasn't strong enough to do the right thing. Maybe he believed in me more than I ever believed in myself. Maybe my birth mother was right to abandon me because I was worthless anyway. I wasn't going anywhere; I had no ambitions.

As my thoughts darkened, I felt the strong arms of depression pulling me into the abyss.

I gently grabbed the spider with a tissue and tossed her out the window. I watched her land on a bush. After taking a second to assess her new situation, she disappeared into the greenery.

If it were only that easy for me to start a new life.

I reached for my athletic shoe by the foot of the bed. I slipped two fingers inside and pulled out a small plastic bag of five pills of Vicodin I'd stolen from Brooke's medicine cabinet. She started locking up her bedroom as a safety precaution after I told her how the watchdogs used heroin to control us in the brothel. But what she didn't consider was that picking a lock was a skill I'd also acquired. Hector had kept all the chocolates and sweets locked up in the kitchen, and on days when we desperately craved sugar, we had to learn how to steal without getting caught.

Ignoring the voice of reason in my head, I opened the bag and placed two pills onto my tongue. I didn't know how else to stop the pain in my brain. So, I did what I knew worked.

As I sunk into the welcoming effects of the drug, someone knocked on my door. My fingers tightened around the plastic bag, and I tossed myself back onto the mattress, pulling the covers over me.

A knock echoed again. "May I come in?" Brooke poked her head around the door. "I drew you a hot bath. I put bubbles in it too."

"I'm such a failure. I'm so sorry for the mess I made," I said in a low voice, on the verge of crying.

Like a mother hen, Brooke flung the door open wide and hurried toward me. "No. No. No. Don't say that. What happened isn't your fault. I should have consulted with you before I hired that creepy woman." She shook her head. "I thought it would be a nice distraction for you, but clearly, I didn't consider what summoning Julia's spirit would do to you."

I sat up and crossed my legs, sitting on my hand with the pills in them to hide it from Brooke. "I feel her presence all the time. I'm not sure it's my imagination or if she's truly here. I feel like she's trying to tell me something." I was talking with more emotion than the situation warranted. I noticed it before Brooke had a chance to pick up on it, and I toned it down. "It's scary, you know, seeing her spirit and thinking I may be losing my mind."

It was the first time I'd allowed my actual age to show. I'd been focused on playing the part of an educated, confident woman. Dropping my guard felt good. But one wrong word, one slip-up, and Brooke would find out that I had betrayed her trust. She would kick me to the curb like the previous adults in my life. They all say they love us, but their love has conditions. We are only considered loveable if we do what we're told. But if we dare step out of line or act out, we're labeled a "troubled kid" and prescribed meds. Adults always say they want to help. Teachers. Social workers. The government. All of them use the same empty words, but nobody truly listens. They don't want to hear about our pain. We are only sad little projects for them to post about on social media. Make them look good. Julia was the first person in my life who genuinely cared and listened to me. And now Brooke, who had assumed her role as my protector without ever asking anything from me in return.

Shame descended on me, and I could no longer look Brooke in the eyes. I was scared she would see right through me and read the lies in my eyes—that I was nothing more than a druggie, a thief, and a liar.

Brooke sat down at the edge of the empty bed frame. Without the weight of the mattress, it slid back a little. "You are not crazy. We all have our own ways of processing grief."

She looked away from me. When her eyes returned to me, they were glossy. It was my moment to redirect the conversation to her.

"Have you ever lost someone you loved?"

Her eyes dropped to her lap, where she pinched her hand with her fingers and started to massage it. "I was married once to a wonderful man." She smiled, but it wasn't an expression of joy— rather a sadness. "We were young. Very young," she emphasized.

"I didn't know," I lied, feigning amazement as I recalled the face of the man from the pictures I'd dug up in her office two weeks ago.

"It didn't last long," she explained. "Fate intervened. Death stole him from me." She swallowed hard and looked at me with squinting eyes. "We were in a bar celebrating my twenty-seventh birthday when Bobby got into an argument with another guy. I don't even remember what started it. It was something stupid and banal, I'm sure. But when Bobby had enough of the nonsense and turned away, the guy hit him on the back of the head with a beer bottle. We didn't know it then, but the strike had caused internal bleeding in his brain. Security kicked the aggressor out of the bar, and we left shortly after that. Bobby was complaining about a headache. When we were home, I told him to lie down and rest because his face looked ashen. As he was walking to the bedroom, he fainted and fell to the ground. I called 911 right away, but I was too late to get him help. He died two hours later at the hospital. Just like that," Brooke concluded with an emotionless face as if the story had been told a million times and had lost its shock value to her.

Even though I didn't know her husband, his tragedy touched a nerve. Nobody I loved had ever died in my arms, although I'd seen enough friends beaten to within an inch of their lives.

"My God, that's awful! Did the police ever catch the guy who did it?"

"Nope. Never. He's still out there drinking in bars, dancing with women, enjoying life while Bobby is gone, taking all our hopes and dreams with him. Losing him was as if someone had stolen my future from me."

"Why didn't you tell me about him before?"

"It's not a happy story. I didn't want you to think that because I never found the man who killed my husband we'd never find Julia's killer."

"But it's a possibility. Isn't it? We may never find the killer."

"Anything is possible. I promised you I'd do everything in my power to help you find the bastard, and I stand by that promise. But I'm worried about you. I think you take this investigation too seriously. That's why I hired the medium. I wanted you to lighten up a bit. This whole surveillance of Tony is consuming you. There is life beyond revenge."

I shook my head. "Not for me. Not now. At least, not yet."

Brooke rubbed her right eyebrow, looked down, and sighed. "I spent most of my adult life going to group therapy for people who have lost loved ones. That's how I met Valerie. That's how I know she won't let us down tomorrow when Tony sees her for counseling. She lost her son in a motorcycle accident. Valerie and her husband were driving behind their son and watched him get hit by a car. He died in his mother's arms from a broken rib that punctured his lung. She never recovered emotionally from the loss of her child. Even after all these years, she'll often sit by her son's grave from sunrise to sunset. She does maintain a few clients, enough to pay her bills, but apart from that, she has no life."

"Why are you telling me this?"

"You're still young. You have your whole life ahead of you. I understand that finding out what happened to Julia is important to you; it's important to me as well. But don't let it consume your whole life. I had hoped the séance today would offer us some answers. I was wrong. That woman was fake."

I laughed. "Yeah, she totally moved that tabletop."

"Yeah, fake witch." Brooke laughed with me.

Our laughter slowly died down. "Well, Tony may open up for Valerie tomorrow, and then we can put an end to all this misery."

Brooke's face became serious. "What will you do if we find out it was Tony who tried to kill Julia?"

"Oh, there's no question about it. I'm going to kill the fucking bastard."

Brooke answered my statement with silence, taking her time to offer a conclusion to our discussion. "All right. Go and take a bath before the water gets cold."

She walked out of my room, leaving me alone with my thoughts. "I could totally kill Tony," I assured myself. "I totally could."

*   *   *   *   *

Out of all six bathrooms in the house, the bathroom Brooke offered me on my first day in the house was my favorite. It was open and bright, radiating purity. She had worried that the white tile on the floor and walls, the white vanity, and white porcelain sink and tub would make me feel as if I were in a hospital, but I assured her that compared to the washroom in the brothel, this was heaven.

The steam had already fogged up the mirror when I slipped out of my clothes and sunk myself into the foamy water. As the heat enveloped my body, my worries began to melt away. The Vicodin was taking effect.

Brooke left a lit candle on the edge of the sink because the tub's rim wasn't wide enough to hold it. The scent was vanilla, which wasn't my favorite, but I considered it a sweet gesture anyway. It had taken me a few weeks to allow myself to enjoy a bath, not just jump in, scrub off, and jump out. Here, nobody was knocking on the door, telling me to hurry up. No foreign pubic hair was floating in the water. No blood smears on the floor. Only cleanliness so tangible I could nearly taste it.

I took a deep breath and submerged myself completely, my fingers gripping the edge of the tub. The air bubbles popped in my ears, and my nostrils filled with water. The combination of sensations made me ticklish, but I felt relaxed as the tension slowly left my body. I could have stayed underwater forever, but something cold touched my hand. The sensation was sudden and severe enough for me to jolt out of the water into a sitting position. I sensed someone's presence in the room. I snapped my head around the spacious room, but there was no one there. I was alone. An eerie silence like a thick fog descended on me. The only thing I heard was my own breathing.

I looked at the mirror, where drops of condensation ran together in clear lines. I could make out the letter "B" among the lines. I rubbed my eyes, thinking that the hovering steam in the room was playing tricks on me. When I opened my eyes again, I glimpsed the shower curtain move in the corner of my eye. I jumped in fright, sending water out of the tub.

"Brooke!" I screamed, my heart hammering against my ribs, but received no answer.

There were small puddles of liquid on the white tile near the far end of the bathroom where the splashed water couldn't have reached. There was no physical explanation for it.

"Brooke!" I screamed again.

A slim figure appeared behind the white shower curtain, its silhouette sharp and visible. I sunk underwater to hide—perhaps not physically but mentally.

The soap bubbles were mostly gone from the surface of the water, and when I opened my eyes underwater, I saw a face leaning over me.

Kicking and tossing my arms as if I were being attacked, I splashed out most of the remaining water from the tub. I hit my head, and the impact stilled me. I stared at a crack on the ceiling, unmoving, as if I'd been paralyzed. A powerful jolt pulled at my chest and slowly moved me into a sitting position. I was no longer alone in the bathroom. A woman was standing in front of me, water dripping from her hair and clothes. Worms hung from her clustering locks, and there was dirt underneath her fingernails. This figure was ghastly, but I recognized her. It was Julia. She lifted her arm and pointed at the mirror, which displayed the letter "B."

Utter shock choked the words in my throat. I had no voice. I knew Julia wasn't there to hurt me, yet panic gripped every muscle in my body.

I jumped when the bathroom door flung open. "Did you yell for me?" Brooke asked, wiping her hand on a kitchen towel, an apron covered with flour tied around her waist.

I looked back at the spot where Julia was standing.

She was gone.

I crawled out of the tub like a maniac and wrapped my arms around Brooke's legs. "Sh-she was here!" I panted. "Julia…her spirit! She was here. I saw her!"

Brooke grabbed a large bathroom towel from the hook, wrapped me in it, and helped me to my feet. "What are you talking about?"

"The séance must have worked. Julia's spirit was here in the bathroom with me. Look!" I turned toward the mirror to show the letter "B" written on it to Brooke, but my words slurred when it wasn't there anymore. The writing was erased by a wide messy smear as if someone had cleaned the mirror with a towel.

"What is it? I don't see anything."

As I recognized how my behavior must appear to Brooke, I forced myself to dial it down a bit. "Never mind. I think I'm exhausted. All I need is a good night's sleep."

Brooke rotated me by my shoulders to bring me to look at her. Her probing eyes searched my face. "Did you use?"

I pulled away from her. "No, I didn't use. God, Brooke. When will you stop accusing me of that shit? I'm not a drug addict."

Brooke sighed and flung the kitchen towel over her shoulder. "I don't know, Annie. Maybe it wouldn't be a bad idea for you to go and visit your parents."

Here we go again, I thought. Once I start acting out, people want to get rid of me.

"You know I can't go back. Hector could find me there. I'd only put their lives in danger. But if you want me out of the house, you only have to ask."

She rolled her eyes. "I don't want you out of the house. Don't be melodramatic. I'm merely suggesting that you should get out of this environment for a while and spend some time with people who love you."

"If they loved me, how come they never came looking for me?" I snapped, grinding my teeth.

"You know that's not fair. The world is a big place. They had no idea where you were."

The best way to get someone to leave you alone is to agree with them and do what they deem an appropriate response. "All right. I'll call my mother, but first, I want to see if anything comes out of the meeting between Tony and your shrink friend tomorrow."

Brooke clapped her hands. "All right. Good enough for me. How about you get dressed and come down to the kitchen? I made us pancakes. From scratch."

Although the mere thought of food made me nauseous, I couldn't hurt Brooke's feelings again. No one had ever made me pancakes at ten o'clock at night. "Pancakes sound pretty damn good right about now. I'm coming."

Once left alone, I rushed out of the bathroom to catch Brooke down the hallway. "Do you mind if I sleep with you tonight?"

"In my bed, or do you want to put your mattress in my room?"

"My mattress will do."

She gave me the thumbs-up as she walked back down the stairs. I was too scared to go back to the bathroom, so I dressed as fast as I could in my room, avoiding every mirror along the way. Then I bolted after Brooke, chased by the chill running down my spine.

18

"What time is your friend supposed to be here?" I asked, leaning my shoulder against the door and scratching at the green paint on the sign that read "Dr. Valerie Hawkins."

Brooke smacked at my hand. "Stop that! How many times do I have to tell you? You act so childishly sometimes."

I'd become accustomed to people smacking me around, but it was the first time from Brooke. She must have noticed my shock because her shoulders drooped, and she sighed. "I'm sorry, Annie. I shouldn't have snapped at you."

I'd already forgiven her. Neither of us had slept well last night. Both of our minds were racing and on edge.

"Can't you call her?" I suggested, irritated. "Tony will be here in an hour. What if he shows up early and finds us standing in the hallway like two idiots?"

She threw a hand in the air, rolling her eyes. "She's probably at the cemetery and lost track of time." Brooke made the call, and I used the time to scroll down Helen's Facebook page for any new developments. Ever since I'd convinced her not to post the screenshot of Brooke sitting at Julia's table during The Newlywed Game, Helen approached me with caution.

Her fellow Facebook group moderator, Jeff, had identified three party guests using his facial recognition software, but Helen hadn't called me to let me know. I found out the news from her Facebook posts. The latest photo album of still images from the video revived members' interest. In one week, five new pictures popped up on the wall—all possible sightings of Julia. They were all fake, of course, but I couldn't tell the group. The truth about Julia's tragedy in Mexico would have brought closure to all members and taken the wind out of their sails. Letting them believe Julia was still alive kept them going. More importantly, we had a killer to catch, and I could use any help I could get.

"She's inside, in her office. She just didn't hear us knocking," Brooke said as she slipped her phone back into her oversized black bag. It was the same bag I'd stolen off her chair and ransacked months ago. Though we didn't know each other then, guilt swept over me for my past actions, and I looked away as the lock clicked and the door opened.

"Stop staring. It's rude," Brooke whispered, following her friend to the main room, where she handed her a yellow envelope.

"I told you, I don't want your money," Valerie said, pushing the envelope back to Brooke.

As if this wasn't their first time playing this game, the two women moved on with their conversation without mentioning the money again, the envelope remaining on the table.

"Okay, so it's clear what you need to do, right?" Brooke asked.

Valerie shook her head and touched her thick, dry lips. "You need me to have him admit to his crime. But as I said earlier, people lie, even to their therapist. Nobody likes to admit their failures or mistakes. And I'm not a priest, so people don't usually tell me their crimes."

"I know, but do your thing," Brooke insisted, making hand gestures. "Build his trust. Maybe rile him up a little. All we need is a slip of the tongue."

Valerie shuffled to the corner, where she opened the cabinet door. Inside was a mini-fridge. "Sprite? Water?"

I could have used something stronger, but I settled for a can of Diet Coke.

During the next forty-five minutes, we went over a list of things that irritated Tony: The career Julia stole from him. His frustrating life of living in her shadow. The bitter feeling of dependence on his wife's money.

At a quarter to three, Valerie showed Brooke and me to the bathroom, and I locked the door behind us. Brooke closed the lid and sat on the toilet.

I leaned against the sink, waiting for Tony to arrive. I thought about telling Brooke about my visit to Valerie's house a few days ago, but I decided against it. There was no need to complicate things between us. Brooke could be quite possessive. "How did you get Valerie to agree to this? She could lose her license."

Brooke's watery dark eyes landed on mine. "When your grief is so profound and deep, and you have no reason to go on, the strangest things can keep you going."

"So, she doesn't care if she loses her license, or worse, goes to jail for this?"

"Maybe she wants to get some sense of justice? I don't know. Look at all the illegal things I'm doing for you."

I bobbed my head. "Can't argue with that."

A confident knocking on the door silenced us in the bathroom.

"Shush. Listen!" I held my breath until I heard a familiar voice. It was Tony.

I pressed my ear to the crack between the door and the frame to hear better.

The first fifteen minutes of the session was a basic introduction. Tony was sharing information about himself and his current situation. He was a widower with a six-year-old boy. Yada, yada.

"Your wife disappeared over three years ago, correct?" Valerie asked. "Did you seek professional help during those years to help you with your grief?"

"No, I didn't. I was managing it well enough. I didn't think I needed any help."

"So, what brings you here today?"

The quiet moment that followed felt like an eternity.

"Something strange has been happening lately," Tony spoke at last. "I can't sleep at night. I hear things. I think I may be going crazy."

"What things do you hear?"

"Voices…?"

"Whose voices?"

A pause. "Julia's."

"I see. And what is she saying to you?"

"Saying? I…well, she isn't saying anything specifically or asking me anything. It's like she's trying to scare me. Or like she's haunting me?"

"Do you believe in ghosts, Mr. Rose?"

"I don't—I mean, I *didn't*. I'm not sure anymore."

"Do you also see your deceased wife's spirit, or do you only hear her?"

He must have shaken his head because there was no audible answer.

"Is it possible that your guilt is projecting itself onto you?"

I turned to give a thumbs-up to Brooke as my approval for her friend's manipulative skills. She smiled back at me.

"Guilt? For what?"

"I don't know. Do you maybe feel responsible for your wife's disappearance in any way?"

A sigh. "I do," Tony said, and I looked back at Brooke with a huge grin, but my joy soon vanished because her face assumed a mask of skepticism.

"I blame myself every day. I don't know what you've read in the papers, but she was drunk at the game and I let her wander off alone. I...I was so *angry*! And disillusioned about her behavior. She'd said mean things to me at the game. And she humiliated me in front of all those people, and I wanted nothing to do with her, so I went back to our cabin...I know now I shouldn't have left her alone in that state of mind."

"But you didn't know she was alone, right? Weren't there other members of your family on the ship with you two?"

"My family was already upset with my wife. The money, the fame, they changed Julia. She tried to fix everybody's life around her. She wanted to tell people how to live their lives, and most people don't like that."

"Mm, did Julia and you see eye to eye when it came to your family?"

"I understood where she was coming from, sure. But I think the way she went about it hurt people."

"Do you think she felt alone?"

Again, Tony paused before answering. "I don't know."

"Did you feel alone in your marriage?"

"I suppose I did."

"I remember reading about Julia's case in the news. At some point, the police considered her disappearance a suicide. Do you believe she wanted to hurt herself?"

"No! Never! The police...! That's bull—all of it. She *loved* Sam! She would never have intentionally left him."

Why would Tony say that? If he were the killer, then having people believe his wife killed herself would have been a perfect cover story. I started to nibble on my lower lip from the confusion I felt at Tony's words.

"So, what do you think happened to her?"

I pressed my ear closer to the crack.

"Why is this…? Why do you want to know?"

"Well, if we can identify the root of your hallucinations—is it guilt, grief, loneliness, or something else—then we can target that emotion to help you."

"You think I'm hallucinating?"

"What do you think?"

Tony took his time to answer again. I felt the anxiety building within my chest.

"I asked my father to sleep at my house last night. I called him this morning to check on him. He didn't hear anything."

"I see. And what did your father say when you mentioned the voices to him?"

"I didn't tell him about the voices!" Tony snorted. "I told him I heard a rat or a mouse in the walls. I asked him to stay for the night to see if he heard it too before I called an exterminator."

"Do you lie to your father often?"

"No…I mean, I don't think so. But you know how it is, he's my father, and I want to make him proud. But I couldn't tell him that I'm hearing Julia's voice in the night, though, could I? He'd think I'm crazy!"

"Maybe he heard the voices but thinks the same way you do."

Tony chuckled at the irony, and I wished I could have seen his face, not just hear his voice. "I guess I see your point," he said.

"Tell me, did something happen in the past few weeks that may have brought on these hallucinations? Anything new or a stressful event in your life? A tragedy? New people? Did you look at old photos of Julia?"

"Well, sort of. I mean, there was someone. A woman."

My heart sunk at his statement. How could I miss him meeting a woman?

"We met—not in a romantic way. In a professional capacity," Tony continued. "There's something about her that reminds me of Julia, and it...it disturbs me. The way she talks and walks. She even looks like her. And she had this ring. Julia wore the *same ring* when she disappeared...I don't know, but she's driving me crazy. I can't get her out of my head."

My whole body erupted in fire. My palms became clammy, and beads of sweat gathered on my forehead.

"Have you been engaging in any self-destructive behavior since you met this woman?"

"I don't think so. I drink sometimes—but I'm not a drunk. Why do you ask?"

"I just wanted to see if this woman is a trigger for you to go down a slippery slope."

Tony sighed. "I guess I do feel I'm losing control of my emotions and behavior at times, maybe."

"What I'm going to ask you next may be a little too personal, so please forgive me. But it's important we talk about it. Have you been intimate with this woman?"

"No! As I said, our relationship is business only."

"All right. Were there any others? Have you had a girlfriend or lover since you lost your wife? Any intimate relationships?"

"No." His answer was short and to the point, making me think he was lying.

"All right. So, how about this for an idea? My advice is for you to go out tonight. Meet new people. Meet a woman, perhaps. It's not healthy for a young, healthy man like yourself to commit to a life of celibacy. Many grieving men feel that they will betray their deceased wife's memory if they open up their hearts to a new partner, but three years is a long time to be alone for anyone. I'm sure Julia would want you to be happy."

"What? Are you telling me to go out tonight and *hook up* with someone?"

"Why are you surprised? You don't think you deserve to enjoy yourself? To love again?"

"I…I don't know…I suppose you're right. I never thought about it."

"Would you do it for me? As an experiment?"

"At this point, I'll try anything to stop the voices in my head."

"Sometimes, our raging hormones do crazy things with our minds. I believe that refocusing your attention away from yourself and to someone else would be a healthy choice. How about that professional-relationship female friend you mentioned?"

"I don't know. She's young and…beautiful. Full of life and opportunities. What would she want with a grumpy guy like me?"

"If you start talking down to yourself, you will continue to spiral down the path you're on."

Minutes passed; they were still talking about me. I should have been flattered, but my mind swam in anger. I didn't want Tony to go out and hook up with other women. How stupid of the therapist was it to suggest it? She had one job: to get Tony to admit his crime. Why was she trying to heal his battered soul instead?

My anger had nearly boiled over when Valerie opened the bathroom door to where we were hiding. The moment the door opened, I swooped down on her like a hawk.

"Why would you suggest to Tony to go out and look for sex? We had a good thing going here, and you ruined it."

"Sweetheart, I understand your frustration—"

"I'm not your patient, so don't play your mind games on me!"

Brooke put her hand on my shoulder, and I shrugged it off.

"If you didn't notice, he spent a lot of our time together talking about you. So, why don't you find out if he's going out tonight? If he is, find out where he's going and surprise him there! Alcohol is a great tool to loosen someone's tongue."

"This could work," Brooke chimed in. I shot her a disappointed glance.

I rubbed the back of my neck with trembling fingers. "This is not what I wanted to come out of this. This was all a waste of time," I grunted and walked out of the office. My mind kept playing images of Tony making love to some random redhead. The mere thought of it set my insides on fire.

Brooke caught up with me by the car. When she popped the door open, I got in without a word, huffing and puffing angrily. Sitting in the passenger seat, I scooted closer to the door and looked out the window, refusing to talk to her.

She didn't take the hint. "Do you think that was a fair way to treat an old, broken-hearted woman who'd just done us a huge favor, by the way?"

I ripped out a few strands of eyebrow hair with my fingertips to feel pain. When I turned to Brooke, my eyes twitched from the nerves. "She didn't help us."

"She did! Tony booked a second appointment with her. We knew from the beginning that this could take time."

"So, you're siding with her now? Please enlighten me because I'm obviously too dumb to see the bigger picture here. How again is Tony fucking other women, or me, supposed to help us?"

Brooke's face went ashen. "You're kidding me, right?"

I scowled at her. "No, I'm not. I don't like complicating things."

"No one said anything about you sleeping with him. But I should call him and find out if he's going out tonight. Get ourselves invited? As friends."

"No!" I snapped. "It's stupid! I'm going home and back to bed, or to watch TV, whatever. I've had enough bullshit for one day."

The more I tried to convince Brooke, the more I knew I was overreacting. But why? I wasn't attracted to Tony Rose. How could I be?

When we arrived at home, my anxiety was overwhelming me. All I could think about was what I was going to do about my raging emotions.

19

"I thought you said you were going to make spaghetti," Brooke scolded, standing at the door of the surveillance room.

"I will. I already started on it, but I wanted to check on Tony quickly." I put out my cigarette in the ashtray. The smoke hung in the air between us.

Brooke glanced at the wall of screens, then back at me. "You left the water boiling." Brooke's tone wasn't lecturing. It was more disappointed, worried even.

"Sorry, I forgot." I switched off the power button to the console, and all monitors went black.

"I'm worried about you." She crossed her arms. "When I agreed to this illegal surveillance of my client, I never imagined you'd become so obsessed with him."

I shot out of the chair, and it rolled back to the wall. "I'm not! Stop saying that!"

"When was the last time you saw Tony in person?"

I clicked my tongue. "I don't know. At the sushi restaurant?"

An argument was brewing between us, and it felt like fate had given me an opportunity to get out of the house without arousing Brooke's suspicion.

"You need to get off my back!" I snapped, bumping Brooke with my shoulder as I passed her. I walked briskly down the hallway toward the kitchen. She took the bait and followed me.

"Look at you! We can't even discuss a simple matter without you freaking out."

I flung the cabinet door open. "I'm not freaking out!"

"Yeah, I can see that."

I slammed the box of spaghetti on the table and turned to face Brooke. "What do you want me to do, then?"

"How about setting up an appointment with Tony to sign the new contracts? That would move our investigation along. Not this…" She had one hand on her waist and the other gesticulating. "Not this nonsense you've been doing. Sitting in that damn room, day and night, spying on the man."

As if invisible forces had led me to turn up the heat, I found myself motioning at her fervently. "I don't care about helping him resolve his legal issues. I need to catch the bastard in a lie. I need evidence against him or to clear him. I need to know the truth about him. But we have nothing."

"And staring at a monitor will get you that?"

I shook my head and turned my attention back to the ingredients. I attempted to unscrew the jar of spaghetti sauce. "Why can't you leave me alone about this?"

Seeing my failed attempt, Brooke took the jar from my hand, tapped the edge of the top against the counter, and opened it with one smooth, swift movement. "I'll get off your back when you start acting like a responsible adult. You started out like a professional and on point, but lately, it seems like you're losing control."

That moment presented me with the excuse I needed to get out of the house without being the one at fault. My adoptive father was the master of using this tactic to see his mistress while leaving my mom at home, marinating in self-blame.

"You know what? I can't listen to how bad I am at everything anymore. I'm going for a run." I turned off the stove, spun around, and stormed out of the kitchen like I used to do when I was a spoiled teenager. I dashed along the hallway and burst into my room to change. Tony was following the therapist's advice and was going out tonight. I'd watched him shower, shave, and try on half a dozen outfits on the monitors in the surveillance room. If I called a car now, I could catch him before he left his house.

I threw on a pair of trainers, a long-sleeved tee, and a hoodie and slipped into my Nike running shoes to deflect any suspicion. Brooke was waiting for me by the library door where I'd left her, a burning cigarette wedged between her shaking fingers. "Are you seriously going for a run? Now? It's already dark outside."

"I don't care. I wanted to stay home and cook for us, but you messed that up. I can't stay here and listen to you bitching at me all evening."

"I didn't mean to bitch—" she started, but I slammed the entrance door behind me before she could finish her sentence.

The chilled, early April temperatures sucked the heat from my body the moment the main door closed behind me. I zipped my hoodie to my chin, punched the passcode into my phone, and clicked the Uber app. I rushed down the stone steps, feeling anxious as I ordered a ride. Once I left the protection of the covered coach entrance, I stepped into the gloomy evening air, heavy with mist. At the end of the long driveway, I looked back at the house. Brooke was standing in the window of her study, cloaked in soft golden light and lifting a glass to her lips. I bent over and touched my toes to pretend to stretch. I pressed my feet against a moss-covered rock by the side of the road and flexed my toes. From underneath my armpit, I could see Brooke watching me. I bent to the side a few times to stretch my arms and upper body. Then I launched into a jog.

Ten minutes after eight, I walked along the vaguely lit main street in the general direction of Tony's house, following the Uber driver's movement on my phone. When he was a mile away, I sat on a bench at a bus stop, waiting for the Toyota Prius to reach its destination.

I kept glancing over my shoulder to make sure Brooke hadn't followed me. The street was nearly deserted, and all I heard was the echo of lonely dogs' barking and the sloshy sounds of car tires driving over puddles. I feared the dark, especially a dark street. I kept seeing figures stepping out of the shadows: Hector, Ornelas, Julia, some of my previous clients. Would this pounding fear ever leave me?

I picked up a stick from underneath the bench on a pile of wet debris and grasped it hard as if my life depended on it.

Sitting still for long minutes, I noticed how fast the moisture in the air began to settle on the ground. The landscape was giving me the creeps as the fog slowly rolled in. A small critter rustling in the undergrowth behind me pierced the stillness, and I popped up from the bench like a jack-in-the-box.

A pair of headlights broke through the thickening fog, and I glanced at my phone. The sight of my Uber ride gave me relief, and I dropped the stick.

The navy-blue Prius stopped in front of me, and I opened the door and jumped into the backseat with the haste of someone being chased. The driver leaned back to check on me. For the first time since I began using driving services, I felt afraid of being in a car with a stranger. Behind the wheel was a middle-aged man with a thick, round beard, chubby cheeks, and a receding hairline. The smell in the car was bringing back old memories I had long buried. As a reflex, I closed my arms and legs, trying to make myself as small as possible.

"Did you order a ride?" he asked, checking his phone. "Annie Adams?"

Yes, that's me, I wanted to say but bobbed my head instead.

To cancel my ride now would have been rude, and without a legitimate reason, Uber would downrate me, so I stayed.

Soon the car was in motion.

A text from Brooke came in, and I clicked on it:

I don't like it when we argue. Please come home so we can talk

She didn't deserve to be left marinating in self-blame, so I texted back:

I don't like to argue either. Let me finish my run first. I need to cool off, but I'll be home in an hour

In a second text, I wrote:

I'm sorry—just for good measure.

I disappeared on Brooke once a week after I moved into her home. One night after we'd decided to place spy cameras in Tony's home, my thoughts wouldn't quiet in my head and allow me to fall asleep. To exhaust myself physically and mentally, I snuck out of the house and went for a run. Two hours later, Brooke found me sitting on a stone marker, crying, at the end of a random dead-end street. I was lost.

But that night, I was safe. I had a cell phone with GPS navigation, I'd learned my home address, and I'd smoothed things out with Brooke via texts. She had no reason to drive around the neighborhood looking for me.

Near Tony's house, I asked the driver to pull over at the side of the road, where I had an open view of the driveway. The interior lights of the house were shining through the front windows and onto the BMW parked in its usual spot. I let out a sigh of relief when I realized that I hadn't missed him leaving his home.

With the Prius's engine idling—which was nothing more than a faint humming and nearly impossible to hear—I set my eyes on Tony's house. Every time a car drove by, I ducked my head—a reaction that raised my driver's eyebrows. "Is everything okay, miss?"

"Oh, yeah," I said, tucked between the two rows of seats. "I just dropped something."

He knew I was lying.

Five minutes before nine, when I was beginning to consider whether Tony had taken a taxi and that I had missed him, a dark car turned into his driveway. Tony's mother, Barbara, stepped out of the vehicle. She pulled a small suitcase as she approached the main door, making me believe she was there to look after Sam while Tony was out for the night.

A wave of irritation swept over me at the thought of Tony going on a hunt for a female companion. I blamed myself for allowing Valerie to mess with our plan. I needed Julia's husband to be miserable and in a mood for confession, not blissful and sexually satisfied. I wished I could think of something to stop the night from unfolding.

I'd chewed the nail on my left index finger to a bloody mess when, ten minutes later, Tony's BMW rolled out of his driveway and onto the main road.

"Sir, could you follow that car, please?" I said to my driver urgently, smudging blood onto the leather cover on the back of his seat.

The puffy-faced man locked eyes with me in the rearview mirror, then, moving slowly, he put the car in gear. His slow-motion movements sent me to the edge of insanity.

"Please, hurry. We can't lose him."

"I hope you're not trying to involve me in some illegal activity," the man said, glancing at me again in the rearview mirror.

I watched Tony's car take a right turn and go out of sight. I wanted to punch out that round face of the man and take control of the wheel. It could have been a good plan if I knew how to drive.

"No, nothing like that." Panic interfered with my ability to think. "He's my...boyfriend...uhm...I think he's cheating on me," I stuttered to get him going faster.

My pleading worked, and the driver offered me an empathic look before hitting the gas.

At last, we were moving with speed, and we caught up to Tony's BMW, leaving me feeling slightly victorious.

To my surprise, Tony didn't take the exit toward New York City. Instead, he drove along the highway, heading to downtown Montclair.

"It seems your boy is in the mood for a good time," my driver remarked, talking to me over his shoulder.

"What makes you say that?" I inquired, watching all sorts of people laugh and talk on the busy sidewalks as if they hadn't a care in the world.

"You're not familiar with this area? All the nightclubs and restaurants are jammed together here." He pointed out his window with one fat finger. I shuddered at the feeling of seeing those blotchy fingers so close to me. Please don't touch me, I thought. If you touch me, I'll claw your face off.

"Oh, look, your boy's stopping. What do you want me to do?"

I pulled the hood over my head. "I'll get out here. Thank you."

The driver twisted his torso and put his hand on the backrest. I tried not to look at his fingers. A flood of bad memories from my life in the brothel was not what I needed tonight. "How about a piece of advice from an old man, sweetheart?"

I looked at him with a blank face. "Shoot."

"If you feel the need to spy on your boyfriend, then he's not the right guy for you."

I snapped my fingers at him. "I'll keep that in mind."

Once my Uber rolled back into traffic, I ducked between two cars and watched Tony pass a group of bystanders in their mid-thirties, walk up to a double glass door, and enter a brick-fronted building. I tried to follow him, but the bouncer stopped me at the red rope. "This isn't a gym, sweetheart." *Why was everybody calling me sweetheart?*

Holding the mountain of a man's gaze, I pulled the zipper of my hoodie down far enough to expose the upper line of my lace bra. Pressing my boobs against his muscular torso, I slipped a hundred-dollar bill into his hand. "I thought it's what's inside that mattered," I whispered into his ear, blowing warm breath onto his skin. "Maybe I can show you more later?" I leaned away a little and winked.

"Uhhh, coming in hot, I see. Go ahead, sweetheart, but ditch the hoodie." He nodded at me to keep moving.

With a renewed sense of power and accomplishment, I passed a group of giggling girls in tight jeans and heels and entered the club, considering Brooke's cash well spent.

Neon lights ran along the floor and the ceiling, turning the brick walls the color of poison green in the rustic hall. A DJ was spinning records behind a booth at the far end of the large room. High-octane music pounded against my chest, giving me the same rush as if I were high on something. I'd never been to a vibrating and loud place like this before. All the noise and strobing lights were disorienting and painful against my eardrums.

Panic gripped my heart when I realized that finding Tony in this crowd could be difficult. I kept my hands in my pockets as I passed tall tables and laughing guests sitting on barstools. I couldn't have been more out of my element. As I squeezed myself through the dense group of people, I felt everyone's eyes on me. Were they wondering about my outfit or something more sinister? Did someone recognize me from my old days? Was a member of the Mexican cartel here to drag me back to the mud by my hair?

The walls were closing in on me. I felt trapped. I kept glancing back to see if someone was following me. Not able to get a grip on my anxiety, I cornered myself against a wall, feeling its safety behind my back.

"I don't think I've seen you here before," said a tall guy with a round face and beer on his breath.

I moved away without a response, my heart beating in my throat.

"Bitch!" he called out after me before the crowd had swallowed him whole.

There were too many people in here, all too close to me, rubbing against me, touching me, bumping me.

My head started to spin. I couldn't understand why Tony came to this chaotic place for fun. There was nothing fun here.

A girl with purple hair and a lip ring blocked my view of the dance floor. "I like your style. Who needs a sexy dress, am I right?"

"I'm sorry, I can't do this," I said, pushing her to the side to escape. I needed to get out of there. I didn't even know what I was doing in that crowded bar in the first place. To stop Tony from hooking up with some random stranger? I didn't think this through. How would I do that anyway? Beg him not to kiss the girl? This was all a horrible idea. I was stupid to be so impulsive and follow Tony here.

I reached the exit, where I stopped and hesitated. My legs refused to cross the threshold. Pestered by a strange nagging feeling, I looked back at the crowd.

"Julia?" I heard someone yell. I didn't know why, but I responded to the call by searching for the direction of the voice.

My eyes landed on Tony standing by the VIP area, cloaked in neon-green light and holding two drinks.

I froze.

He was going to recognize me and realize I wasn't Julia.

He moved toward me, and I stumbled backward. Driven by panic, I raced along the red carpet, took a hard left into a narrow hallway, and burst out of the building, knocking over the bouncer who allowed me into the club earlier. "I'm sorry!" I offered, as I dodged my way through traffic and across the street.

"Julia, stop!" Tony was on my heels.

Pulling my hood into my face, I began running down the street, slamming my way between pedestrians.

"Julia, it's me, wait!" He was running after me.

I double-backed and crossed the street again, almost getting hit by a silver convertible. The long and loud honking made my heart race at record speed.

I glanced back. Tony was watching me from the curb.

I put my head down as I leaped between cars. The air rang with the constant sound of car horns.

I made it to the other side of the road again and rounded the corner.

More people. More traffic.

I forced my way through, bumping into evening strollers. I was out of breath. I needed to find a quiet place to hide.

Across the street stood a three-story office building under construction. A chain-link fence wrapped around the property suggested it wouldn't be easy to access the building. From a distance, the boarded-up double gate looked impenetrable. I scanned the area with my eyes, looking for another option. The alley next to me was a dead end. If I tried to hide there, I'd be a sitting duck. If Tony found me squatting behind a trash can, how would I explain myself?

"Julia, wait!" Tony's thundering voice swept over the crowd like a roaring engine, cutting me to the bone.

Crossing at the red light, I reached the other side of the street and came to an abrupt halt in front of the construction site gate. Against my better judgment, I rattled it, but it didn't budge.

Tony's head popped above the crowd on the other side of the street. *What do I do? Where do I hide?*

I noticed a bunch of porta-potties to my right arranged in a neat row by a construction site. A few giant steps got me there. I leaped behind the blue boxes and hunkered down in the dirt. I could barely draw a breath I was so scared. I told myself to remain still, but my pulse pounded in my ears and my mind wouldn't stop racing. *Why would Tony think I was Julia?*

I rubbed my face with my hands, hoping it would calm me.

It didn't.

My heart beat faster than ever. I needed to get out of there. I needed to be home in bed, putting this night behind me.

I banged my head against the back of a porta-potty in exasperation. The pandemonium on the streets slipped over me like a blanket, enclosing me in a confined space of fear.

I closed my eyes, trying to focus on differentiating the sounds of the night. Squeaking of car tires. Honking. Laughing. Talking. Music. It was all confusing, yet somehow in harmony—until my ears tuned in to a series of thuds that sounded like approaching footsteps pounding the pavement. The sound didn't come from a woman's heels. These shoes made a dull and heavy thump. The thought of Tony finding me here sent a new shock of panic through me.

Out of reflex, I gripped a piece of jagged rock. The sharp edges pressed into my skin, but the pain was nothing compared to the madness that reigned in my head.

The footsteps faded and soon were gone, drowned out by the boisterous noises of party people. I loosened my grip on the rock. My muscles relaxed a little as I understood that the rushing footsteps didn't belong to Tony, or if they did, that he must have run past the stinking boxes of shit where I was hiding. Yet, distress, like iron weights, kept me pinned to the ground.

Tony can't find me here, I kept telling myself.

After sucking in and letting out a long breath, I rolled onto my knees and scooted to the edge of the potty. I poked my head out to have a look at the street, but my blood ran cold when my eyes caught a man standing on the sidewalk only a few feet away from me.

It was Tony. No doubt about it. He was standing with his back to me, arms akimbo.

My body stiffened, and I gasped. My hand slapped against my mouth to muffle any sound I might have made. I inched back into my hiding spot, the pebbles scraping my knees.

My heart thumped in my throat. My racing thoughts made me dizzy. Why was Tony still here? Why didn't he give up chasing me? Did he truly believe I was Julia? If he caught me hiding here, then everything I'd been working for would be lost. What should I do? Attack him and run away? Kill him?

I reached for the jagged stone again when my phone started to chime and vibrate in my pocket. I pulled it out as fast as I could. I pressed the button on the side to mute the call. My chest began rising and falling uncontrollably. I feared Tony might have heard the ringing. Holding my breath, I slowly looked at my phone to check the caller ID.

The name Tony Rose glared on my screen.

20

My iPhone kept ringing and ringing in my hand in silent mode. I felt as if I were holding a countdown device for a bomb that was about to explode. I couldn't think of a single reason Tony would be calling me at this late hour. He certainly wouldn't have been able to recognize me with my hoodie up when he saw me in the club. Yet, he thought I was Julia and yelled after me. The only explanation that made sense was that his brain had caught up with reality. His wife was gone, but Brooke's new assistant looked just like her. He was calling me to see where I was, but I wasn't falling for his trick.

I didn't answer the call.

When the screen returned to sleep mode, I waited for a voicemail notification to appear, but nothing arrived. Maybe Tony was texting me, apologizing for calling me so late. But I didn't receive any text messages either.

I rolled onto my knees and peeked around the corner to see if Tony was still typing or leaving a message for me on his phone.

He was gone. Night owls and partygoers passed through where he had been standing on the sidewalk.

He must have left, but I couldn't exclude the possibility that he was still searching the area for me.

As my heartbeat slowed, I weighed my options to stay hidden for a little longer or use this window of opportunity to make a run for it, call a car, and get home.

I pulled back into the cover of the porta-potties to contemplate my choice, but the smell of feces and urine mixed with a strong disinfectant was so unbearable that it made it difficult to concentrate.

The night was getting colder, and whenever I glanced at the long dark alley near the construction site, I felt the urge to get the hell out of there.

I gathered my strength to scan the street for Tony once more before leaving my hideout when a sharp squeaking sound near me made me jump in fright. A disgusting, fat rat was barking at me like a dog from the shadows behind the porta-potties as if letting me know I was intruding upon his territory. I backed away as fast as I could and jumped to my feet. There were plenty of rodents in the brothel, but that didn't mean I'd ever become used to them.

I pressed my back against the chain-link fence to order a car when I felt someone's eyes on me. A figure loomed in the dark alley. I thought we locked eyes, but I couldn't be sure. I didn't see a face, nor a body, only a silhouette of something that resembled a human frame.

I took off running down the street, heading away from the construction site. I couldn't stop looking back over my shoulder as the entertainment district of the city dwarfed in my eyes.

When I was a couple of blocks away, I maintained a hurried pace as I pulled up the Uber app on my phone to order a ride. Looking down while moving, I bumped into a young woman walking toward me with her friends, and my phone fell from my hand.

"Whoa! Slow down, sister," she said, crouching down to retrieve her my phone.

"I'm sorry. I didn't mean—" was all I could say as the woman handed me my phone. My voice seemed to be lost.

I started running again. I didn't stop until the lights and music had faded behind me into the darkness of the night.

I soon found myself standing alone next to a woodsy park as I waited for the car to arrive. As strange as it seemed, I felt safe standing there alone in a secluded area where no one could hear me scream if someone snatched me.

*   *   *   *   *

It was nearly eleven o'clock at night when I tiptoed my way into Brooke's house, holding my shoes in my hand. My first stop was the kitchen to grab a glass of water because my throat was so dry that it ached to swallow. I gulped down two glasses of water, but the feeling lingered.

To wind down and take my mind off the evening's events, I opened the cabinet door above the refrigerator and pulled out the bottle of Smirnoff. I took a swig, then another, wiping my mouth after every gulp as if it were my last. I stopped counting after the fifth mouthful, yet a feeling of unease still lay heavy like bricks on my chest.

This house wasn't the brothel. Ornelas and his watchdogs weren't going to punish me for my disobedience. Brooke would never hurt me, yet I feared the consequences of my actions more than anything. I was disappointed with myself for acting so foolishly, for betraying Brooke's trust again. Why was it so hard for me to do the right thing?

I poured water into the vodka bottle to make up for the missing amount and swirled it around to mix the liquids. I rearranged the minibar to its original state. Then I rinsed my mouth.

My next trip was to Brooke's bedroom. Holding my breath, not wanting to make a sound, I quietly opened her door. A soft wheezing and the mound under the blankets suggested that Brooke was sleeping.

I crept closer to her bed and looked down at her in the dark. She looked peaceful, innocent even—and very defenseless against an intruder.

Brooke always kept her front door unlocked. Anybody could have come in here during the dead of night and kill her. Why did this woman have no fear of evil?

I thought of the letter "B" that Julia's spirit drew in the condensation on the bathroom mirror. Was she trying to warn me about Brooke?

An orange prescription medicine bottle and a half-empty glass of water rested on the nightstand. Brooke must have taken her sleeping pills. I sat down on the edge of the bed, next to her head.

Her breathing didn't change.

I could have killed her too. Maybe she wanted that. She might have wished someone would end it all for her and end the pain.

I massaged my face with both hands, trying to break free of my disturbing thoughts.

As I sat still, allowing my body to get rid of the extra adrenaline, an overwhelming wave of fatigue descended over me.

I brushed my fingers along Brooke's forehead, stood up, walked to my room, where I swallowed two Vicodin, and washed them down with a hard seltzer.

I spread myself out on my mattress, anticipating the effects, but my mind refused to go numb. I was thinking about Tony and why he thought Julia was still alive. Did he imagine his missing wife coming back to him one day? Was it the hope of her return that kept him from engaging in a relationship these past three years? Or was it possible that Julia's ghostly voice at night was messing with his head? I thought it was messing with all our heads.

I shut my eyes to stop the noise in my head, but the sudden darkness just made me dizzy. The whole room began to spin around me as hot drops of sweat swelled up and rolled down my forehead and spine. I was hot and bothered.

Not able to suppress the uncomfortable sensations, I crawled out of bed and made my way to the surveillance room, sliding my shoulder against the wall as I moved to keep myself upright.

After three attempts at punching in the passcode, I gained access to the room.

The monitors were on, displaying a series of night vision images. Brooke must have spent her evening spying on Tony, or me, or both of us, and forgotten to turn off the system before she went to bed.

I couldn't blame her for losing trust in me because I was losing faith in myself.

As I yawned, I spotted movement in Tony's living room on the sofa. I leaned closer to the screen and zoomed in on a pair of naked butt cheeks, tucked between two long and toned legs ending in high heels, thrusting and thrusting, hard and violent. A hand was clamped over the woman's mouth. I watched the performance in shock.

When the man pulled away from between the woman's legs, I saw it was Tony.

He flipped the woman onto her stomach, bending her over the back of the couch. He brushed her long blond hair to the side over her shoulder, removed her bra, and stuffed it in her mouth. With one leg pressing into the cushion of the couch, he mounted the slender woman and pounded her from behind, her double Ds bouncing painfully.

The act was too much for me to stomach. I looked away and puked on the floor.

21

The sour smell of my vomit filled the small, confining room—the stench was as if I'd fallen into a dumpster behind a Chinese seafood buffet restaurant at the end of a hot weekend. I wiped my mouth with the back of my hand. The taste of my half-digested dinner mixed with vodka and Vicodin lay stubbornly on my tongue.

A glance at the monitor was enough to make me feel sick again. I couldn't bear to watch Tony engaging in sexual intercourse with a stranger.

Instead, I set out to find a bucket and a washcloth to clean up my mess before Brooke saw it.

My head throbbed, and my stomach swam with queasiness on my way to the laundry room, where I retrieved a bucket and a clean cloth from underneath the sink.

Keeping the lights off, I turned on the faucet and filled the pail with warm water and added some soap. The old pipes creaked and moaned in the walls, adding to the creepiness of the moonlit room.

When I turned the water off, something in the house continued to rattle and knock against the wall for a few seconds. If anything was waking Brooke up tonight, this was it, but I was confident in the strength of her sleeping pills.

When silence ensued, I waited, listening for the sounds of footsteps or a door opening.

Nothing.

The house remained deadly quiet.

Holding the handle of the full bucket with both hands, I stepped out into the dark hallway. The moving shadows of the bare trees outside cast a sinister light show onto the walls. I felt a chill rise over me as a small branch tapped lightly against the window.

I'd reached the end of my endurance and flipped the light switch on to illuminate my way back to the surveillance room, risking waking Brooke.

As if someone had cut power to the house, the switch didn't work.

"What the…?" I said, my breath leaving my mouth in a stream of white fog.

I let go of the handle of the bucket with my right hand and brought my palm against my mouth. I breathed a hazy, thick vapor on it. I shivered from the sudden paralyzing cold. I remembered from science class that condensation occurs at forty-five degrees Fahrenheit, or something like that, which made even less sense. There had to be an open window somewhere in the house, letting in the cold draft, but I couldn't see much in the moonlight.

Freaked out now, I pressed on, but I was barely moving. My legs, like blocks of lead, scraped along the floor. Every step was a struggle as if someone held me back.

I felt a slight cold touch on the back of my neck. I jumped and slammed my back against the wall, dangling the bucket in my hand and spilling water onto the hardwood floor. Panting clouds of white, I looked in the direction I'd come from and saw a pale translucent figure floating a few inches off the ground. Without a doubt, I knew it was Julia. I recognized her icy-blue eyes that stared at me, unblinking.

Gripped with fear, I dropped the bucket. It landed on its side and flooded the floor around me. Standing in a puddle of water, I watched tiny maggots roll out of Julia's damp hair.

Julia was my friend, yet her ghostly image petrified me.

Her lips moved inaudibly. She smiled at me, and I felt the warmth of her gesture fold over my heart like warm fingers. She needed me to be brave.

I turned to face the apparition. "What do you want from me?" I whispered. The words from my mouth rode down the hallway on my icy breath.

Julia's mouth opened. Her pale lips stretched wide. "*Bbbbbbbb!*" she screeched in a bloodcurdling voice as she flew toward me and then through me.

I felt my heartbeat stutter.

As I touched my chest, I fell forward and onto my face as darkness and silence overcame me.

*   *   *   *   *

Judging by the amount of sunlight bursting through the stained-glass window in the hallway, it was early morning when Brooke found me lying on the floor.

"Now look at yourself, Annie," she said with pity and sorrow in her voice.

"What's going on?" I asked, wiping the drool off my left cheek.

Brooke handed me a soft beige towel. "Someone's here. Didn't you hear the knocking?"

I pressed the palm of my hand against my forehead and moaned. My brain felt raw and aching. "No, I didn't. Why am I on the floor?"

"Oh, I'd like to know that too." Her worrying eyes lingered on me a bit longer, then she ran her fingers through her hair and tightened the belt around her bathrobe. "I'm going to see who's at the door. You better clean yourself up, and the surveillance room too. It smells like a toilet at a sorority house after a party."

Resting on my side and trying to get the feeling back into my fingers, I watched Brooke walk out of my view.

The washcloth was right next to me. I picked it up, dragged the bucket to me, and started wiping up the spilled water.

On weekends, there was always music in the house. Brooke had an iPhone connected to a Bluetooth speaker that played her favorite radio stations when she was at home, but there was no music this morning. She must have wanted to spare me the headache.

As I squeezed the water into the bucket, I heard the door open, followed by an exchange of heated words. I went to the window in the reading room to see the person behind the angry voice.

Justin Rose, dressed in gray joggers, stood on the doormat, assuming an aggressive stance and yelling at Brooke.

"I know it was you, Brooke. Don't try to deny it!"

"I don't appreciate your coming to my home this early and yelling at me, Justin."

"You didn't approve when Julia hired me to handle her finances, and now you've been whispering your poison into Tony's ears. Well, congratulations, my brother wants to kick my sister and me out of the company once again. You just couldn't stop until you achieved what you wanted, could you?"

"I did write the contract, if that's what you're alluding to, but it was Tony who requested it. He's my client, and I'm his lawyer. Did he tell you about the negative balance on the company's books? Or about the pending IRS audit?"

Justin flung his arms up in frustration. "I don't believe a word of that bull!" He pointed his index finger at Brooke. "You started this, and now you'll stop it."

Brooke took a step forward, pushing her chest against his finger. "Even if you had a say in the matter, I will not tolerate you coming to my home and bullying me."

Justin stuttered, put his hand down, and stepped back a foot. "I didn't mean to threaten you, Brooke, but you must understand my frustration. If Tony goes through with this, I'm done for."

"You'll still have your company. You have other clients, don't you?"

Justin didn't reply. He looked away and pulled down on the back of his neck with intertwined fingers.

"May I come in for a cup of coffee?" he said at last.

"It's not a good time, Justin. I'm sorry."

"You need to help me, Brooke. I don't know what I'll do if Tony takes the money. I'll have nothing left."

Brooke's arms remained folded over her chest, holding the bathrobe together. "Let's not freak out just yet, all right? Why don't you set up a meeting with Tony and Sylvia? I promise Annie and I will be there too. We'll find a solution to the company's problems. You need to trust me."

Justin bobbed his head. "I don't know. Tony seems hell-bent this time on carrying through with his decision. It all feels too familiar."

"You need to let me do my job and protect all of you. But if you don't mind, I need to get ready. I have an engagement that I can't be late for."

At the first sign of Justin's willingness to leave, I returned to the bucket and carried it into the surveillance room to clean up my mess.

Brooke joined me as I was picking out half-digested food particles from the control panel.

"What happened last night?" she asked calmly.

"I think the better question is what is Justin Rose doing here?"

"Did you hear us?"

I pursed my lips. "Of course I did. He was yelling."

"Then you know. Our plan is working. Somebody in the family will break soon."

I understood the words that came out of her mouth, but seeing Julia's brother-in-law on the doormat of Brooke's felt fishy and intimate. What gave Justin the right to barge in on his brother's lawyer like that?

"You don't even look surprised. Is it normal for him to show up at your house, especially early on Saturday?"

Brooke sighed and scratched her forehead. "We're upsetting a lot of people around us. Desperate people do desperate things. And what causes the problem is either money or love. What do you think caused Julia's tragedy?"

I plopped down onto the rotating chair. "I don't even care what happens to me. I just want to find out the truth."

"Are you going to tell me what happened here last night?"

I looked her in the eyes for a long deliberating moment, deciding whether to tell her the truth or lie.

I settled on partial truth.

"I saw Julia's ghost in the hallway. She went inside my body."

Brooke looked away, shaking her head. "Enough, Annie. I can't take much more of this nonsense."

"What nonsense? You invited the witch here to conjure up her ghost. So why don't you believe me when I say she appeared to me?"

She buried her face in her hands, looking tired. "I can't do this right now. Not today, okay?"

I hurried after her. "What's today?"

She stopped but didn't look back at me as she put her head down. "Today marks my twenty-second marriage anniversary with Robert, and it's never a good day to be around me."

22

I didn't know what had gotten into me, but I was messing everything up. Every aspect of my life was going wrong. Helen no longer trusted me. Ever since Jeff isolated Brooke's picture from the video on the night of The Newlywed Game, she had this notion in her head that Brooke was hiding the truth from us because she was the one who pushed Julia over the railing. Helen went so far as to convince herself of my involvement in helping Brooke get away with murder. I should have argued more with her on the phone, pleading Brooke's innocence, but I was no longer sure of it myself.

As of that morning, I was still a member of her Facebook group. I checked at least three times. Helen hadn't kicked me out.

Yet.

But I had a feeling I owed my continued membership to Jeff. Jeff was the rational one between the two moderators, while Helen allowed her emotions to get the better of her.

Ruining my reputation with Helen wasn't my only failure. My attempt to discuss the incident of Justin Rose showing up at the house with Brooke turned out to be fruitless as well. I'd been around Brooke's office long enough to know that her clients never spoke to her with unbridled venom, yet Justin Rose had no problem talking to Brooke as if they were squabbling siblings. What brought on Justin's behavior? Were they lovers in the past? What was Brooke hiding from me?

But Brooke wouldn't talk to me as she got dressed. She just left the house without so much as a glance my way. Her way of ignoring me hurt me more than her yelling or nagging.

As the day advanced, it became harder to escape Helen's words and my own self-criticizing train of thought.

To keep busy, I engaged in a series of chores, hoping the mindless work would quiet the voices in my head and speed up the time. I aired out the house, vacuumed, dusted, took a long bath, and got dressed—not for any specific occasion but because I needed to get out of my pajamas and appear presentable.

Still, restlessness ate at me all day.

And on top of everything, the awful smell in the house drove me insane. The stench of my vomit seemed to cling to the walls, and no matter how many windows I opened or how many times I washed up the floor, the foul smell continued to linger. I kept drenching rooms in air-freshener to mask the smell, but it only made the house stink like throw-up-scented potpourri.

When I reached the edge of madness, I broke into Brooke's medicine cabinet and stole a few more of her Vicodin. I popped one pill and stashed the rest in a Ziploc bag inside my shoe underneath my bed.

I paced around the house some more, fighting the devil on my shoulder urging me to swallow more pills and have a drink to take the edge off. I refused to listen—for now.

Then I remembered that Brooke also used CBD oil to calm her anxiety naturally. I decided to give it a try. I found the vial among the bottles of vitamins in the kitchen cabinet and placed a few drops underneath my tongue.

I circled the kitchen island a few times before settling down in the library. I read five chapters from Julia's diary to get my mind back on track—to focus on why I came here in the first place. There was one entry that scared the hell out of me—that made me doubt Julia's memories. Rather, it seemed she didn't trust her memories either.

Entry #7

I concluded today that I am insane· Maybe the injury to my head is to blame· Or maybe the drugs that Hector forces into my veins have upset the chemical balance in my brain· I don't know· I've been overwhelmed by these crazy dreams lately that won't stay in the night· They cross over into the day, haunting me, mocking me· I dream about murders and deception· Ugliness and hatred· I see monsters lurking in the shadows, but I can't be sure if the monsters are out there to get me or if I'm the monster· I don't know· Maybe reading the book I wrote in another life is messing with my head· It's a book of fantasy, after all· Full of supernatural powers, mystical creatures, villains, and heroes·

I wish there was a way I could separate reality from fantasy· I wish someone here could help me with that·

London keeps nagging me, so I keep up with this diary, but I can't trust what I write· On some days, it all feels hopeless, maybe even imagined·

I try not to cry in front of the others. They look to me for strength. I'm the oldest, or maybe second oldest after Kitana, and the youngsters need me for support.

But I do cry. Mostly late at night while sitting on the toilet. When nobody is listening. Those nights when I feel hopeless, I think a lot about dying. I look at everyday items like shoelaces or toothbrushes, and I ponder how I could turn them into a weapon of my own destruction.

The only thing that stops me from ending it all is that tiny scar on my lower belly. When I touch it, I feel a connection to a child. I feel it deep inside of my heart. It's a gut-wrenching feeling, not knowing where your child is. It's painful, but it's the only thing that gives me the will to keep moving. I have to find a way out of here and back to my former life. There has to be someone out there who could help me catalog my memories. There has to be someone out there who cares if I live or die.

Reading Julia's words made it more evident that I was failing in every aspect of my original plan. I hadn't tortured Sylvia yet, and I was thinking about Tony way too much. Sylvia, or even Justin, were much better suspects. Going after them made more sense. Yet, I couldn't let go of pursuing Tony. This need of hearing the truth from his mouth had become an obsession of mine. I was wasting time. I also kept disappointing Brooke. Even a blind man could see that I was turning into a colossal failure.

I was so disappointed with myself that I absentmindedly scribbled words in the margin of Julia's notebook: *Worthless. Useless. Die.* When I realized the damage I'd done to the precious artifact, tears began to well up in my eyes. I rolled into a ball on the sofa, my entire body trembling, weeping at the sad disaster my life was slowly turning into.

I must have fallen asleep because it was four o'clock in the afternoon when I opened my eyes to a dark house, with no memory of the past few hours.

I flipped on the light switch for the standing lamp and called out for Brooke. My voice bounced off the cold walls without receiving a reply.

I closed Julia's diary and placed it back in my secret place on the bookshelf, fear playing with my nerves. Never before had I let the house fall into darkness when I was home alone. I should have listened to Brooke and adopted a dog from the local shelter months ago. He could be my ears and my eyes watching out for intruders, could love me unconditionally, be my companion...

With cold, shaking hands, I called Brooke's number, but it went straight to voicemail. Next, I tried her office in Manhattan, but when the answering machine picked up, I remembered it was the weekend and the employees were off until Monday.

I gathered my knees to my chest and huddled against the backrest of the reading sofa, staring into the black hall. "Come on, girl, stop being a baby! Get a hold of yourself!" I encouraged my mind to give the order to my body to move.

As if someone sent me a sign, my phone beeped, signaling me that the battery was down to five percent.

"Shit!"

I called for Brooke's cat, but she never was a people's pet, and she didn't answer my call now.

Four percent.

"Shit! There is no one here. The house is empty!" I kept telling myself. "There's nothing to be afraid of. Let's go!"

With a big gulp of air, I jumped off the sofa and leaped to the light switch in the hall. I ran to the kitchen, turning on every light along the way.

In the bright kitchen filled with knives, I felt safe enough to microwave some grilled chicken with parmesan and marinara sauce.

While I ate, I wondered if Brooke had an annual tradition to remember her late husband and their marriage, and if so, who would know about it.

The only person I could think of was Tony, but I dreaded the idea of calling him after what I'd witnessed on the monitors last night.

Still, I had no other option. I had to make sure Brooke was okay.

To see if Tony was home, I headed to the surveillance room with the false confidence lent to me by the brightness in the house.

Tony was in his kitchen, sitting on a barstool by the breakfast island. His mother was massaging his shoulders.

I checked the other monitors. His lady friend from last night was gone.

I called him on my cell phone. I watched him lean over his phone to check the caller ID. "I need to take this," he said to his mother.

She glanced at the screen and shook her head. "Oh, is that your girlfriend?"

"Mom, don't start." Tony pulled away.

"Oh, look at you, rushing to answer her call like a sad little puppy. Woof! Woof!"

Tony walked out of the camera's view hidden in the kitchen when I heard his voice on the phone. "Annie, how's it going?"

"Hi, Tony. How are you?"

"Hanging in there. I'm looking forward to our meeting to sign those papers."

"Everything is prepared. We only need to set a date for the signing. But that's not why I'm calling. I can't get hold of Brooke. She isn't answering her phone. Earlier, she mentioned something about today marking the marriage anniversary of her and her late husband, Robert? Do you know if she does anything special on this day? Or where I might find her?"

Tony showed up on the hallway camera. "Oh, yeah. I'm aware of the date. But if Brooke didn't tell you where she was going, then she probably doesn't want to be bothered."

I clenched my teeth. Then I released them slowly. "Do you know where she is?" I asked in my sweetest voice.

"I do."

I sucked in a deep breath. "Look, I need to talk to Brooke. It's important. It can't wait until Monday."

Tony looked back from the doorway at his mother, then put more distance between the two of them. "I don't know. It's not my secret to share. Brooke will be upset with me if I tell you."

"Tony," I said softly. "Please don't make me beg."

I watched him drop his head back and bite his lower lip. He punched the air a few times. "All right. But you didn't hear it from me. Brooke goes to The Drunken Crab every year on this day. It's a pub run by Julia's brother in NOHO." I could detect tension in his voice.

"What's NOHO? I've never heard of that." Tony already knew I was a West Coast girl, so I had no reason to play the New Yorker.

"Oh, it's north of Houston Street in Manhattan."

"All right, I'll google it. Thanks, Tony. Hey, look, I'm really sorry for putting you in this position. You've done me a huge favor. I owe you one."

"Just don't be surprised when I come to collect."

I smiled to myself. But my joy metamorphosed into a frown as I recalled the previous night. In particular, seeing a call from Tony on my phone while I was hiding from him at the construction site.

"One more thing. I had a missed call from you last night. Was there something you wanted from me?" I asked because usually people returned missed calls from their clients, which I'd failed to do.

He pretended to bang his head against the wall. "I must have butt-dialed you," he laughed uneasily, and I leaned closer to the screen and put my finger on his face.

"No worries. Thanks again for helping me out."

*   *   *   *   *

An hour later, I made my way to the pub in NOHO that Tony was talking about so I could confront Brooke about her disappearance. I also owed her an apology for last night. It would have been wiser to let her mourn in peace and wait for her at home. But I was too scared to be alone in the house.

The Drunken Crab happened to be a speakeasy built in the basement of a four-story historic building, with an old iron fire escape mounted on its facade. Once again, I had to warn myself not to stare like a tourist as I exited my Uber.

On the sidewalk, I leaned against a wrought-iron cage enclosing a tall, slender tree to remove a pebble from my heel, smiling at a group of young men vaping outside in the chilly wind.

Following the signs, I descended the stairs and entered a gift shop that displayed items from T-shirts and beer mugs to stuffed animal heads mounted on wooden plates that one would use for decorating a home bar.

"It's called a jackalope," a rocker-looking guy informed me when he caught me staring at a mounted jackrabbit head with antlers.

I glanced at his leather wristbands and elaborate arm tattoos.

"A what? Is that real?" I asked, pointing at the mystical-looking creature.

"Yep. Google it if you don't believe me." He smirked.

I returned his smile and looked around a little, confused, when I noticed two guys and a girl walking out of a contraption that looked like a confection booth, drinks in hand, and laughing as if they were leaving a comedy show.

"Is that the bar entrance?"

"It is, but don't tell anyone." He crossed his lips with his index finger. This slogan must have been some clever marketing trick to get people talking about the place.

As soon as I entered the authentic Irish-style pub, I spotted Brooke by the bar, talking to a male bartender. Although I recognized her, she looked like a different person, broken and lost. Her back was hunched as she stooped over her drink with her hand supporting her head and her elbow pressed into the wooden counter.

I locked eyes with a female waitress approaching me, then walked across the low-lit room and sat down on a barstool next to Brooke.

She eyed me through her thick glasses. "What're you doing here?"

"I came here to be with you!" I yelled over the music that seemed to be a little too loud for an intimate bar like this. "I didn't want you to be alone today."

She turned to me, and I noticed a cigarette tucked behind her ear. "I don't need your pity."

"I don't pity you. I just want to hear about the love Robert and you shared."

She looked at me for a few seconds. "Bring us a pitcher of Paloma," Brooke told the bartender.

He sized me up. "Sure thing, lass."

Brooke pulled out the cigarette from behind her ear and sniffed at its entire length as if it were a fine cigar.

"Why do you care about my love life?"

"You don't have a love life."

She scoffed. "Touché."

I touched her hand. "Look, Brooke. It's pretty obvious Robert was special. The love of your life. And the police never caught the bastard who killed him. And these feelings of failure and disappointment have caused you so much pain. I've been acting selfishly lately, but I'm here to talk if you want. Or just listen, if that's what you need."

"What we had wasn't simply love. We were soulmates," she mused. "It was a savage love. Passionate. The kind of love where you can't get enough of each other. When all you think about is making love, endless love." Her head dropped down, and her nails scraped over the wood. "I don't think I should talk about sex with you. Considering—" She stopped herself before finishing her train of thought.

"Considering my background?" I finished her sentence for her.

"I don't want to rub salt in your wounds."

I smiled at her. "You're not. I still believe in love. It's good to hear that you were lucky to experience it."

Brooke spun on her chair, faced me, and grabbed both of my hands. "Many men would be happy to have a beautiful young woman like you." Then she seemed to bite her tongue.

I'd had many men who were happy to have me. Whether I was willing or not.

She released my hands. "That came out wrong."

"People are more resilient than you think. I've been hurt and hurt badly, but I don't want to be a victim for the rest of my life."

She offered me a pained smile. "I feel guilty for keeping you here, denying you the life you need."

"You're not denying me anything. Everything I need right now is here with you."

The pitcher of cocktail arrived with two fresh glasses. I filled one for Brooke and one for me.

"Cheers to true love," I said. A bit corny, but the words just slipped out. It was that kind of night when a bitter old attorney and a burned-out former sex slave talked about love.

Brooke clinked her glass to mine, downed her drink, then grabbed the bartender by his collar and pulled him closer. "This is Eric, Julia's brother," she said as the guy struggled to free himself from her hold. "This is my new assistant I was telling you about."

"Nice to meet you," Eric said, smoothing his shirt back into place. He looked to be thirty, but the devil-may-care ragged look might have contributed to that. He kept pushing his honey-blond hair back with both of his hands, exposing his unshaved, round face. There was a lot of pain in his eyes, which made him look both likable and relatable.

"I'm sorry about what happened to Julia. She was a good friend of mine."

He shot me a stunned glance with his almond eyes that sat underneath bushy eyebrows. "You knew my sister?"

"Yeah, in a different lifetime," I said, salvaging the result of my big fat mouth.

Eric stretched his tanned arm over the counter. "What was your name again?"

"Annie. Annie Adams." My initials were AA—alcoholic/addict anonymous. I picked it because it had an ironic ring to it.

"I'm sorry, I don't remember Julia ever mentioning you. I'd like to hear about your relationship with my sister. How did you say you knew her?"

A female bartender with a closely shaven head and a porcelain-doll-like face yelled to Eric. "A call for you."

"Sorry, duty calls. Don't disappear on me now, okay? I want to hear your story." He smiled, but it wasn't sexy. More like pain-stricken in nature.

"He was very close to Julia," Brooke explained. "He still goes down to Mexico a few times a year to look for any signs of her. He's the only one who never gave up hope."

Our glasses were full again, and we drank together.

Brooke slammed her glass onto the bar. "See, love destroys people. It would be much better if we never had that emotion."

I didn't have any grounds to argue. I'd never been in love. Well, I thought I loved Alejandro when I was fourteen, but he only took advantage of my naïveté and innocence to make a buck by selling me to the cartel.

"I mean, look at Barbara's obsession with her youngest son, Tony. She could never accept Tony and Julia's relationship. The mere thought of her baby boy caring for another woman more than her drove the woman crazy. Barbara and Julia would have vicious fights. Barbara even told Tony to get a DNA test on Sammy. Can you believe the nerve of that woman?" Brooke burst out into a raspy laugh. "Especially in light of Tony's cheating!"

"You never told me that Barbara was Julia's enemy!"

"She wasn't her enemy. She was like most mothers-in-law. Way too overprotective of her precious little boy. No woman was ever good enough for her baby."

"Do you think she could have hurt Julia?"

Brooke waved the notion away with her hand. "Nah. Barbara is an old hag. All bark, no bite. I bet she enjoys having Tony rely on her all the time now to babysit Sammy. She likes it when people depend on her and need her help. I guess that makes her feel important or some shit." She hiccupped as she poured a third round for us.

I sipped at my drink, running through the content of Julia's diary in my mind. "I don't know much about Barbara. There's only one entry about her in the diary."

"The bitch wasn't worth wasting any time on," Brooke said between hiccups.

"Why do you hate her?"

"I don't *hate* her. I just don't particularly like her. She was so neglectful with Sammy. Julia hated to leave her alone with him as a baby. She would let her nasty dogs sleep with the baby in the same bed. Julia had her infected appendix removed when she was nine because of dirty dog hair she'd ingested. Yet Barbara always ignored Julia's requests. She always knew better."

"How did Tony handle his mother?"

"He'd had a few arguments with Barbara, taking Julia's side. It made Barbara even more spiteful. I swear to God, she tried to kill that baby a few times."

"Are you talking about the accident at the pool?"

"Yep, that one. Many other 'accidents' happened to Sammy in her care." Brooke used air quotes to make her point.

"I read about the pool story. Julia didn't think there was anything malicious behind it. Barbara had forgotten to close the gate to the pool."

"Whatever, let's drink. I don't want to waste my night talking about Barbara Rose."

We drank again. And we poured again. The combined Vicodin, CBD oil, and now the tequila was beginning to mess with my head.

Brooke grabbed my arm. "Come on. Let's dance!"

I looked at her creased face, her clear-rimmed glasses, her messy short hair, and pictured us dancing. I imagined it a comical sight.

"Come on!" she urged, throwing her arms in the air and shaking her hips to *Lady* from Mojo. Hector used to blast this song all the time in the brothel.

I tossed back another cocktail, swallowed it with a big gulp, the extra liquid leaking out of the corners of my mouth, and rose to my feet.

We danced and laughed as never before. I felt free as a bird. Unburdened. In love. Horny.

Soon we were surrounded by strangers hoping to steal some of our stardust, eager to infect themselves with our good vibes. But I had eyes for only one man, and it was Tony Rose. If he hadn't waved, I might have mistaken him for another one of my mind's projections. But he was there in the flesh, standing by the entrance as if he didn't belong and staring at me with those dark, hungry eyes.

23

Tony Rose stood like a statue on the brick landing of the entrance to The Drunken Crab, dressed in a black leather jacket, a gray V-neck shirt, and black jeans. The neon orange from the light fixtures cast a sheen of bronze on his skin, giving him an end-of-the-summer kind of glow. His usual tousled dark hair was combed and slicked back. And he had eyes only for me. I returned his gaze as I swayed my hips and danced to the rhythm. He wasn't supposed to be here. His presence revealed him as my informant to this place. Nevertheless, I was glad to see him. Was he here to see me?

The song ended, another began, the beat faster and with more bass. I felt the pounding in my chest, electrifying me. I tried to smile at Tony, but my lips wouldn't comply. My guilt was stopping me from being nice to the man who was married to my best friend.

My head began buzzing with flashbacks of last night. I kept reliving the moment when Tony molded his naked body over the blonde on the couch. My blood burned in my veins from the disturbing memory.

I needed a drink. No, I needed something stronger to suppress the outrageous yet sexy images in my mind.

I broke our stare and forced my way through the crowd and back to the bar. The drinks and the pitcher I shared with Brooke were gone.

"Here," Julia's brother set a fresh cocktail in front of me. "Can't leave your drink unattended."

"Why?" I yelled over the loud music.

Eric gave me a stunned look. "Because someone may slip drugs in it! Did you grow up in a bubble or something?"

"Something," I said in a low voice before grabbing my drink and taking a sip.

I watched Eric's eyes move over my head and sweep across the dance floor as he polished a glass with a towel and bobbed his head to the beat of the music. Then the movement of his head ceased, the grin vanished from his lips, and his shoulders dropped. "Hell no!" he exclaimed, then slammed the glass onto the ground and jumped over the bar.

I staggered back, and the Paloma in my hand spilled over my shirt as Eric's feet caught me as his legs flew over the polished wooden top.

I lost him for a second in the crowd, but he resurfaced by the entrance, near Tony. As if anticipating a hostile encounter, Tony backed himself against the wall and put his arm up to protect his face. Eric still managed to land a punch on his right cheek. Then he gripped Tony's collar and started to drag him away from the wall.

The tipsy thirty-somethings jumped away in fright, creating a boxing ring for the two men. But Tony wasn't fighting back. He remained stationary, taking hit after hit, only holding his arms up to guard his face.

Overwhelmed by a powerful feeling of injustice, I cut my way through the horde of people to get to Tony and protect him. Most dancers didn't realize what was going on a few feet away from them, but those who were close by had their cell phones out and were recording the incident.

By the time I reached the scene of the beatdown, security had dispersed most of the thrill seekers.

I wedged myself between the two men, pushing Eric away from Tony. I didn't particularly take Tony's side. First of all, I had no idea what had instigated the fight—Eric may have had a legitimate reason to bash in Tony's face. Second, I'd been telling myself for months how much I hated the guy. But he was also the one whose face was battered and bloodied and needed protection. Something inside me answered the call.

Eric staggered back, his expression one of pure rage. He looked at me, then back at Tony, and raised a finger at him. "That piece of shit isn't welcome here," he grunted, his lips trembling.

"What's gotten into you, Eric?" I asked, my hand pressed against Tony's chest. I could feel his racing heart underneath his shirt.

"This bastard killed my sister and got away with it!" Eric blurted into my face, spraying saliva with every syllable. He then leaned to the side to confront Tony behind me. "I told you! If I see your smug face here again, I'll kill you."

Like a tiger ready to pounce, Brooke burst out of the crowd and grabbed hold of Eric's shoulders. "Calm down, Eric. Let's not make any threats here in public," she urged, pulling the raging man away. "Take Tony home," she instructed me over her shoulder.

Security had managed to restore order by dispersing the gawking crowd that had assembled around us. Only a few scandal-vultures lingered, taking pictures and murmuring theories to each other.

"You're bleeding," I said to Tony.

His expression was blank—the face of a man who cared about nothing or no one.

"Wait here!" Never taking my eyes off him, I slammed a twenty onto the bar and asked for a double shot of vodka on ice. While I waited for the bartender to pour me the drink, I grabbed a handful of napkins.

A few people remained in hopes of witnessing another event unfold. I shot them a piercing glance as I passed by them.

"Let's get outside," I told Tony, and he turned away from the wall and started walking.

The gift shop attendant watched us leave, mouth agape. "Are you trying to catch flies?" I hissed at him.

I'd left my coat inside on the stool by the bar, and I felt an instant chill the moment we emerged from the narrow steps out onto the street. A sea of yellow cabs churned in front of us, but judging by the unlit cab lights on top, they were all occupied.

I needed to get Tony away from this place in case Brooke wasn't able to calm Eric down and he came outside for round two.

"My car is parked over there." Tony pointed down the street at nothing in particular.

My eyes lingered on his face for a moment, taking in the damage Eric had done to him. The skin over his right eyebrow was split open a quarter inch, and blood trickled down his cheek. His lips were swollen and bruised. A red blotch spread over his left cheekbone, and a few other smaller cuts disfigured his face.

"I don't think you're in any condition to drive."

"I'm fine," he said indifferently.

We started down the busy street, passing piles of dog waste and plastic trash.

Tony didn't need support, but I walked with him, holding the glass of vodka and the napkins, like an impromptu nurse in a battlefield.

He noticed my shivering and draped his leather jacket over my shoulders. I tried to resist, saying he needed it more than I did, but he insisted I hold onto it.

I should have been thrilled to see him get his ass kicked, but I only felt pity.

At the backlot of a tattoo parlor that was closed for the night, we got into the backseat of Tony's BMW. I dipped the cluster of napkins into the vodka and started cleaning the blood off his face. Alcohol dabbed onto open wounds stings like hell—I'd had my share of experiences with this method of disinfecting—but Tony didn't flinch.

Feeling uncomfortable and nervous, I held out the glass to him. "You want a drink?"

He shook his head no, so I drank the rest with one gulp.

I moved my hand back to resume cleaning his face, but he grabbed hold of my wrist. My pulse pounded underneath his fingertips. He held up my hand for a few moments, saying nothing, doing nothing, as he gave me a calculating and attentive stare.

As his penetrating eyes got under my skin, my lower hips began to tingle. My chest and arms felt as if they were flushing with warm blood. I should have ripped my hand from his hold, stepped out of the car, and run back to Brooke. But I didn't do any of those things.

The moment was suspended between us. Tony's breathing had become more audible. His chest was rising and falling at an increasing rate.

He pulled me on top of him.

I didn't fight it.

He waited again, studying my face. I tried to remain calm and collected, but I couldn't hide my racing heart. My mouth opened, and the sound of my rapid raspy breathing filled my ears.

With one confident movement, Tony ripped open my blouse, buttons popping on the dashboard and landing on the leather seats and floorboard. He stopped and waited again. I should have felt naked, vulnerable, but I didn't feel any of those emotions: I wanted him to continue.

He removed my bra and kissed my breasts, my neck, my chin, my cheek. At last, his mouth latched onto my lips. Our tongues touched. I tasted blood. His kiss was aggressive, wet, and warm as if he wanted to devour me.

His hands slipped down the side of my torso and gripped the flesh above my hips. He tossed me back onto the seat where I had been sitting only a few moments ago. He yanked at my pants, and I helped him get them down. He leaned away. He remained unmoving, watching me again with those hungry eyes.

He waited.

I watched him breathing with his mouth open. I knew what he wanted—what was about to happen. And I should have stopped him. How many times in the past eight years did I promise myself that no man would ever touch me again?

Sex is pain. Sex is submission, humiliation, deviant power. That was what I learned in the brothel. My body was never going to be someone else's pleasure toy again.

I kept telling myself to kick this man off me and run.

But there was a wild, savage animal unleashed inside of me. A feeling so raw and natural, it made me blind to reason.

Against my better judgment, I grabbed Tony's shirt, yanked it off, and pulled him onto me.

The cabin of the car quickly warmed with our hot bodies. My naked back slipped on the moist leather seat. Tony's lean, muscular arms bulged underneath me as he cradled me. I had feelings inside of me I'd never felt before. I was scared to make a sound, but my voice had become its own master. For a moment, I feared someone in the parking lot would hear me moaning, but soon I was swept up in a feeling that made my head swim and my body tremble.

I didn't know how long our act lasted. It was an out-of-body experience, and this rosy-cheeked confident girl couldn't possibly be me. It was as if she were my alter ego in a parallel universe where I had stayed in high school and went to college and pursued my dreams. This was the London White I would have been if only I had said no to Alejandro—a girl with a normal life.

As our united trembling eventually ended, Tony straightened up and smoothed back his loose hair. His chest glistened from perspiration. He set those secretive eyes on me again and said nothing.

I should have covered my breasts and looked away, but I held his gaze, unyielding, content.

"I shouldn't...I shouldn't have done this. I don't know what I was thinking. Did I hurt you?" he asked.

I sucked in my throbbing lips and shook my head.

He offered me his hand, and I took it as if it were a peace offering. He pulled me to his chest. My skin touched his warm, moist body, and the scent of his cologne slithered into my nostrils. I closed my eyes as he buried his face into the hair behind my ear.

"You have no idea how much I've wanted to do this," he whispered.

I didn't reply. I relished the calm of this moment. Thinking of something witty to say would have dragged me out of this sea of tranquility I was lost in.

The windows were fogged over, encapsulating us in our own little world. As if nothing and nobody existed outside our piece of heaven.

I caught a glance of my reflection in the rearview mirror, but the face didn't belong to me. It belonged to Julia.

I gasped and jolted away from Tony.

There was somebody who mattered, and I had desecrated her memory.

The realization of what I'd done came hard and fast. The shame I felt made me dizzy and sick to my stomach. I couldn't breathe. I needed to get out of the car and run far away.

But I was trapped in the car—in my enemy's car—unveiled and exposed. My bloodstained blouse lay ruined on the floorboard, buttons ripped off. Where can I go looking like this?

I crossed my arms in front of me, trying to hide my nakedness. Tony handed me his shirt, and I pulled it over my head.

"Are you upset with me?" he asked, buckling up his belt.

Words wouldn't form, so I shook my head again.

"You want me to take you somewhere?"

Where? To Brooke's? That could never happen. I panicked.

"I'm going to call for a car."

He put his hand on my phone. "I'll drive you. Seriously, it's not a problem. Just tell me where you want to go."

"I'm hungry," I said out of the blue. "I think I had too much to drink tonight." I didn't know why, but I also offered him a smile. Why was I being so nice? I was supposed to hate this man.

"I've got an idea." He cocked his head with a mischievous sparkle in his eyes. "Grilled cheese sandwiches!"

My stomach rumbled, and I laid a hand on it to dampen the sound.

"I don't want to force you, but you must know that I can make a killer grilled cheese sandwich. I put ham in it and horseradish. And I drench it in salted Irish butter. Who can say no to that?"

"You're right. I can't say no to salted Irish butter."

He gave a slight nod with his head, his lips curling up on one side.

He turned over the engine, and the fans defogged the windows. He switched on the seat-heater for me, and I curled up in my seat.

Although I wasn't a virgin—far from it—I felt like I'd lost my virginity. Nobody had ever touched me with such raw passion yet gentleness. Tony's body trembled with mine. His breathing mixed with mine. If this was what making love felt like, then I understood why Brooke had such a hard time letting go of her memories of Robert.

The drive was long, but we didn't fill the journey with small talk. I mostly looked out of the window, marveling at the night lights of New York City, because I was afraid to look into any of the mirrors.

At times, I turned back to Tony, wondering what he thought of me. What thoughts were turning the motors in his brain? The only thing I could read in his eyes was concern. I remembered that look all too well. Julia used to look at us younger girls with those same eyes.

We parked underneath an oak tree and not at his usual parking spot. With my shoes in my hand, I stepped out of the car barefoot and hopped on the cold, wet grass toward the house.

I didn't get far before Tony's arms swooped me off my feet, and he carried me to the door.

"What if your mother catches us?" I asked, eyeing Barbara's car in the driveway.

"Don't worry. Ma always sleeps like the dead." He pulled me to him and kissed me.

24

The furnace must have kicked in because I felt the warm air drifting from the duct and bristling the tiny hairs on my skin. I detected the faint fragrance of the fishpond and the potted flowers from the yard in the draft. I sat on the kitchen countertop, smiling like an idiot, my head still in a daze.

As I watched Tony prepare our late-night snack in the glow of the kitchen light, a ravenous appetite came over me. My belly kept rumbling. I drank a big glass of water to dilute the acid in my stomach. It always worked in the brothel.

"I know this is weird…you and me in my kitchen making sandwiches at one o'clock in the morning," Tony said as he buttered the bread next to me. "But I'm glad you're here."

If he only knew how weird indeed. I'd been watching him lingering in this kitchen for weeks on the monitors without his knowledge, plotting my revenge. Brooke had warned me not to mix business with pleasure, so what was I doing here? What was this raw desire that kept me close to this troubled man—the magnetic pull I had succumbed to? If not for the guilt I felt by betraying Julia's memory, I may have enjoyed this stolen moment. But I did feel guilty.

To silence my conscience, I kept telling myself that I was in Julia's house with her husband to find out new information about her murder. It was my job to play the part.

That fabricated self-assurance did little to convince me that I was in Tony's house for the right reasons. Yet I was too impaired by the combination of alcohol and prescription meds to admit to myself that I only stayed because I enjoyed being with Tony.

I sat on the counter without pants, barefoot, smelling of sex, and wearing Tony's shirt. The lines blurred between London White and Annie Adams and who I was at the moment. Brooke had warned me about putting myself in a compromising position. Why was I so awful at listening to her advice?

Tony handed me a package of sliced cheese and asked me to put a slice on each piece of bread.

Unsure whether to talk or stay quiet, I resorted to smiling whenever Tony glanced at me.

When he caught me scrutinizing his bloody lip, he touched the cut. "I think my face looks worse than it feels. You don't need to worry. I want you to know that I don't regret going to the bar tonight to find you."

He must have expected me to say that I was glad too, but I didn't give him the satisfaction.

"Why did Julia's brother attack you like that?"

Tony's eyes shrunk, and the spatula stopped in his hand. "I'm not his favorite person in the world."

"That's pretty obvious. But why? Does he blame you for Julia's disappearance?"

"He thinks I killed her." He said this as a mere statement without revealing how he felt about his brother-in-law's accusation.

I stretched his shirt down to cover more of my thighs before I allowed my eyes to meet his again. "Did you?" I breathed the words.

He swallowed hard. "Are you scared of being alone with me?"

A chill ran down my spine. "Should I be?"

He turned his hips toward me and wiped his hands on a kitchen towel. "Well, if you followed Julia's case in the news, which I'm sure you did, then you know the police arrested me on suspicion of killing my wife."

"I did read something like that, yes."

"Do you believe I'm capable of killing the mother of my child?"

The tension in my chest grew. "I don't know you at all. I have no idea what you're capable of doing."

He looked away and shook his head. "The tabloids tried to paint me as a monster. They published half-truths and speculated without fact-checking. When Julia disappeared, I was their scapegoat—somebody to blame, a suspect the public demanded. But when the evidence didn't support their theory, they turned on Julia. It was despicable. Can you imagine what it would do to Sammy if he ever read what those blogs and papers wrote about his mother?"

"He doesn't know about any of it?"

"No. We did everything we could to keep Sam out of the spotlight. You can't imagine how difficult it was to live through those years. One day we were an average family, trying to balance our work and personal life. The next, the whole world wanted to know every little detail about us and our marriage. Every aspect of our lives was dissected like a frog and published for all to see. The media and the public crushed my life and tore my guts out until there was nothing left for them to take. As if it wasn't enough that I'd lost my wife, I also had to explain to my son why his mother would never tuck him in bed again and why she would never kiss him good night again. But I wasn't allowed to grieve because I had to deal with the police accusing me of her murder."

He sighed and wiped his nose with the back of his hand.

"The first year was the toughest. I wanted to stay in bed all day and pretend it was all a horrible dream. I lost my will to live. But

Sammy was here, and I had to find my strength for him. I couldn't have done it without my mother's help. People took my strength as a sign of guilt. I received death threats." His whole body shook as if a chill had run through him. "Do you know there are Facebook groups dedicated to destroying my life?" He swallowed audibly again. "Sometimes I wish I could turn back time and prevent Julia from writing those damned books."

"What do you think happened on that cruise ship? Do you think she jumped? Or was she pushed?"

Tony's expression turned pale as if all happiness had left him. "Your guess is as good as mine."

I studied his face, looking for any signs of him lying—a twitch in the eye or perhaps a fleeting glance to the left. But there was nothing.

"I loved my wife. Our marriage wasn't perfect, but I never dreamed of hurting her," he said convincingly.

"I never said you would."

"But you thought it. That's why you brought it up."

He looked dejected as he talked, and I was choking up, feeling sad for this broken man. For the first time, I indeed saw the devastation Julia's disappearance had caused him.

The fan kept humming, and I sat there, helpless and lost, as if the purpose of my life had been ripped away from me.

"I'm sorry for bringing up your wife; I was wrong to do it. I didn't mean to rip the bandage off your wound."

Tony said nothing.

I jumped off the countertop. "I think it's better if I get going."

He put both his hands on the counter, the plates of sandwiches in front of him, his head hanging over them.

I extended my hand toward his back to comfort him but stopped halfway.

I picked up my shoes from the floor, attempting to walk away from this kitchen, this house, this man.

"I don't want you to go." Tony's gentle voice echoed in the stillness.

He sounded desperate.

My heart gave a strange twitch.

I glanced up at the spy camera hidden behind the grate of the duct in the ceiling, assuring myself that staying would be a big mistake. It was madness to be here in the first place, but I couldn't bring myself to leave him alone.

Before Julia appeared in the brothel and assumed the role of a mother hen, the worst thing I remembered was being alone with my pain and not being able to share it with anyone. All that hatred and resentment kept building up inside of me, turning me into my own worst enemy. I had Julia, but who was there for Tony?

I felt his hand touching my hand and turning me around. He went down on his knees in front of me and pressed his face against my belly. His hands drove the shirt up on my waist and he kissed my naked skin. His fingers folded over my back, and I buried mine in his hair. I slid down in his embrace until we were face-to-face. He helped me out of his shirt.

"I want to see you," he whispered, and I held his gaze because I wanted to see him too. I craved to watch his eyes fill with pure desire for me. He wasn't there for my body or to take advantage of me. He wanted my soul, my heart. He wanted the whole *me*.

His right hand pressed against my chest. His touch was warm on my skin. "I don't know what it is, but I feel connected to you. I know you have your doubts about me, or maybe you're scared of me, but I'd never hurt you. I'd never hurt anyone."

I desperately wanted to believe him and attempted to push the bad memories from my mind so I could be in the moment. Breathe it in. Soak it up.

He kissed me on my lips with short, teasing pecks, escalating into a devouring passion that connected our mouths as one.

Soon I found myself on his lap, moving up and down, taking him in and uniting our bodies.

His eyes never let go of mine. It was the most intimate thing that had ever happened to me.

With a confident grip, he seized my hips and tried to lift me. I fought him, not wanting to be in the view of the spy camera.

I pushed him onto his back in the concealment of the kitchen island and laid my body on top of his.

He struggled to give up control, and despite my efforts, I soon found myself on the countertop with him between my legs.

The spatula flew onto the ground as we climaxed. The clanking sound echoed in the stillness of the night.

I collapsed in Tony's arms, and he locked me in the embrace of his trembling body. We both held our breaths, listening to the sounds of the night as the squeaks of a bed rose above the silence, followed by stifled footsteps.

"My mother's coming," Tony whispered, gazing over my shoulder at the staircase. "You want to meet her, or would you rather leave the introduction for another day?"

"Oh, God. She can't see me like this," I said, jumping off the marble countertop. I scrambled to gather my clothes and huddled behind the massive kitchen island.

Watching Tony buckle up his pants, I pressed my back against the furniture, trying to control my breathing to help me slow down my heartbeat.

Tony's hair was disheveled, and his chest had a sparkling sheen visible underneath the lighting fixture. A grin formed on my lips as I watched him stack the bread slices with conviction.

"What are you doing, Tony?" I didn't like Barbara's voice. She sounded angry and disappointed, prompting me to say something. I put a hand over my mouth to stifle any sound.

"I'm making something to eat."

"In the middle of the night? Have you lost your mind?"

"I got home and was hungry. Sorry if I woke you, but it's all good. You can go back to bed."

"It's too late. I'm already up."

The sound of a barstool's legs scraping over the tile warned me to ready myself to change position in case Barbara decided to join her son on my side of the island.

"I'll be only a minute. Go back to bed."

"Why are you so eager to get rid of me? And why do you look like you just finished a marathon? Oh, my God. What happened to your face? Is your lip bleeding?"

I saw Barbara's hand reaching for Tony's face, but he pulled away and ran his hands over his hair, fixing it. "It was a crazy night. Things got out of control."

"Did you get in a fight over someone? You and your money-hungry whores."

Tony stiffened. "Mother!"

"Don't 'Mother' me! You know exactly what I'm talking about. You always let women control your life. Look at what being married to Julia did to you! You're still living in the shadow of your deceased wife, sucking the same tits you did three years ago. What are you trying to do now? Bring home another milk cow? Or pick up someone who only wants our money? Why don't you focus on getting a job of your own, so you don't have to be at the mercy of that dead woman?"

"Mother, enough! Her name is Julia, and it's my money, not ours. But I'm not discussing this with you now."

"Truth hurts, doesn't it, son? I told you not to marry that ambitious woman, but you didn't listen to me. Julia turned you into a helpless man—a lap dog. You have a son upstairs who needs a strong father, yet here you are, partying and drinking, maybe even doing drugs, trying to latch onto someone else instead of getting your life in order."

"I'm not listening to this again. You need to leave now! Pack your stuff and leave my house. Go home!"

"It's the middle of the night. I'm not going anywhere."

"I won't tolerate you dishonoring Julia's memory. She was my wife and the mother of my child."

"Yeah, your wife, who turned you against your own family and tried to destroy us all."

"Enough! I said I'm not having this conversation with you."

"Why are you doing this?"

"Doing what?"

"You've been doing so well lately. Focusing on Sam and being the good father I raised you to be. Now, look at yourself! Partying for the second night in a row like a frat boy and whoring around the city. You are just like your father was."

Staying hidden was becoming difficult. Tony needed someone to take his side against his raging bitch mother. Was she on drugs? Or drunk? What the hell possessed her to talk to her adult son this way?

"You are the one to throw stones," Tony scoffed. "And I'm not my father, so stop trying to compare me to him. Understand? You're my mother, not my wife. It's none of your damn business who I sleep with or where I go. Now either you go upstairs and back to bed, or get out of my house. I finally had a great night out; you won't ruin it for me because your life is miserable."

"Don't you dare talk to me this way! I'm your mother!"

"Then act like a mother! Now go!"

My phone vibrated in my purse. I rolled onto my knees and gently pulled it out and opened the new message. It was a single black-and-white picture from Brooke—a screenshot taken on the monitor showing Tony holding my naked body.

Fuck! I thought, staring into the spy camera, thinking Brooke was still watching me.

With my jaws clenched tight, I closed the message before Tony could see it. But he was no longer in the kitchen. I peeked over the corner to see him ushering his mother upstairs. I quickly gathered my belongings, and when both of them had disappeared onto the second-floor landing, I bolted to the front door and left.

25

It was dark, and a sharp, damp wind whipped the trees outside. I didn't remember hearing the tapping of the rain when I was in the kitchen with Tony, but it was coming down hard now, soaking through the flimsy T-shirt and the jeans I just pulled on my cold, wet legs.

I didn't know what to do; I only knew what I was supposed to do. I needed to get home and make things right with Brooke. I just wasn't sure if I was welcome in her house anymore after the picture she had texted me.

I screwed things up really bad this time, and I had no idea how I would fix it.

A dog howled in the distance, and I shuddered, reluctant to leave the safety of Tony's house.

An elongated rectangle of warm yellow light appeared on the concrete driveway coming from one of the bedrooms upstairs. I stepped down from the entrance, my heart racing in my throat. Tony would soon return to the kitchen and find me gone. I had to get away from this place before he came looking for me.

Skimming between the evergreen bushes, barefoot and soaking wet, I hurried toward the street like a burglar leaving the scene of the crime.

Outside of the gate, I put on my shoes. Farther down the street, I retrieved my cell phone from my purse and looked at the black-and-white picture of Tony's naked body intertwined with mine on the kitchen counter.

"You stupid idiot!" I grunted, slamming the phone against my forehead at least half a dozen times. But who was counting?

Kicking myself for my stupidity, I opened the recent call log menu on my phone and scrolled through the names of the few people I'd met since moving to Montclair. There were only a few names: Brooke, Helen, Jeff, Tony, Justin, Sylvia, and Kevin. Brooke was the only person with whom my relationship was intimate enough to call at this time of the night. But in light of tonight's events, I wasn't that brazen to call her for help.

I chose the second-best option, Brooke's brother, Kevin. According to Brooke, he had a thing for me. I hoped his feelings for me were enough to take pity on me and come to my rescue in the middle of the night. If he didn't answer or turned me down, I could always run home. It wouldn't have been the toughest thing I've done in my life, but that didn't mean I was looking forward to making my way across town in the pouring rain.

Then there was option three: calling for a car. But in my current state, disheveled and wearing a soaked-through shirt, I was reluctant to get in a car with a stranger.

I was about to hang up after six rings when a deep, drowsy voice answered. "Annie? What's wrong?"

Kevin was right to think that something was wrong. I'd only called him one other time, two months ago to inquire about Brooke's favorite restaurant to plan a surprise birthday dinner for her. Never before, never since.

"Sorry for bothering you so late, Kevin, but I had no one else to call."

"Is Brooke okay?" He sounded more awake now.

"Uhm, yeah, she's fine. It's me who needs a bit of help."

"What's going on?"

"Could you please pick me up at the corner of Highland Avenue and Edgewood Terrace?" I said timidly, knowing he'd recognize the area.

"Now? What time is it?"

"One thirty-five."

"Jeez! Are you on a stakeout? Is Doucheface up to something?"

"I'll tell you in person, but could you please hurry? It's raining, and I'm freezing my ass off."

He yawned noisily. "All right. I'll be there in ten."

Kevin Russell couldn't have been more the opposite of his sister, Brooke. He was laidback and scruffy-looking, but not in an unwashed, unkempt way—more like a hipster. He used to work for the harbor police before he started his own security company with a substantial cash loan from his sister. Thanks to the high-end clients Brooke sent his way, Kevin's business took off, and he was able to repay the loan earlier than expected. Even though he no longer owed money to his sister, he didn't shy away from helping her set up the illegal surveillance at the Roses' house. I always wondered if he was hoping to get something out of our arrangement or if he was simply doing his brotherly duty. But if there's one thing I've learned in life, it's that nothing's for free.

As I stood on the corner, waiting for Kevin with my shoulders pulled in to preserve whatever body heat I had left, I felt guilty for dragging him out of bed. I didn't know much about his private life, but I knew he wasn't married and didn't have any children. Although I doubted a charismatic, smart man like him slept alone in a cold bed every night. Had my late-night call caused drama with a possible girlfriend? Why did I always act first and think later? Hadn't I learned my lesson with Hector? How many more men was I willing to sacrifice to get what I wanted?

Brooke was right. I was turning into a damsel in distress. I owed it to Julia and myself to do things differently this time, to be self-reliant and resilient, but that wasn't happening as planned.

Fifteen minutes later, as I was beginning to wonder if Kevin was going to show up, a white Chevy truck broke through the curtain of rain. I turned around to face the headlights that blinded my eyes.

"Climb in," Kevin said through the rolled-down window as he leaned over to the passenger side and opened the door for me.

I dropped my purse on the floorboard and plopped onto the seat. The water was dripping from my hair and onto my shoulders. My jeans made sloshy sounds as I wiggled into place and put on my seatbelt.

"I'm not even going to ask," Kevin said with disdain, his judgmental attitude ripping at my guilt. He reached to the backseat and pulled a blanket to the front. "Here you go. Dry yourself off before you catch a cold."

I nodded with pursed lips as I tried to fabricate an adequate explanation for my appearance. But Kevin wasn't stupid. Far from it.

"Where to?" he asked as he turned the heater on full blast.

"Home, please," I said, twisting the water out of my hair with the blanket.

As he drove, Kevin peered at me a few times before he said anything. I was grateful for his lack of interrogation, but he didn't stay silent for long.

"You know, I already told Brooke that I don't want to know anything about your illegal surveillance of Tony Rose, but you guys can't leave me out of it, can you?"

"I know we asked a lot of you, but you need to know that we appreciate your help, and it's for a good cause. We couldn't be doing any of this without you."

He frowned. "Whatever. I hope all this snooping around is worth the trouble."

"Do you think we're crazy for doing it?"

"I think you should all move on with your lives. I told Brooke the same thing. I warned her that she would end up in a ditch somewhere if she didn't stop her self-destructive behavior. Before it was Robert's tragic passing, then that woman—the shrink, Valerie—who kept Brooke in mourning with those group meetings. Now it's you and that wicked family reviving her need for revenge. She lives for justice to be delivered."

My skin felt hot and prickly. As I watched the windshield wipers rubbing back and forth over the glass, my heart crawled into my ears. I heard every heartbeat pounding against my eardrums. "What are you saying? I'm a bad influence on your sister?"

Kevin flinched as he turned onto Brooke's street. "Not you specifically, but in case you haven't noticed, Brooke has a self-destructive side. She was mocked as a child for her height, for her thick glasses, and her awkwardness. Robert was the only man in her life who showed her any affection. After she lost him, Brooke buried herself in her work. She built her wealth, almost obsessively. Everything in her life was measured by money. She lost her ability to love people, but somehow, she connected with Julia and you. I don't know if you guys will ever succeed in finding who pushed Julia over the railing—if someone pushed her over at all. But I'm afraid if Brooke doesn't find Julia's killer, it will break her. For good this time."

We pulled up to the dark house, a single coach light our only guide up the long curvy driveway. Kevin put the truck into park, but he didn't turn off the engine.

"What do you want from me?" I asked, staring blankly out the windshield.

"I want you to stop fooling around and do your damn job," he sneered. "Put an end to this madness, even if you have to put a gun to Doucheface's head or intimidate that clown of a woman, Sylvia. I don't care, just get the truth out of them before Brooke drinks herself to death."

My face felt hot and flushed. "What do you think I've been doing?"

He cocked his head and rose an eyebrow. "From the looks of things? You're fucking around."

I felt as if a mule had kicked me on the chest. I peeled the blanket off me and handed it back to Kevin. "Thanks for the ride."

"Keep it." He looked away. I put my hand on the door handle to get out when I sensed an arm reaching over me to open the glove compartment. "Here. Give this folder to my sister."

"What's this?" I asked, taking the thick file from him.

"She asked me to find Tony's mistress—the one Julia mentioned in the video."

The thickness of the folder suggested that there was plenty to find.

"Thanks again," I said as I stepped out of the truck.

I was halfway to the front door when Kevin called after me. Holding the folder tight against my chest, I turned and wiped the rain from my face. I was sure he was going to apologize for talking to me with so much hostility; I was under the impression he liked me. Instead, he said, "Don't call me the next time your lover kicks you out of his bed."

And he drove off.

26

Feeling humiliated and angry, I snuck into Brooke's home. I set my purse and shoes on the floor and sat down by the door. Weakened by ravenous hunger, exhaustion, and humiliation, I placed my head in my hand, staring down at the brown folder. Did I want to know what secrets it held? I was too scared to open it.

A bone-chilling draft swept through the hallway. I shivered as it touched my damp skin. This unexpected biting cold had been a sign of Julia's forthcoming apparition, but this time I couldn't bring myself to care enough to look. If anything, I would have welcomed her company. I wished she would simply tell me the answers to all my questions.

Kevin was right. This pathetic attempt at revenge was destroying all of us because we sucked at it. *I* sucked at it. I kept glancing at the brown folder, but I couldn't bring myself to see what was inside just yet.

Brooke's cat ran out of the guest bathroom and curled under my legs. I reached between my knees to pet her and waited for Julia's translucent ghost to appear, but there was nothing. No strange visions. No unusual sounds.

I lifted the cat and looked at her cute face, desperately needing to feel something kind inside, a warmth to remind me that I was human. Instead, the cat hissed at me, clawed her way out of my hands, and ran into the shadows.

I winced at the pain and put my knuckle in my mouth to suck at the blood. When I dropped the folder, a sheet of paper partially slipped out. I took it as a sign and flipped open the cover of the folder to see what information Kevin had managed to gather on Tony.

I found page after page of profiles on beautiful women. I recognized only one face: the self-entitled, arrogant receptionist at Russell & Associates.

Barbara was right. Tony was a whoring piece of shit.

As rage and disappointment filled my stomach, my hunger for food vanished. I shoved the papers back into the folder and marched toward the bowels of the house with a purpose. My need to sob created a ball in my throat, and I tried hard to swallow it, but it remained there like a stubborn tick. My mind was fixated on one thing—to wash Tony off and out of me. I felt betrayed and used, like the fool I was. His sweet words, "I want to see you," and his smooth talk had worked on me as it had for so many others. He was not the husband Julia wrote about in her diary. Was she indeed that blind to Tony's infidelity, or had her mind blocked out the bad memories to save her from more pain? Our brains weren't any better than a computer if trauma could wipe away certain parts of our consciousness and memories. Why would a mind betray itself in such a way? Was it survival? To ease the pain? Or something else?

I stormed into the closest bathroom and went straight to the shower. I turned on the hot water, feeling borderline hysterical. I stepped into the shower and collapsed to the bottom, my knees pulled tight to my chest and my arms wrapped around my legs. And I cried like I hadn't cried in a long time.

I didn't notice Brooke enter the bathroom. I only saw her shape through the fogged-up glass, holding the folder open and browsing through the pages. I sucked my nose and washed my face while she set the folder on the sink counter and moved toward me. She opened the glass door and stepped into the shower in her nightgown. I reached for her with both arms.

"I messed up everything," I sobbed.

She lowered herself to me and took me in her arms. There was so much I wanted to apologize for and tell her. The emotions all but bursting out of me. But I said nothing. I only held onto her with all my might as the warm cascade of water beat down on us. I came here to find justice for Julia, to bring down the people who hurt her, so why were we the ones who seemed to have lost everything?

27

Julia Rose's Diary

Entry #22
It's unbeknownst to me why whenever a memory
comes back, it's always something traumatic· I'm
beginning to think that writing this diary wasn't a
good idea· It started well· In the past few weeks, I've
penned about my life in this Mexican shithole, where
I'm forced to pleasure sick bastards· I wrote about
the beatings, about the broken spirits of my fellow
prisoners, about Hector's revolting infatuation with
me· But the more I think about this diary and try to
recall my past life, the more I suffer from horrible
nightmares· When will the pleasant memories come
back? Do I even have any?

Entry #23
I've been trying to stay away from writing because
every time I sit down to jot down events from my

day, I'm bound to relive the pain and humiliation· Yet some invisible force keeps making me pick up my pencil· I think I secretly hope that one of us will be able to break free from this prison and use my diary to get the word out about our suffering·

I also hope that if I die in this place, at least I'll leave a piece of me behind for those who loved me—if somebody loved me at all·

I've been having a reoccurring dream—a nightmare really—that makes me believe I wasn't a good person, and now I'm being punished for my sins· It's easier to accept my current predicament when I tell myself I deserve it·

I'm ashamed of the memory, though I'm not entirely convinced it's a memory at all· It could be a miserable projection of my current mental state· My hands shake as I write these words· But I can't stay silent anymore because I fear if I never tell anybody about this stain on my past, then I may die with this dark secret and won't find peace in the afterlife either· These destructive thoughts and images are eating me alive· I've lost my appetite· Hector warned me that if I don't start eating, he'll force-feed me like a goose and I won't like it·

I can't put this task off any longer· I need to face my demons because I can no longer sleep at night· I feel as if everything around me is radiating heat, burning me alive· My skin prickles and itches as if armies of insects were crawling on me at night· I

can't shake them off. I've scratched my limbs bloody
with my jagged nails, but the feeling remains.
The last few nights, I've tried to sleep on the bare
floor to get away from the other pulsating and warm
bodies in the room, but I can't seem to get far
enough away. And the disturbing thoughts are spinning
in my head like a merry-go-round.
I need to write down my nightmare. I need to face
the mistakes I've made, even if there is the possibility
that my sick mind fabricated these memories. I can no
longer trust my mind, as it wouldn't be the first
time it has played tricks on me.
Hector thinks that I have the stomach flu, and
between pages and paragraphs, I flush the toilet and
make gagging sounds in case he's listening outside the
bathroom door.
I could have waited until nighttime to write about
this particular memory, but I needed an uninterrupted
environment for myself. I didn't want someone
noticing the flickering light of the candle and report
me. I'm friends with most of the girls, but you never
know who will sell you out for an ounce of heroin or a
fresh slice of tres leches cake in a place like this.
The dream always begins the same. I'm lying in a
hospital bed. A heart monitor is beeping next to me.
A handsome young man named Tony is holding my
hand. He has messy dark hair and mesmerizing brown
eyes. His eyelashes are long and nearly touch his
eyelids as he watches me. His eyebrows are full and

form two arched lines—so perfect a painter couldn't have painted them better.

He tells me that everything will be all right. That we are doing the right thing because the Adderall I was taking, and the drinking and drugs, surely damaged the fetus. I tell Tony that I feel conflicted about what I should do, and maybe we should look into the possibility to test the fetus to determine if the baby has suffered brain or other damage due to my substance abuse. Still, I fear the doctors' and nurses' judgment, so I decide not to say anything about my drug abuse.

I see myself chewing my nails as the rapid heartbeats beep on the monitor. I seem to be bothered by the sound and ask Tony to turn off the equipment.

I start crying and bang my head against the pillow. "I'm so stupid!" I repeat on a seemingly endless loop. Tony steadies my shoulders. "We didn't know. You can't blame yourself."

"How could I not know? How did I not notice missing my period for two months?"

Tony runs his hand over my matted hair. "We're doing what's best for this baby. Don't beat yourself up for it. We'll have beautiful children together. As many as we want."

"You truly believe we're doing what's best for the baby, or what's best for us?"

Tony stiffens and leans away from me. "I already told you. Whatever you decide, I'll stand with you. If you want to keep this baby, I'll support you. If you want to abort this pregnancy and try again later, when we're clean and healthy, I'll support that too."

"So, it's all on me now, isn't it? I decide if we kill our child or let him or her live?"

Tony's eyes turn dark. "I give up. You women are always saying that it's your body, your decision. I'm here to support whatever decision you make. Yet somehow, I'm the bad guy?"

"I didn't say you were the bad guy."

"But you think it! You blame me for this pregnancy as if you weren't part of it. What measures did you take to prevent it, huh? It's always the guy's fault. Everything is our fault. I'm not surprised that so many guys decide to stay single."

Tony grabs his phone from the bed and turns toward the door. "I'm gonna get some coffee. I'll send Justin in."

My body visibly shudders at the slam of the door. I let go of my belly that is as flat as an ironing board. In my dream, I remember thinking that my body betrayed me. It gave me no sign I was carrying a new life inside of me. No warning at all.

I remember those nights in the college, studying, popping Adderall to keep me focused, and drinking gallons of coffee to stay awake. And then there was always someone's birthday or an anniversary or a national holiday to give us a reason to drink and party. I can even recall my diet, or rather, the lack

of it. Microwaved burritos. Or the embarrassing
amount of Ramen noodles and cheap junk food I
gorged on. I doubt I had eaten anything healthy in
those years that didn't come out of a package.
The dream continues with the hospital room door
opening. Another man enters the room. He's taller
than Tony and more muscular, but they have the
same face and unruly hair.
"My brother told me to keep you company," he says
gently as he quietly shuts the door behind him. He
gives me a pitiful look, and I quickly wipe off the
tears, as if I'm embarrassed.
He kneels by the bed, ignoring the chair set out for
visitors, and takes my hand. In the dream, I don't
look surprised, but I'm stunned now, recalling it. Why
would another man approach me so intimately? And
why would I let him?
"I'm begging you not to do this, Julia."
I pull my hand away. "Please don't start this again,
Justin."
"I know it's my kid. I feel it in my gut."
I prop myself up on my elbows; my face is a shade of
red. "No, it's Tony's baby. Not yours."
"How do you know?"
"I know."
"I want a DNA test."
Leaning forward in offense, I say with venom. "I'm
terminating this pregnancy because I've made stupid
mistakes, and it was a complete lack of judgment on

my part, but it's time to grow up, Justin, and face the music. It was one night—you and me—one stupid night I regret. Nothing more. We were both drunk. I was upset about my exam. You were there to comfort me. But Tony must never know."

I stopped writing because this scene has been in my head for countless nights. I still can't comprehend its content, but the realization that I was by no means a perfect human being is daunting. I had to set the diary on the floor, make a series of gagging sounds, and flush the toilet for Hector. It took me a moment to pick up the notebook again, and I just stared at it on the floor for a while. But I need to finish my story. If you want people to know you, you have to share the bad with the good.

"Do you think I'll let you fool my brother? He needs to know the truth."

"No, he doesn't. He doesn't need to know anything about us. You and me—that was two months ago. Our relationship wasn't exclusive at that point. Do you think Tony wasn't seeing other girls besides me? If you tell him, you'll only hurt him and ruin your relationship with him. He'll never forgive you."

Justin stands up. "I'll take my chances."

My fingers grab the sheet, and I pull both hands into tight fists as I grind my teeth. "If you tell Tony about us, I'll say you raped me. A girl under the influence can't consent. Let that marinate for a minute, big guy."

A veil of red descends on Justin's face. "If you kill this child, you'll pay for it."

"Don't you dare threaten me, Justin."

He raises a finger at me. "You'll go to hell for this."

"I'm not killing any child!" I rage. "This, inside of me, is the size of a pea."

"Well, I guess you're lucky your mother didn't think the same way about you."

The door creaks open, and I catch Tony's troubled face as he carries in a tray with three Styrofoam cups on it.

"Coffee, bro?"

Justin shoots him a sharp look. "No, thanks. I'm amped up enough," he says and storms out of the room.

Tony's eyes linger on the door before he looks back at me again. "What's gotten into him?"

I shrug, unable to come up with a plausible lie. Then the doctor enters the room, robbing Tony of the opportunity to grill me.

That's when I wake up, drenched in sweat, my heart racing. I'm a cheater. An addict. A liar. A murderer. But I remember having a son—a cute blond little boy with rosy cheeks. I also have a Cesarean scar to prove I gave birth. Did I go through with the abortion? I may never find out.

28

The next morning, I woke in my bed alone to the scent of eggs and bacon. I winced as my head swam with dizziness from the combination of a lack of sleep and my low blood sugar. Although I was beyond exhaustion, I'd hardly slept through the night. I kept thinking about how to approach the situation of handling Tony and the rest of the Roses.

I couldn't recall when Brooke left my bed, but she was with me most of the night, holding me in her arms. She had every right to be angry with me, but she'd reserved her judgment for another day. All she did was soothe me and be there for me, and that was what I needed—someone to tell me I wasn't the terrible person I believed myself to be.

I'd made countless mistakes in my life. I was a lousy daughter to my adoptive parents. I fell for my birth mother's honey-trap when she returned in my life. I had foolishly donated my bone marrow to her so she could live. I was desperate for her love and an explanation of why she had abandoned me. Enamored in those thoughts, I had missed the warning signs of her hidden agenda. In hindsight, I see it now—the way she discarded me a second time like an unwanted piece of clothing. I should have been focused on school and my emotional health. Instead, I flung myself into the arms of the first sweet-tongued stranger who made me feel special. I should have known better than to blindly run away with

Alejandro at the age of fourteen without leaving any breadcrumbs behind for my parents to find. We weren't connected biologically, but they put food on the table, bought my clothes, cared for me when I was sick, and loved me. So why did I prize a stranger's *good* intentions over theirs?

I didn't want to be that foolish girl anymore. I came to New York City with big plans and was determined to do the right thing for the first time in my life. I was doing important work, and I thought things were on the right track. Yet I ended up playing the same record again like a fool.

In the past ten years, I'd been called a lot of different things: lazy, ungrateful, stupid, whore. All names I hated. So why did I keep justifying the stigmas and give those degrading names life? Why couldn't I break the cycle?

Brooke was outside on the patio. The table was set for two. One glance at the basket of croissants, the platter of cheesy scrambled eggs, and the crispy bacon strips was enough to activate my drooling.

Brooke pulled out a chair. "Come, sit with me." She poured me orange juice. I took the glass and gulped down the whole thing. I sat down opposite Brooke, where an empty plate was waiting for me. Without making eye contact, I loaded my plate with a little bit of everything, my greedy hunger pushing away my guilt.

"I need to tell you something, and you're not going to like it," Brooke said.

I stopped chewing my bite of warm croissant and melted chocolate.

"I've been reflecting on our past few months together—the goals we achieved, the challenges we failed to meet. I've concluded that we need to put an end to our crusade for revenge."

I tried to swallow, but I almost choked on the food. "I know you're mad at me for last night, but to give up everything? Now?"

Brooke tightened the front of the cardigan over her chest. I felt the brisk morning wind on my body and wished I had on another layer too.

"Trust me. I've given it a long and serious assessment. Everything that's happened with us and between us these last few weeks, and mostly to you, led me to the conclusion that it would be better for both of us if we turned all the evidence we've collected over to the FBI. We'll make them reopen the case."

The moment I stepped on the patio, I sensed something was off with Brooke. She was quieter than usual, grimmer. I attributed her reserved demeanor to the latest in my series of disappointing actions. My sleeping with Tony was the ultimate betrayal of Julia's memory. I couldn't blame Brooke for not wanting to see me anymore or be associated with me in any way. I thought of what Kevin had said to me in the car. *"Put an end to this madness, even if you have to put a gun to Doucheface's head or intimidate that clown of a woman, Sylvia. I don't care, just get the truth out of them before Brooke drinks herself to death."*

I put down my fork and slipped my hand over hers. "I know I've made mistakes, big ones, but I never meant to hurt you. I may have…" I removed my hand and looked away because I couldn't bear facing her without breaking down again. "I'm not what you think I am. I'm a failure, a liar, and a cheat. I messed up everything like I always do. You took me in and treated me like family. In return, I betrayed your trust."

I stopped talking for a moment to gather my strength for the things I had to say. Then I blurted it all out, needing to pour clean water in the glass at last. "I'm still an addict. I'm not clean. I've stolen some of your Vicodin from the medicine cabinet. I also used drugs with a guy I met in a bar."

Brooke's mouth opened, and I braced myself against the nasty words she had every right to spit into my face. But her voice didn't follow, so I continued speaking.

"There is no excuse for my behavior last night; I know that. But I want you to know that I was high and drunk. My judgment was seriously impaired."

"By your own fault. By your own choice."

I looked away. "You're right. Entirely."

I craved the eggs and a cup of strong coffee to tame my headache, but it no longer felt appropriate to take anything else from Brooke. I got up from my chair, ready to leave the table. Brooke didn't stop me. She was gazing out onto the belt of green pasture as if I weren't there.

Driven by self-hate and desperation, I went back to my bedroom. I dragged the mattress out of the corner of the room and dropped it back into the bed frame. I sat down, waiting for Brooke to show up at my door and accept my apology.

She didn't come.

I took a deep breath filled with desolation and pulled my travel bag out of the closet. I started packing, removing my clothes from the drawers and tossing them into the suitcase. Almost everything I owned was from Brooke. She bought my clothes, my shoes, even the tissue I was using to wipe the tears from my eyes. It didn't feel right taking any of it.

I put most of the stuff back into the closet and drawers. I kept the clothes I bought for myself with stolen money at Walmart when I first arrived in Texas after crossing the border. From the cluster of clothes, one particular piece stood out—a beige scarf I had used to wrap around my head and face as protection against the cold as I passed through a Texas rancher's land near the border. I lifted it to my nose to check if the scent of London White still clung to the fabric. It was still there: sweat, tobacco, cheap perfume, and dust.

"You never told me about your journey across the border." Brooke's voice startled me, and I dropped the scarf as if I were embarrassed to be caught with it.

"I did tell you," I said quietly, looking for signs of her intention in her expression. "A coyote helped me get across."

Brooke pushed away from the frame and stepped inside my room. "I know, but you never told me the whole story in detail. I want to know how you managed to escape the brothel and make your way here."

"In light of everything that's happened, this is what you want to hear about?"

She picked up a framed photograph of Julia that I'd cut out from an article and studied it for a moment. Then she placed it back on the bookshelf. "I have some big decisions to make today, and I told myself if I had all the pieces to the puzzle, I could understand you and your motivations better. I read Julia's diary, but now I realize that there's more to the story. I respected your privacy enough that I chose not to ask about your experience being locked up or how you escaped. But I think I'd like to hear it all now."

"You can say it out loud…my experience as a sex slave. What I was is no longer an open sore; shame no longer has the power to hurt me."

"Very well, your experience working as a sex slave. And if you don't want to talk about how you managed to get away with Julia's diary and make it here to me, that's fine—I can accept that. But I want you to know that I'm here to listen to your story. I'm here to understand, not to judge."

"Why? Do you need an excuse for why I stole from you and lied to you? Why I can't shake my addiction?"

"I don't care about the pills. I do care about you ending up like me. Broken. Wasted. Opioids might be your slippery slope, but I battle with addiction too…Bitterness. Anger. Resentment. Hatred. I was never able to let go of those demoralizing feelings. I know I'm an alcoholic. I've drunk pretty much every day since Robert died. It will kill me, I know it. But it doesn't mean that you should end up in the same place as me."

"You've accomplished more than most people dream for themselves."

She flung her arm. "What? This? None of it matters when you're a miserable old cow like me. What's the point?"

I pat the bed next to me, inviting Brooke to sit with me.

Instead, she pulled out the chair from the desk and settled into it. "So, tell me the story. I need to hear it before I make my decision today, for both our futures."

Only a moment ago, I was packing, ready to leave this house with no place to go. To be honest, I didn't want to leave, but I thought I had no choice. Now, Brooke had come to make peace. She was calm and collected. I felt emotionally closer to her than ever before. She deserved to know what happened in Mexico.

She had the right to know that a murderer was living under her roof.

29

I felt my body release adrenaline into my bloodstream as I teleported my mind back to Ensenada.

Back to the place of my nightmares.

Brooke was already familiar with the ill-fated events of how Julia ended up with us and how we became friends. She read about the acts I performed daily on disgusting men and the indescribable cruelty I endured from them.

This story started on the day Julia died.

* * * * *

It was early in the morning when Julia's soft moaning aroused me out of my sleep. I rubbed my eyes as I crawled over to her mattress to see if she needed anything. I found her sheet drenched in sweat and crumpled underneath her unmoving body. Her face was drained of color; her hair lay in sticky clusters. I touched her cheek. Her skin was on fire. I asked her to open her eyes, but she didn't respond. I tried to shake her awake but to no avail. I rushed out of the room to get help. I found Kitana sleeping on a cot in the kitchen by the sink.

"Come quickly! It's Julia—I think she's sick! She's so hot and won't respond."

Kitana groaned as she rolled out of bed, bracing the aching bones in her lower back with both hands. This wasn't the first time one of the girls was sick. If we were lucky, Kitana would find a bottle of Tylenol in the cupboards, but most of the time, there was no medicine to be found in the basement. A few girls had a bad habit of self-medicating with the bottles of painkillers, so Hector stopped buying them.

Kitana's face stretched with worry as she removed her rosy lips from Julia's forehead. "Help me quickly. We need to put her in the bathtub."

I grabbed Julia's legs, and Kitana lifted her from the front. Two more girls, Trinity and Najeri, woke up to the chatter of our voices and rushed to help us carry her.

Perez was sleeping in the hallway that led to the bathroom. We managed to sneak by him without waking him.

We laid Julia in the bathtub, fully clothed, and Trinity started the water. "Not too cold," warned Kitana. "We don't want to shock her." Trinity adjusted the water temperature to a bearable lukewarm while Kitana soaked a towel and laid it on Julia's forehead.

"What do you think's wrong with her?" I asked, feeling despair taking hold of me.

"Must be some infection. I don't know. Did Julia complain about any pain to you?"

I shook my head. "You know Julia. She never complains."

"You need to find Hector. He cares about her. Maybe he'll break the rules and call a doctor this time."

I chewed at my lip, fidgeting. "I don't know. He'll have my head if I wake him."

Kitana looked at me with a long and sad expression. The other two girls were staring at me too.

I caved in.

Emboldened by my willingness to help my best friend, I slipped out of the bathroom and crept past Perez. I tried the door handle for the main room, but it didn't budge. If I wanted to reach Hector, I had to ask for help from his faithful watchdog.

"Hey, Perez," I whispered, gently squeezing his arm.

"What? What!" He jumped and grabbed his handgun. I fell back against the wall. When he realized what was happening, he aimed the barrel of the gun at my forehead. "What the hell you doin', puta?"

"I need to talk to Hector."

He pulled back his hand holding the pistol, threatening to hit me with it.

"Get back to your room, or I drag you back by your hair."

"Please! It's about Julia—she's very sick."

Perez ordered me to lead him to the bathroom. From one glance at Julia's unconscious, pale body submerged in water, he started to bang his gun against his forehead, murmuring profanities.

"Please," I begged. "She could die."

Hissing and cussing, he pulled out his cell phone and called Hector. He didn't answer, so Perez made us swear to behave until he got back. I watched him unlock the main door and leave.

Thirty minutes later, he returned, trying to keep up with Hector, who was walking down the hallway with a sense of urgency. Our little boss burst into the bathroom, his face bright red, his voice laced with worry.

He gave Perez an order to usher us back to our room. Our resistance met Perez's brute aggression as he threatened to use his gun if we didn't obey.

As the four of us girls exited the bathroom, I looked back from the door. Seeing my unconscious friend in Hector's arms, her skin transparent and showing the veins underneath, broke my heart in two.

For the next month, I harassed Hector for information every chance I had. But he pushed me away or punched me in the stomach to stop my constant inquiries. Without any reliable information, I found myself keeping my insanity at bay by whispering theories and murmuring half-truths with the other girls.

Where did Hector take Julia? Was she okay? Would we ever see her again?

There was one ominous sign of Julia's fate: Hector slowly let himself go. He lost weight and grew out his beard and mustache, giving him the appearance of a beggar. I overheard Guerrero telling him to clean up before Ornelas, the boss, came to visit. Hector discarded the warnings without any care.

Two more months went by, and I was losing hope of ever finding out what happened to my dear friend.

Then one evening, Hector jerked me to the side as I was leaving a client's room.

"Where is Julia's diary?" he asked, and at his words, my knees began to tremble.

"What diary?" I asked, playing dumb.

His fingers rolled into a ball as he lifted his fist to my face. "I don't have time for silly games. Do you have it or not?"

By then, I was so used to lying to save my skin that I had become a master storyteller. But there was something in Hector's eyes, a hint of sadness and hopelessness, that told me this time it was different. This time, telling the truth would save me.

It's not like it mattered what happened to me anyway. I no longer cared if I lived or died. When Julia disappeared from my life, she had taken a part of my soul with her.

I checked the area to make sure we were alone and said, "I hid it in my pillowcase."

"If I get you out of here, will you promise me to take it to her little boy?"

"What? No! Her son can never find out his mother survived the fall and ended up in this pit."

Hector grabbed the strap of my lace bra and pulled me closer to him. "This is not a negotiation. If I get you out of here, you do as I say, or else. Understood?"

I straightened up and looked into his desperate face, allowing him to see my defiance. "I'm not doing anything for you until you tell me what happened to Julia."

Hector closed his eyes. His fingers loosened over my bra. Then he let go of me altogether. "She's gone."

"Gone where? Tijuana?"

His eyes found mine again, and they lingered as if he were deliberating what to say next. "No."

I gasped. Even though I had suspected for a while that Julia was dead, hearing the words out loud from the mouth of the last person to see Julia alive made it real. I remembered losing power over my limbs and collapsing to the ground. I slammed against the wall. The back of my head bounced off the plaster. If I knew that the last time I would see Julia was in the bathroom, I'd have said goodbye.

There was no funeral. No flowers. No casket. No proof of Hector's words. Others had disappeared from our midst. But we always knew those girls were dead and buried in the farmlands. Julia only had a fever, so how did she die? Didn't she see a doctor? What was wrong with her? I had so many questions, but Hector offered me no explanation.

I agreed to Hector's plan because it offered me a chance to seek justice for Julia, and it was my only way to escape that terrible place.

Hector was going to ask Ornelas for my transfer from the brothel. I had just turned twenty-two. I should have been sent to work the streets of Tijuana years ago.

The preparation for my relocation took another month. In the meantime, Hector coached me on our escape plan. Once he introduced me to the middleman in Tijuana, the man who watched the girls for Ornelas there, we'd kidnap him at gunpoint, take his money, and run.

Hector was going to take me to the US Embassy and get me my passport. He promised me enough money to find my way to New York City. It wasn't a bulletproof plan, but it was the best we had.

After three new young girls arrived at the brothel, Ornelas gave his blessing for my transfer.

Hector drove me and another girl in her late teens up to Tijuana. I didn't even get a day's rest in the safe house before I was expected to work that night.

That was when everything started to fall apart.

I barely had any interaction with my pimp, but I was watched twenty-four/seven, eliminating any chance of escape. Hector couldn't stay longer than two days to avoid suspicion. Three months of humiliating and painful work followed, most of which I spent in an opium haze before Hector could return to Tijuana for a second crack at our escape.

He hired a local fool to pick me up at the corner. We drove to an abandoned alley with Hector hiding in the backseat.

I used my assigned burner phone to call my pimp, Ramos, for help. He and his two faithful servants were always nearby if a john needed a beatdown. I only had to say that the guy didn't want to pay me for Ramos to appear out of nowhere and take care of business.

Hector and I didn't count on Ramos bringing four goons with him instead of the usual two. A petrifying terror pinned me to my seat as I watched the four brutes dragging my client out of the car, punching and kicking him in the process.

Hector popped up from the backseat and started shooting at them. Bullets flew, and the alley rumbled with echoes of thunder. I covered my ears with my hands, screaming with fear.

"Get down!" Hector yelled.

Watching the bloody battle ensue around me, I had a moment of clarity. Clenching my purse, I rolled out of the car and dragged myself toward the trunk to join Hector.

I screamed when a bullet hit him on his right thigh, bringing him to his knees. I cried when I watched him jerk back from another shot to his left shoulder.

The four attackers were lying on the ground, unmoving in their own pools of blood. The john was dead too, but Ramos was still on his feet, and he moved toward Hector with his gun held sideways in his hand. He was bleeding from his stomach, but that didn't seem to stop him from trying to finish off Hector. I didn't doubt I'd be the next one to die for setting him up.

"If I don't make it out alive, make sure you save yourself," Hector said weakly. "Julia's boy deserves to know the truth."

Amid the chaos, I remembered the knife Hector had given me before I called Ramos. I had to shuffle through bottles of hand sanitizer, tissues, lipsticks, and condoms before I felt the smooth wooden finish of the blade's handle.

I crawled underneath the car. As Ramos walked by on the other side, I reached out and cut across his Achilles tendon with one swift move. The tough abuser of women and children bellowed like a wounded animal and collapsed. Hector dragged himself to Ramos, leaving a bloody trail on the asphalt, and put a bullet into his skull. It was, however, too late. Ramos's gun had already fired, and a bullet tore a hole in Hector's chest.

Choking on my fear, I rushed to Hector's side and pressed down on his spurting wound. Without him, I was lost. How was I going to find my way back to US soil alone?

"H-here…t-take the money. If the embassy doesn't h-help, call…this number," he said, coughing and spitting up blood. "He's a coyote…down s-south. Ornelas…he won't find you there."

The sirens of police cars wailed in the night. I took the blood-soaked envelope and the piece of paper with the number on it from Hector's hand.

"Go! Now!" Hector urged with his last breath, coughing a few times before he lay silent.

I quickly grabbed my knife and got back to my feet. My nylons were ripped over my knees, my hands were red, but at least the blood didn't show on my black dress.

Retreating from the scene of the massacre, I caught sight of one of Ramos's men twitching and groaning. If Ornelas found out I was here, he'd blame me for everything. I'd never be safe again. If I wanted to survive, I had to eliminate the last witness.

I knelt by the side of the bulky, fat man, feeling nothing but emptiness.

"Help me!" he begged, holding onto his chest where blood oozed in earnest. I clenched my jaw and gripped the handle of the knife with two hands. Then I cut across his neck with a shaking hand, my eyes closed.

And the man became still.

* * * * *

"Now you know the truth. I'm a murderer," I told Brooke, who had been listening to my story, her only reaction to blink. "I'll understand if you want to call the police."

"From what I've heard, it was self-defense. Besides, no jury on earth would find you guilty, considering your past and what you've gone through."

"I didn't have to kill him…I *wanted* to."

"Based on what you described of his wound, he looked like he was going to die anyway. From where I'm sitting, you did him a favor by ending his pain."

"You can't be serious."

"I am serious. If I were in your shoes, I'd have done the same thing. At least I hope I would have had the strength to do the same thing."

"The strength? I was a coward."

"No, Annie. You're the bravest person I've ever met. You never gave up."

The ball in my throat grew bigger, and I could barely hold back the tears. Like I said before, I've been called some nasty things, but never brave.

I reached to my nightstand for a tissue to hide my tears. Brooke's words followed. "What happened after? Where did you go? Did you go to the embassy?"

"No. I couldn't. Not after what I'd done. I feared I would end up in prison. Besides, I went to Mexico with Alejandro on my own accord. I thought the cops would blame me for what happened to me."

Brooke stood up and sat by my side. She brushed the hair away from my face. "I'm so sorry I wasn't there to help you."

"You're here now."

She nodded.

"I need a glass of water. I'm also hungry. I haven't eaten much for days. Would you mind if I finish the story while I eat?"

"No, of course not, honey."

Back sitting at the table on the patio, I stuffed forkfuls of eggs in my mouth while Brooke watched.

"Using the money Hector had given me, I bought a bus ticket to make my way southeast," I said with a full mouth. "I had to take half a dozen buses to Tamaulipas. The Gulf Cartel controls the borders on the west, and Hector thought we had a better chance to cross there without Ornelas finding us. Of course, by then, I was alone. Hector died in Tijuana. When I arrived in Tamaulipas, I checked in to a small motel and paid for it with the blood money. I called the number from the paper Hector had given me and arranged a meeting with a coordinator. He was a Mexican-American man who spoke perfect English. He must have studied in the US. He never revealed his real name. We both used aliases, so that was okay."

"Was he nice to you, or did he try to hurt you?"

"No, he didn't touch me. He was expecting Hector to be with me, so I had to lie. I told him that Hector couldn't travel with me, but he'd be here in a couple of days. I think he thought I was Hector's girl, therefore off-limits. I was in that motel room for about a week, waiting for the right circumstances to leave. It was early in the afternoon one day when I got in a van with twenty other people. Most of them weren't from Mexico. They came there from Honduras, Guatemala, and a few were from Asia.

"We drove for about four hours to a small village near the border. We were told to eat and drink as much as we could because we might have to hide in the bushes for hours or run for our lives and ditch our belongings, including snacks and water. The food was terrible—dry rice and spicy beans—but nothing I wasn't used to over the past few years, so it didn't bother me. I crammed all my belongings into a backpack, dressed in layers, wrapped a scarf around my face, and waited with my group.

"When it was dark, around eight o'clock, which was when the border patrol had a shift change, we walked to the Rio Grande with our coyote. He didn't reveal his name, so we called him boss. He wore a baseball cap low over his brow and a bandana to cover his face so I wouldn't be able to recognize him in a lineup."

I drank some orange juice and bit into my toast. "He led us to a part of the river where the water was barely knee-deep, and we waded through without having to use rope or a floating device. Once we made it to the US side, I paid four thousand dollars to the coyote. A Texas Ranger was waiting for us. He realized I was an American and invited me to his home to rest. I took the food and water the kind man offered to our group, but I didn't stay. I left alone from there the next day. I made it to the first bus stop and took a Greyhound to San Antonio. I got myself a motel room there and fresh clothes from Walmart. I was so hungry for American food, so I gobbled up two Big Macs and downed a large chocolate shake. I remember lying on the bed in the motel all afternoon to ease my stomach pains, watching some silly sitcom on TV. It'd been eight years since I left California, and I couldn't believe I was back in my home country. Maybe not in Cali, but I was still in my homeland."

I put down my fork. "You know the rest. How I looked you up online and traveled here."

Brooke poured me another glass of orange juice. "I'm glad to hear your whole story finally. I'll need some time to wrap my mind around a few things." She gently brushed her fingers along my jawline. "But, please, promise me you won't leave."

I swallowed the mouthful of berries and said, "Where would I go?"

She gathered her plate and utensils from the table and carried them back into the house. She looked back at me from the door.

"While you were sleeping, I booked a yacht for this Wednesday."

"A yacht? For what?"

"I'm going to invite the entire Rose family for a cruise."

30

"I'm not sure I like the idea," Helen said on the phone.

After breakfast, I called Helen, following Brooke's advice to invite the moderators of the "What Happened to Julia Rose" Facebook group to the cruise the coming Wednesday. The basis for Brooke's suggestion came from her sense of righteousness. After the numerous years the group had dedicated to searching for Julia's killer, both Helen and Jeff deserved to witness the finale with the Rose family.

I couldn't agree more. It was also an opportunity for Brooke and me to clear our names.

"I thought this was what you always wanted?" I countered, reluctant to let Helen off the hook.

Helen sighed. "You know it is, Annie. You know me. I opened up like a book to you." I could sense an air of judgment in her tone. "But being out on the open water with people I don't trust and with no place to hide if things go south isn't exactly how I imagined this ending."

"That's the point! The whole family will be trapped out on the ocean with us. We'll have an opportunity to confront them and expose who we truly are. Brooke said she has a few tricks up her sleeve that I hope will help us persuade the Roses to tell us the truth."

"I don't know. It sounds kind of silly to me. You think one of those psychos will admit to pushing Julia to her death because we're on a yacht, asking nicely?"

I looked at Brooke, who'd been listening to our conversation on the speakerphone, for help.

"Hey, Helen, it's Brooke."

"Brooke? Hi! How are you?" Helen sounded surprised to find out that our conversation wasn't private.

"I'm hanging in there. How about you?"

"You know. Same old, same old." As soon as I noticed Helen clamming up, I regretted bringing Brooke into the conversation.

"I'm not going to try and talk you into coming on this boat trip, but we could use the backup," Brooke reasoned, hunching over my phone. "I have a few plans for persuading them, but there will be five of them and two of us if you don't come. I'd feel a heck of a lot better if you and Jeff were there to watch our backs."

"And who will watch our backs?"

"Don't start, Helen," I interjected.

A bubbly chuckle came through the receiver. "Why? Let's be honest here. Brooke is still a suspect, right? She was there on the night of the murder too."

"Brooke's already explained why she didn't tell us she was on the cruise ship that night," I said, holding Brooke's gaze.

Helen reprimanded us with a moment of silence. "Liars always have an explanation for their lies once they're caught," she said with a sudden change in her tone. She sounded contemptuous and judgmental.

Brooke, looking frustrated, pushed away from the dining table. "All right, Helen. My offer stands. You and Jeff are invited on the cruise. I'll have the folder with the information of all the known lovers of Tony Rose there with me. You're welcome to it, but I won't beg you to come. I've been protecting all of you. I cooperated with you in your investigation. If you think you're better off without us, then feel free to take that chance. But if you can put aside your suspicions and dislike toward me, then we'll see you at the dock at four p.m. sharp." She reached down and disconnected the call.

"Why would you do that?" I snapped.

"There's no reason to waste another breath talking to her. She'll be there. So will Jeffrey." Brooke removed her glasses and cleaned them on the tail of her blouse. "Do you honestly believe that after dedicating three years of their lives to watching videos, analyzing pictures, and hunting down witnesses, they would miss the opportunity to meet the whole family? I don't think so."

Later that afternoon, my increasing worry about facing Tony again left no room for me to stress out over Helen and Jeff. Dozens of messages from Tony sat unread in my mailbox, taunting me. I'd chewed down four of my nails as I debated reading them. But I couldn't trust myself, especially if he asked me to see him, so I refused to open them. My gut told me that if I took a peek, I would want to see him.

When Brooke found me marinating in my dilemma, I blamed my sour mood on Helen's recent hostile behavior. If she thought I was lying, she didn't show it.

On Monday, Brooke took me to her office as a well-dressed sidepiece of hers. She expected me to shadow her all day. Like Batman and Robin, we patrolled the dangerous waters of the law firm together. Brooke might have thought she was being clever, involving me in the company's business by making me feel like I belonged, but I saw through her plans. She intended to keep an eye on me all day as if I were a misbehaving teenager with no integrity. After what she saw on the monitor Saturday night, I couldn't blame her for wanting to keep me on a short leash.

Most of the day I was confined to the privacy of Brooke's office, where she ordered me to sit in her posh leather chair as she made the calls. She rang Tony, Justin, Sylvia, and Barbara and invited them on the boat trip to sign the new business contracts and trust documents and also to commemorate the third anniversary of Julia's disappearance.

Out of the four, Tony was the only one who thought the idea was very thoughtful and agreed to meet us on such short notice. He sounded composed, maybe even a bit excited.

Justin said his schedule was booked for Wednesday and turned down our invitation.

Sylvia complained about stomach problems.

Barbara blamed her husband, Bill, for their refusal. He'd already made plans for the two of them to play golf with friends, or so she said.

With each rejection, Brooke sunk deeper into an emotional abyss. After the final call, not even the fancy coffee creations and glazed doughnuts with nut pieces the receptionist brought in could lighten her mood.

An hour later, as Brooke and I were running out of ideas to get the Rose family on board, Tony called Brooke's cell phone and said that everybody would be there at four on Wednesday, without exception.

It was a short call, a statement without an explanation, leaving us to wonder if Tony had offered money or made threats to get everybody on board.

While I nibbled on a doughnut and browsed my phone for local news about Ensenada, Brooke finished the final version of the new trust for the Rose estate.

While Brooke printed a copy of the documents for every family member and shoved the packages into her trusted briefcase, I fantasized about pushing the irritating Sylvia Rose overboard. I pictured her shrieking as she fell into the abyss, holding on to her fake boobs to save them. She was tall yet fragile-looking, like a flamingo. It would be easy to overpower her.

Then I thought of the possibility of Bill, Tony, and Justin uniting to overpower us. We wouldn't have a chance. I didn't fully understand Brooke's plan and how it was going to benefit us, but she asked me to trust her, so trust I did.

For lunch, Brooke took me to the same coffee shop where I'd stolen her purse and rummaged through its contents in the bathroom months ago. As I watched her eating her sandwich, I played with the idea of telling her about those first days when I stalked her. Since we'd been sharing so many secrets lately, coming clean with each other seemed like a good idea.

"Remember when we first met," I started, planning to ease into the nasty details. But Brooke immediately shut me down, saying today was not the time to be nostalgic.

We didn't return to the office that afternoon. Instead, Brooke drove us to a fancy spa in SOHO. To say I was shocked to witness the staff welcome Brooke as a frequent customer was an understatement. Judging by her rough outer shell, I would have never taken Brooke for a woman who pampered herself with fragrant oils, mud baths, and massages.

The last glow of daylight was fading into the night as we arrived home. For reasons I didn't understand, I felt like a stranger in the house. I looked around with an air of detachment as if I were seeing the rooms and the furniture for the first time.

When Brooke excused herself to retire to her room to change, I sat down in the family room with a heavy heart. Watching an ant crossing the polished wood floor, I realized that our day together had a feel of farewell to it. It was Brooke's way of saying goodbye to me.

The more I rolled that idea around in my head, the more I believed that after the boat ride on Wednesday, Brooke was going to part ways with me. I knew she wouldn't kick me to the curb empty-handed. No, she would give me money to start over and help me get on my feet. She would offer me help to find a job. Maybe give me a few business cards and phone numbers of people she knew were hiring. I'd get a job as a secretary. Or perhaps a receptionist. The image of my future self, typing away on a keyboard day in and day out without purpose, screwing clients for attention, like Brooke's receptionist did with Tony, made me feel dreadful.

Dressed in a tracksuit, Brooke crossed the hallway without looking at me. She may have missed me sitting there in the dark, so I followed her into the kitchen. My presence startled her, and she dropped the empty bowl she was carrying. She looked distracted when we both bent down to pick the bowl up.

"Are you all right?" I asked. She pushed her glasses up higher on the bridge of her nose and grinned at me.

"Why wouldn't I be?"

I could tell she'd already had a drink or two, which she seemed to have consumed too fast. Her face was flushed with a rush of blood, and her eyes were glossy.

She wandered into the pantry, grabbed veggies from the fridge, and started chopping them up for a salad. There was something distressing about her face, as if she wasn't mentally there in the kitchen with me. As if her mind had taken her to a faraway place.

I offered to help prepare dinner, but Brooke asked me to pour her a drink instead. I grabbed a light beer from the refrigerator for her. She took a sip, then slid the bottle toward me on the countertop. I wrapped my fingers around the bottle but didn't lift it to my lips. Instead, I sat there listening to the wind whistling through the trees, thinking about how much I'd miss this place and Brooke's company.

Without an appetite, I poked at my salad. Brooke's mind had not returned to the present, making me feel lonely in her company.

After dinner, I returned to my room, where I swallowed the remaining two Vicodin I kept stashed in my shoe. It was unusually hot in my bedroom, so I stripped down to my underwear and crawled onto my mattress on the floor. As I lay there, I had a perfect view of the gray T-shirt Tony had given me in his car. I stretched my body to reach it and pressed the crumpled soft fabric to my nose to see if I could smell him on it. His scent was still strong, soaked into the fabric. Spicy. Masculine.

Cursing underneath my breath, I grabbed my phone and began reading Tony's text messages. I was only halfway through them when I felt an itch—an irritating feeling in the back of my mind that I couldn't scratch. With each of his admissions about missing me, wanting to see me again, wanting to apologize, I told myself I didn't care. But I was faltering. I was losing ground.

I told myself that I was pathetic—a girl who always chose wrong, a girl desperate for someone to love her. Then I suddenly had a lucid moment. I understood who I was and where I stood in life. To break the cycle, I had to do one honorable deed. I'd have to finish one damned goal I set for myself. Then and there, I realized that this evening, I was going to end up at Tony's house once again.

31

I knew what I had to do. I didn't stop thinking about it during the entire trip in the squeaky-clean Toyota Camry that had picked me up near Brooke's house.

Once again, I secretly left home without telling Brooke. But she was already done with me; I had played all my cards and lost. Playing it safe now would bring no redemption. I had to take chances. I owed it to Julia, Brooke, and even Helen.

The driver dropped me off a block away from the two-story colonial masterpiece. Like a dark angel of revenge, I moved stealthily across the long driveway, staying in the shadows to avoid the cameras.

To stop my obsession over Tony, Brooke had disconnected our monitors in the surveillance room on the night she caught me being intimate with Julia's husband, so I was going into the house blind. For the second day, I had no idea what Tony had been up to, who visited him, or what he was doing. Not knowing his whereabouts and activities created a hole in my chest. I felt as if I'd lost my favorite comfort animal, leaving me without solace or resolve.

The grass was still wet from yesterday's storm, and my shoes sloshed under my weight as I rounded the corner of the house and crept near the fishpond. If Tony happened to be watching the monitors of the home security system, he might have spotted my shadow whizzing through the dimly lit yard, but it was a chance I had to take.

As I passed an open side window, I heard music. It was foreign. French, I think. It sounded like the type of music in a movie where people in Paris sat at coffee shops.

A long rectangle of bright white light spread over the patio steps and the evergreen bushes in decorative pots. I stopped to see if a shadow would cross the projection on the ground. There seemed to be no movement in the kitchen.

I crawled on my knees to the patio door and peeked into the kitchen through the glass panels. The place was vacant and pristine as usual. No bowls or cutting boards on the counter. No pots on the stove.

I tried the handle. It opened. I felt my heart suddenly tense in my chest as if a hand had reached in and seized it.

I slid inside and gently closed the door behind me.

Staying low, I crept around the island and into the hallway. The music was coming from the far side of the house. I spotted a door ajar—to a guest room, if I remembered correctly.

Before I'd left Brooke's home, I'd considered texting Tony to let him know I was coming, but I would have wasted the element of surprise. I was going to corner him and pry the truth out of him even if I had to extract the words by force.

Rounding the staircase, I found myself within an arm's reach of the open door. The brightness inside painted a sliver of gold onto the tile floor in the hallway. The singer's voice was more intense now, passionate and feisty.

I poked my head around the doorframe, blood pulsating in my ears, expecting to see Tony in the company of a woman.

Since our last encounter, I'd learned I was just another sucker who believed his sugary words. He was an adept lover and a perpetual cheat. He had long perfected his game of getting into young women's panties, and I foolishly fell for his trickery.

Beating myself up for being so gullible, I took a deep breath and peered into the room. At the sight of the scene, a feeble squeaking noise escaped my mouth. It wasn't a nest for lovers. Far from it. It was the showcase of someone's guilt—a killer's remorse.

32

A room full of oil paintings was revealed to me—about a dozen large canvases, all different but essentially similar, portraying the same scene.

I stepped inside the gallery, feeling the painter's agony and remorse. I lifted the closest frame from the floor. The technique was amateurish, somewhat abstract, but the image was unambiguous. The stern of a boat, a wooden railing, a woman falling, a set of hands pushing her, and an ocean so dark it was nearly black.

Goosebumps broke out all over my body. If this wasn't proof of Tony's guilt, then nothing was. There was no doubt left in my mind that Tony was Julia's murderer, and I had fallen for his deception. I had begun to see him as a sensitive, innocent victim. I'd given myself over to him. I let him touch me, my body and soul.

My disgust turned to bile and rose into my throat.

Staring at the paintings, I no longer believed Tony had remained a bachelor for these past three years because he held out hope for his beloved wife's return. His heart was a stone that didn't yearn for love. Some say killing another human being kills a part of you too. Murdering the mother of his child must have transfigured his soul. Tony wasn't human anymore. He was a monster.

As if it were burning my hands, I hurriedly placed the painting back on the floor and leaned it against the wall. I pulled out my cell phone with shaking hands and took a series of pictures of the room. My intention of rushing back to Brooke's and showing her these images urged me to get out of this cursed house. My knees wobbled as I snuck down the hallway, my eyes set on the patio door and to my escape beyond it.

My hand rose instinctively in front of me as a powerful force slammed into me. There was a pressure on my right hip and over my breasts. A scent I recognized attacked my nostrils. I knew I had to free myself, but he was much stronger than I was, and he pinned me to the wall.

"You came," he breathed into my ears, and my mind was transported back to Ensenada, back to the brothel. Back to hell.

I didn't reply, but Tony didn't need any encouragement. He turned my head and kissed my neck. His other hand groped underneath my shirt. I wanted to scream, but my voice recoiled so far back into my throat that I couldn't summon it. When he pulled down my pants, my eyes blurred with tears. His moaning echoed in my head. His words rang like fire alarms.

Tell him to get off you! Tell him! I screamed in my head, but my will remained restrained, like it had been conditioned to do in the brothel. My voice had no power.

He turned me around and looked into my eyes. I was dying to express my disdain, but somehow my face didn't convey my feelings. I might have even smiled at him. I couldn't be sure. I automatically used the same technique to block my mind as I had done for years in Mexico.

I didn't remember much of what happened after that. I blocked the rest of the encounter out of my mind. Tony didn't hurt me physically. I was sure of that. He also didn't mention the creepy art room, leaving me to assume he had no idea I'd discovered his paintings. He was enough of a narcissist to trust in the power of his words and irresistible charm, which he thought had lured me back to his lair. I let him believe that after reading his texts I couldn't stay away from him. I told him I came to his house to surprise him because one night with him wasn't enough for me. I had come back for more.

Despite my wish to escape, we ended up lying in his marital bed, his naked arm draped over my chest when he turned to me. "Whose idea was the boat trip?"

"It was Brooke's," I said, avoiding his eyes. Being in Julia's bedroom, betraying her, crushed me. The sight of her pictures, the bedsheet, and my memories of us were suffocating me.

If Julia's spirit had appeared again and drawn or said the letter "B," I now knew what she meant. She wasn't insinuating Brooke's name. It was her way of calling me a bitch, a despicable human being, and a terrible friend.

"I think it'll be nice," Tony cooed, rapidly blinking. "You and me watching the sunset. I'm kinda looking forward to it."

I bet you would like to have a new model. It must be boring painting the same woman falling overboard again and again.

Tony pulled the sheet over his chest, fixing himself into a more comfortable position. "Should we tell Brooke about us?"

"Us?" Tony's talking about us as an item struck me with a jolt of shock.

"Yes, us. You and me." He smiled.

"No, we shouldn't...Uhm...It would only complicate things right now."

He kissed my forehead. "No need to be so defensive." His grin was as wide as his face. "You're right, though. She's only your boss, not your mother. We aren't obligated to tell her anything." His eyes were honest and his voice sincere. He was a master of illusions. No surprise he fooled me too.

"Would you stay here with me tonight?"

I was too stunned to move. "What would your son say if he found me in his mother's bed?"

Tony forcefully closed his eyes. He opened them again, and his irises were glossy. "He's staying at my mother's tonight."

The last thing I wanted to do was stay with this horrible man for another minute, but I had no choice. If he figured out what I knew about him, I'd never leave this house alive. Ever.

I promised him everything he asked of me. When his limbs relaxed around me and his breathing had become soft and rhythmical, I slipped out of bed, tiptoed downstairs, and left the house in the middle of the night like a runaway.

* * * * *

Brooke was standing outside on the patio, smoking a cigarette and drinking bourbon. She was beyond mad at me for sneaking out that night to see Tony, absolutely furious. I showed her the pictures I took of the paintings depicting Julia's death, but no matter how hard I tried to plead my case, she wasn't interested.

"These paintings mean nothing," she said, grinding her teeth. "Tony could have painted them out of guilt or out of heartache. We wouldn't know the difference. Imagine this: a writer writing about serial killers doesn't mean he or she killed or wants to kill. Art is a form of expression."

"But it proves he saw what happened," I argued, shoving my phone into Brooke's face.

"No. This proves nothing!" she snapped, slapping my phone away from her face.

I gave up and retreated a few steps. I recognized defeat; I had experienced enough of it in my life.

"I don't think we should go on that yacht," I said, lighting a cigarette I'd bummed from Brooke. The gray smoke from my exhale rode far on the night breeze. I felt as if my soul had left with it.

Brooke looked inquisitively over the rim of her glasses at me, studying me. "Did you sleep with him again?"

"No!" I blurted out. "Absolutely not!"

Brooke sighed out loud. "Oh, Annie. Annie. Why are you doing this to yourself?"

Fidgeting on my feet, pacing around in a small semi-circle, I readied myself to defend my statement, but I only got as far as crossing my arms. Brooke immediately saw through me, as if I were made of glass. My conscience no longer allowed me to lie to her. So, I said nothing instead.

"I'll fix it. It seems I have to fix everything." She put out her cigarette in the birdbath before she walked back into the house, leaving me alone with my guilt and self-loathing.

33

On Wednesday at half-past three, Brooke and I rolled up to the North Cove Marina near Manhattan's financial district. The yacht waiting for us in the bay was at least a hundred feet long and shone with the light of the gods as the weather couldn't decide if it was going to be a sunny or overcast afternoon. The weather app forecasted fifty-five Fahrenheit and clear skies, but those online sites were seldom accurate.

I was wearing the replica of Julia's dress with matching red shoes from her last night on the Royal Princess. It was Brooke's way of spooking the Roses one last time, and I went along with it.

I designed my hair into the same loose ringlets Julia wore on Helen's video of The Newlywed Game, and I did my best to imitate Julia's makeup for that night too.

As we readied to embark, the captain, dressed in a crisp white uniform, and four other crewmembers, looking just as dashing, lined up by the passerelle to greet us. To get on board, we had to shake hands and exchange pleasantries. The people responsible for our safety and for ensuring a pleasant trip were Captain Frank, First Mate Patrick, the deckhands Thomas and Ryan, and the stewardesses Stacy and Hannah.

"Please escort the rest of the guests to the salon when they arrive," Brooke instructed the captain. "We'll have drinks while we wait. Thank you, Captain."

A gust of wind got caught underneath my dress, and I rushed to gather my skirt over my thighs to save myself from embarrassment.

The stewardesses led us to our cabins, located in the bowels of the yacht. Following Brooke, I was in awe of the upscale interior and luxurious furniture. Everything was clean and sparkling. All the colors came together into one matching and harmonious design. Brooke's mansion was old-fashioned, where every wood-paneled wall and floorboard creaked and gave off a musty odor. The air in the yacht smelled of roses, and everything was ultra-modern and trendy.

Respecting our privacy, stewardess Stacy left us to refresh ourselves with the expectation of seeing us soon in the salon for cocktails.

We didn't pack much for the trip. Brooke said there was no need to go out of our way packing because this wasn't a vacation, just an overnight cruise.

Five minutes later, Brooke and I met up in the hallway between our cabins and headed toward the salon.

"How are you doing?" she asked.

"Nervous but excited at the same time. I've never been on a boat."

She smiled coyly as if I missed the meaning of her question.

"Right. You meant how I am doing regarding the night with the Roses."

Hannah, the stewardess, passed the hall in front of us, presenting me with the opportunity to mull over my answer a bit longer.

"I think it will be a relief to have some closure; on the other hand, the possibility of our friendship ending tonight saddens me a great deal."

Brooke gently clamped my head with her hands. "You deserve to live your own life, Annie. You deserve happiness. Don't ever stop fighting for it."

Everything that Brooke said to me lately sounded like a goodbye. My heart sunk at the thought, and I felt tears gather in my eyes. I summoned all my strength to hold them back and save my makeup.

Stacy poked her head around the corner. "Ladies, are you ready for your aperitifs? Allow me to escort you to the salon."

The salon was bigger than Brooke's master bedroom in the mansion. Through large rectangle windows, it looked out at the harbor and the Manhattan skyline. Enclosed by beige walls and two rows of white leather seating assemblies, it offered us a place to sit and gather. Everything in the room was either white, chocolate, beige, or teal, and it smelled of money and privilege.

I checked the time. It was nearly four o'clock.

My feet tapped the carpet, and my hand left sweat marks on my knees as I sat in one of the armchairs, staring at a glass of bourbon in front of me. My stomach shrunk, and the mere thought of sending anything down to it promised a return right back up.

On the other hand, Brooke was tossing back her drinks one after the other. She was an old fox. She could hold her liquor, but tonight wasn't the night for making mistakes—she had nailed that much in my head.

I heard the soft thumping of approaching footsteps from the direction of the stairs. My heart jumped into my throat.

"Oh, it's you," I said with a sigh of relief when Helen and Jeff entered the salon.

"Yes, us." Helen rolled her eyes as she pushed back the hair from her puffy red face. "You invited us, remember?"

Brooke gave me an I-told-you-so look perfected with a smirk.

Helen's dress was fitting for the occasion with its nautical style that was tight in all the wrong places.

In contrast, Jeff looked like an explorer from the early nineteen hundreds, accessorized with a bowtie and suspenders.

I got to my feet to meet them. "Oh, yeah, of course. I'm glad you came. It's a big night. I'm nervous. I thought it was Tony or Justin coming." I leaned in to hug Helen as I babbled on. She remained stiff in my embrace. Jeffrey at least made an effort by putting a loose arm around me.

Helen skipped the small talk and went straight to the point. "Where is the folder you were teasing me with?"

Brooke nodded and glanced at the brown package on the coffee table.

Jeff grabbed the treasure first, but before he could examine its contents, Helen ripped it out of his hand. A few sheets of paper fell onto the ground. I rushed to gather them. I kept looking behind me to make sure nobody else had arrived yet.

"Careful," I warned as I placed the papers back into the folder. "The Roses don't know we have these."

"What a piece of shit!" exclaimed Helen. "Look at this, Jeff. You and I combined don't get this much action, and we're both single."

"The best way to emasculate a man is to have a wife who earns more than him. Add some fame on top of that. Voila! You got yourself a bitter cheater," Brooke said, dismissing the stewardess, who stepped in to offer assistance to the new arrivals.

"Fucking hell! I'll never get married," Helen exclaimed.

"What did I miss," boomed the electrifying and confident voice of Tony Rose from behind us.

I caught Jeff hustling to close the folder before I spun around to face Tony. From the swift, sudden turn, I felt the blood drain from my head. I held onto the coffee table for support.

Tony was by my side in a flash and steadied me. "Are you all right?"

I caught Helen's suspicious eyes taking in the scene.

I pulled away. "Yes, I'm fine. I just moved too fast. Thank you, Mr. Rose, for your assistance."

Tony read the room and released my arm. "Tony, remember? My friends call me Tony."

"Certainly." I nodded.

Tony looked behind me at Helen and Jeff. Then he looked back at me with inquisitive eyes.

"Forgive me if I'm wrong, but I feel like we've met before." Tony stepped around me and advanced toward Helen and Jeff by the bar.

Brooke intercepted his approach.

Tony shot her a quizzical look, rubbing his brows. "I know you." He pointed at Helen. "You're one of Julia's fans." He snapped his fingers as he tried to recall the name. "It's on the tip of my tongue."

"I'm Helen Fray, and this is Jeff Durham. We're the moderators of the 'What Happened to Julia Rose' Facebook group."

Tony's face lit up with enlightenment. "Oh, yes, I remember. You came to the memorial service."

"More like a no-body funeral, but yes, that was us."

The air stuck in my lungs at Helen's statement. I expected Tony to strike back with venom, but he didn't reply. He simply shook the hands of the guests.

A ruckus outside directed the group's attention toward the staircase.

"Mother, stop nagging me. I know what I'm doing."

I recognized Sylvia's voice. Barbara murmured something back that wasn't loud enough to be audible in the salon.

"Why does nobody in this family understand that I'm sick? I live in constant pain. Do you know how hard it is to put a smile on my face?"

"Can you two cut it out?" Bill's deep, hoarse voice rumbled.

"Excuse my family," Tony said, appearing embarrassed. "We can be a little loud sometimes."

"Bill, Barbara," Brooke greeted the oldest members of the Rose family. "Sylvia."

"This must have been a costly boat to rent, Brooke," Barbara said, lifting an abstract statue from an end table. "I hope you don't plan on billing our estate for it."

"Honey, stop!" Bill took the statue from his wife and returned it. "This is a fantastic idea, Brooke. Remembering the third anniversary of my sweet Juju's disappearance. It's very thoughtful."

"Where is Justin?" Tony inquired. "I specifically told him to be here on time."

"He's here, sweetheart, relax." Barbara brushed her fingers along Tony's chin. "He had to take a business call outside."

"Don't tell me to relax, Mom." Tony pulled away. "He's doing this on purpose so he can make a grand entrance."

Just as Tony uttered his last word, Justin stepped into the salon. Cheery, vibrant, dressed in white.

"A family gathering on a luxury yacht. You know how to make my heart sing!" He snatched Brooke by her wrists and kissed her cheek.

Then his eyes found Helen. "What's she doing here?"

Tony stepped up to his brother. "We were just talking about that, but you interrupted us with your late arrival. As usual."

Justin punched Tony on the shoulder. "Relax, little brother. This is supposed to be fun."

I noticed Tony's fingers roll into fists. "We aren't here today to have fun, Justin."

Barbara had already helped herself to a drink.

Bill had sat down on the sofa and buried his face in his cell phone as if trying to extract himself from the scene.

"Where's the help?" Sylvia cried out in her irritating voice. "I need a gin and tonic."

"Forget about the drinks. First, I want to know what those two are doing on this yacht with us," Barbara said, pointing at Helen and Jeff. "This was supposed to be a private business meeting."

"I invited them," Brooke said matter-of-factly.

"What's going on?" Justin turned his head back and forth to look at each of us.

"You'll find out soon enough," Brooke said. "Why don't you grab yourself a drink too, Justin?"

"I don't like the tone in this room," Barbara complained. "Family doesn't talk to each other like this."

"Like how, Mother?" Justin sneered. "I thought this was exactly how you liked us. Confused. Angry."

"Don't be ridiculous, Justin," Bill chimed in, waving his pointy finger. "Your mother loves you all."

"Dad, go back to your Wordscapes, okay?"

"Don't be rude to Dad!" Tony stepped in.

I joined Brooke in watching the bickering family with great satisfaction.

"All right, if somebody doesn't tell me what the hell is going on here right now, I'm getting off this boat," Justin warned, reaching for his phone on the armrest of the sofa.

"Too late for that, buddy," Brooke said, pointing out the window.

We all looked outside, taking in the slowly shrinking Manhattan shoreline that was fading into the gray marine layer.

34

"Everybody, calm down!" Brooke said in an authoritative tone. "Today is a special day and a cause for remembrance."

Brooke's unexpected call to order stilled the room.

I noticed Justin's hand shaking as he held his phone.

Brooke moved into the center of the room. "I'd like to ask all of you to take a seat because we'll begin our night with a story."

I stole a glance at Tony, who was alternating his focus between Brooke and me, and I felt the heat rising to my neck and spreading over my face. My role in tonight's theater was specific. Brooke had planned and orchestrated the entire evening, but that didn't mean I was eager to play my part.

"Stacy, would you mind serving the appetizers," Brooke said to the stewardess. She also nodded at Hannah, and they both walked out of the salon.

The boat rocked a bit. I grabbed hold of the bar while the swaying movements prompted the rest of the guests to grab various armchairs and sofas in the room to steady themselves.

Brooke seized her glass from the coffee table before it could spill the two-finger amount left.

"I can't do choppy waters," Sylvia complained, fanning herself with a magazine. "Somebody needs to tell the captain."

"The captain isn't Poseidon, you bimbo!" Helen snapped.

My eyes widened at Helen's statement. I knew she despised Sylvia, and she could be rude at times, but her public name-calling still shocked me.

Sylvia gasped and planted a hand on her heart. I thought she would retort with something nasty, but all she could muster was an incoherent babbling.

"Let's not insult each other this early on our trip. I thought we'd at least make it until dinnertime," Brooke said, taking the brown folder from Jeff, who was unwilling to let it go. His fingers clamped on the documents, and for a second, I thought the whole folder was going to explode on the floor.

Tony got up from his seat. "All right, enough of these theatrics. Are those our trust fund documents?" He reached for the brown envelope, but Brooke pinned it to her chest and crossed her arms over it.

"No, Tony, they're not, but if everybody would finally shut up, I'll explain why we're here today. So, please, take a seat, Tony." There was a nervous edge to Brooke's tone that made me tremble.

Stacy and Hannah walked into the salon, carrying silver trays. "Your appetizers today are smoked salmon on sprouted wheat toast with a dash of cream cheese and sprinkled with capers," Hannah announced as the two women, who didn't look much older than me, set the trays on the main table.

Bill and Helen were the only ones who accepted the invitation to taste the appetizingly arranged spread of food. The stewardesses lingered, ready to serve, but Brooke dismissed them once again. There was a silent agreement between the three women, and instead of annoyance, a clear sign of understanding spread across their faces.

The two pretty stewardesses exited the salon, Hannah closing the double doors behind them. The click of the lock moving into place echoed into the air.

Everyone turned to look at the closed doors as if they were expecting to find an explanation written on them.

"Why are we locked in?" asked Tony as he turned back to face Brooke and me.

Brooke set down the brown folder on the bar and slipped her hand into her purse. She pulled out a silver handgun and pointed it in front of her. "I said, sit the fuck down, Tony!" she hissed between her teeth.

I staggered back away from Brooke. "What are you doing?"

"Well, you wanted these people's attention—now you got it!" she sneered, cocking her head at me. "Go on. Tell them your story."

"What story? Brooke, you're scaring me," Barbara whined, her hands on her heart.

Brooke waved the gun at her. "Good, Barbara. You should be scared. Now that I have all your attention, let me introduce you to London White."

That was my name. My given name after birth. Not the name on my birth certificate, but after my parents adopted me. The name I haven't used since I moved to New York. But Brooke had decided last night that it was time for me to unveil my true self.

I swallowed and stepped into the center of the room.

"You all know me as Annie Adams, the new assistant to your family attorney." I glanced at the gun on the bar top next to Brooke as she lit a cigarette. "I'm not a lawyer. Actually, I've never been to law school. I didn't even finish high school." I shrugged, avoiding Tony's eyes.

"What is this all about?" Barbara's interruption triggered Brooke to raise the gun again, this time at Barbara's chest.

"If you would let her finish, you'll find out."

I wanted to ask Brooke to chill out because she was making all of us nervous with her gun, but I was supposed to be on her side, so I said nothing. I wished she would have warned me about the gun; then I wouldn't have felt so unsettled.

"But I knew Julia," I continued, looking at no one in particular. "We were friends. Well, more like damaged goods, but she was like a sister to me." I smiled. "We were working in the same brothel in Mexico for years. We were practically sharing the same bed—if you can call that dirty mattress with a single sheet and a thin blanket a bed."

"This is outrageous!" roared Tony. "Julia never worked in a brothel!"

As my mind transported me back to my past, I looked at Tony with a long, pitiful expression. If I felt embarrassed at the beginning of this trip for sharing my shameful story with him, now the feeling was evaporating. That was why I was here—why I made the journey from Mexico to Manhattan. I was here to confront Julia's family with the truth and find the one who tried to kill her.

"Yes, did. We worked in a brothel together. In Ensenada, Mexico. For two long years and some change."

"Mexico?!" Sylvia exclaimed.

"Yes, the beautiful, vibrant beach town of Ensenada. Where American tourists go for a cheap vacation. It's a popular place for child prostitution, where men pay big bucks for young girls—the younger, the better. I was fourteen when I was kidnapped and forced to work there for seven years. Then one day, Hector, the man in charge of watching us girls, brought in an American woman the locals had found washed up onshore. She was in a terrible shape. She lay in bed for days, unconscious."

I stopped to consider whether to share a few of the gruesome details. I wasn't keen on reliving the nightmare, but these folks needed to know the truth.

"Though, that didn't stop our handlers from repeatedly raping her. Whenever they felt like it," I said blatantly, pushing the knife deeper into Tony's heart.

Voices of shock cried out in the room. Helen started hyperventilating; Jeff poured her a glass of water.

Bill removed his reading glasses and rubbed his eyes.

Barbara clammed her head with her hands.

Sylvia looked as if she were about to faint.

Justin leaned forward and set his elbows on his knees.

Tony looked at me with his mouth gaping.

"Yep, you heard me right," I continued. "Julia survived the fall and, somehow, by the grace of God, she made it to the shore alive."

I watched everybody's reaction in the room, even Brooke's. I left out a crucial detail about Julia's recovery, her amnesia, hoping that the panic of being exposed would flush the rabbit from the hat.

"Once she began to recover from her injuries, she kept telling us about a vague memory she had of dolphins keeping her afloat on the water," I added for good measure. "Believe it or not. It did make a marvelous story."

"Did she tell you what happened to her? How she fell off the boat?" To my utmost surprise, it was Bill, Tony's father, who spoke first and asked the question I'd been waiting to hear. Of course: the letter "B" Julia had been dangling in front of my face. His name was William, Bill for short.

B.B.B. How could I have missed it? But Bill was a mellow guy, quiet and mousy; his presence would easily be overlooked in a room. He was a loving father who lived a simple life and within his means. What possible reason did he have for pushing his son's wife over the railing and killing the mother of his grandson?

I looked at Brooke as she reached for her gun on the bar, then I faced Bill. "Julia did tell me who pushed her. Why, does it make you nervous she told me?"

Barbara popped out of her seat. "I don't like this. I don't like how you're talking to us, and I don't believe a word you're saying." She gripped her son's arm. "Tony, call for help. We need to turn this boat around."

"My phone has no signal," Tony said.

"Mine doesn't either," Justin agreed.

"I have no reception," added Helen.

"Nobody leaves this room until we find out which one of you pieces of shit tried to kill Julia!" Brooke roared, leveling her gun with both hands, waving it back and forth at the members of the Rose family.

And that was when all hell broke loose.

35

I heard the gunshot, but I didn't see the bullet fly. When Justin and Tony pounced toward Brooke, I sensed danger. I reacted as I always did, closing my eyes and pressing my hands tightly over my ears. It was the worst thing to do if I wanted to survive, but the only way my mind knew how to handle the threat of violence.

Watching a game of crime and punishment unfold in front of my eyes wasn't alien to me, but when Hector had threatened us with his gun, we'd cower in the corner. No one ever dared to challenge him.

The Roses had lost their minds when they decided to defuse the situation by attempting to disarm Brooke.

After the gun went off with a thundering bang, like an explosion, screaming and wailing filled the room. I peeked through my squinted eyes to assess the situation.

Justin was on the floor of the salon, holding his leg and screaming in pain. Blood trickled from his thigh and soaked into the plush white carpet underneath him. When the smell of iron in the air reached my nose, I knew my mind was going to be teleported back to the streets of Tijuana, where I'd killed a man. My stomach turned violently at the sight of blood, yet I couldn't look away. The horror scene petrified me.

Barbara was on her knees next to Justin, pressing a scarf against her son's thigh to put pressure on his wound.

Sylvia had fainted and lay spread-eagled on the sofa like a half-deflated blowup doll.

Bill's mind seemed to have shut down: he stood frozen next to his family with a hand over his mouth, staring at the bloody scene.

Helen hid behind the sofa and was peeking around the edge of it.

Jeff remained in his seat, his knees closed, and slouching, like a five-year-old kid who thought if he didn't move, nobody could see him.

"Now look what you have done!" shrieked Brooke, waving the gun. "Why did you have to charge me like that? I could have killed you!"

Tony rose from beside his brother and inched toward Brooke with a raised hand. "We all saw what happened. It was an accident. Let's all calm down. Give me the gun, Brooke." Tony's approach was calm and confident as if this wasn't the first deadly situation he had to defuse, but his face was awash with panic.

Brooke pushed her glasses up into place, steadying the gun with the other hand. "Get back, Tony!"

Tony took another step toward her.

"I said, GET BACK!"

Ever since Brooke had pulled the gun from her purse, I'd been standing by the bar, dumbfounded, my mind unable to comprehend what my eyes were seeing. Why would Brooke bring a handgun to this meeting? Was she planning to kill someone? We were supposed to be the good guys. When Brooke said that she had a plan to end it all and set me free, holding the Rose family hostage was not what I expected.

I tried to tell myself that Brooke and I were doing the right thing, yet I felt conflicted. I wanted revenge, and I shouldn't care if Tony or anyone else got hurt. But I did care. I didn't want this. I didn't want us to become the bad guys.

"Brooke, don't do something you'll regret later," I said softly.

She glanced at me. Her eyes were red and wild. She wasn't a killer, but she was angry and confused.

I turned to Tony, whose lips were trembling as he switched his eyes from us to his brother and back to us. "Tony, just tell us what happened on the cruise ship the night Julia disappeared, and this will all be over."

He creased his brows. "How many times do I have to say that I don't know what happened to Julia?" His eyes turned dark. His mind seemed to be confused as he spoke. "Is this what this cruise is about? To relive the past? To rip open old wounds?"

"Would you be surprised if I said yes?" I asked coldly, holding Tony's gaze. "Did you kill Julia?"

Tony's jaw clenched, and he looked away. When his eyes returned to mine, there was a new understanding in them. "Was it all a game to you? You and me?"

I poured myself a drink from the bar and offered one to Tony too. I invited him to sit down next to me on the sofa. He told me how he couldn't believe my story because if Julia had survived the fall and ended up in a back-alley brothel in Mexico for years, then how was he supposed to live with that news.

"I have Julia's diary," I said, clasping my glass.

"I want to read it," Tony said in a shaking voice.

"Not until you prove you weren't the one trying to kill her."

Justin's whimpering was dying down. Barbara had managed to clean away the blood, and we could see that the wound wasn't severe. The bullet had only glanced his thigh; it was just a flesh wound.

Bill remained stunned, unmoving. His face was as pale as a ghost's.

Jeff, on the other hand, had found a way to restart his system. He was splashing water on Sylvia's face and lightly tapping at her cheeks. She startled awake with a dramatic flair that evolved into a fit of crying. It was too much for my senses to endure. I turned back to Tony. I could never handle overly emotional adults—too much drama for me.

"All right, look, he's fine," Brooke said after checking on Justin. She had the authority to boss us around, given that she had a handgun we all knew was loaded. "Everybody, back to your seats. You too, Helen!"

I heard the hum of the boat throttle down as if the captain had given the order to slow our speed. The view from the windows was of open water and a glowing orange horizon as the sun set behind gently swelling waves, suggesting we were far from shore.

"You didn't even give us an opportunity to explain ourselves," Tony told Brooke.

"I've been more than patient with you and your lot. I was there that night on the boat with Julia and you. Remember?"

"Of course I remember! You boarded the ship a day or two after us."

"Right. I brought the contracts. Julia thought it would be easier to tell you the bad news while everybody was on vacation. But she miscalculated your greed. I can't forgive myself for going to my cabin and getting drunk alone instead of staying with Julia. I should have protected her."

"I feel the same way, Brooke," Tony said in a controlled manner. "I blame myself every day for not being there for her."

"Stop it!" Brooke cried. "Stop your pathetic mind games on me. Be a man! Take responsibility for what you've done and save your family, or we'll all die here on this boat tonight. None of you deserve to live. You're all parasites. You leeched off Julia. You sucked her dry, and when she had nothing left to give, you killed her."

"What are you talking about?" Tony cried out, losing his cool. "I loved my wife. I loved her when we had nothing! Our marriage was never about money."

Brooke tapped the barrel of the gun against her temple. "You know what I can't understand, Tony? You're saying that your marriage wasn't about money, yet Julia disappeared right before she would have signed the new business documents. She was throwing you all off her money wagon."

"Not me," Tony pleaded. "We were a happy family. Yeah, we had some rough patches here and there, but we were a solid unit."

"So, who was it, then? Your brother?" Brooke bent down to Justin and pressed the barrel of the gun between his eyes.

Barbara whimpered. "Stop it! Please, just stop it!"

Brooke looked piercingly into her eyes. "I'll stop when I find the murderer in the room." She redirected her attention back to Justin. "I read Julia's diary too, you know. Quite a few interesting stories about all of you in there. One was particularly interesting. One that may have given Justin a reason to kill her."

"Nonsense," Justin whimpered. "Why on earth would I hurt my sister-in-law? For money? She made the money, I only invested it. Without her, there would be no money to manage."

"How about the baby you fathered with Julia?"

Justin's eyes widened, and his shoulders tensed as he glanced at his brother. "Are you crazy?"

"What are you talking about?" Tony stepped closer to Brooke, forcing her to readjust her position to get a better angle at them.

"Julia described a situation in her diary in detail, one where she was lying in the hospital waiting for the doctor to terminate her pregnancy. Justin was there. He was pleading for his baby's life. It was a one-night stand, right, Justin? You got her pregnant behind your brother's back?"

"Oh, God, no." Tony sighed and dropped onto the leather cushion of the sofa, laying his head in his hands. "That story isn't real."

"What do you mean it isn't real?" I asked.

He looked up at me with bloodshot, tearful eyes. "Julia was writing a thriller. Her contract with her publisher had her hands tied, she was bound to write young-adult fantasies, but she had this wild story she said she wanted to write. She had used our life as an example and questioned everything in it with a what-if scenario. The abortion and my brother being the father was only a plot twist."

"True or not, it doesn't matter!" Brooke's voice thundered. "Her injuries may have messed with her head, but what happened to her was real." She aimed her gun at Justin again, then at Tony, and finally, the barrel landed on Barbara. "Which one of you tried to kill her?

"We didn't know Julia was forced into prostitution!" Barbara cried, tears washing down her cheeks. "If we did, then we would have looked for her, but the police said—"

"This isn't about those awful things Julia had to do to survive," Brooke sneered. "Tonight is about making the person who pushed her overboard pay."

Barbara whimpered again and sat back on her heels, shaking.

Brooke focused her attention on Sylvia. "Was it you? Were you jealous of Julia because she had everything you never had? She was naturally beautiful and healthy. Her husband loved her." Brooke was talking nasty now.

I finished my drink for courage and joined her quest, despite my conflicting feelings. I was there as her partner, even if I was beginning to feel like siding with the Roses.

"Did you decide to kill your sister-in-law when she told you she wouldn't give you more money for plastic surgery?" I asked Sylvia to show Brooke that I was back in the game. After all, I started this crusade, not Brooke. "Or was it simply a heated argument on the boat between the two of you? She was drunk, unsteady. Did she trip and fall on her own?"

"No," Sylvia sniffed and wiped her nose. "She was like a sister to me; I'd never harm her."

Brooke rolled her eyes at Sylvia's response. It was common knowledge that Julia and her sister-in-law had never gotten along. "But you were angry with her for cutting you off?"

"Well, I was. Maybe. But not enough to kill her. I couldn't harm a fly!"

Brooke pulled Sylvia to her feet. "I heard you calling her an 'emotional, psycho bitch' to your mother. 'A stingy cunt with a grumpy face' you wanted to bash in."

Sylvia struggled to free herself from Brooke's clutches. "I might have been angry, but I didn't mean a word of it!"

"Oh, but you did. You self-absorbed, worthless piece of shit. You're as ugly on the outside as you are on the inside." Brooke punched in a code at the salon door. The lock clicked, and the door slid open, allowing us access to the ship's starboard side and the open deck.

I rushed after the two battling women, fearing the gun would go off again by accident.

Barbara and Tony appeared by my side. My stomach dropped from no longer being under Brooke's protection.

"Help!" Barbara cried out. "Somebody, help us!"

Brooke ignored the likelihood of a crewmember showing up as she forced Sylvia halfway over the top of the railing. "Does this feel familiar to you?" Brooke screamed over the roar of the ocean.

The wind was twisting my hair, and the cold bit into my flesh. "Brooke, please. Don't do something you'll regret."

"It's better me than you!" she yelled to me over the loud clamors of the rough weather.

"Do something!" Tony pleaded. "Please stop her. I swear on my life that I had nothing to do with Julia's disappearance. Yes, it's true that she knew how to touch a nerve in me, and I could have hurt her many times, but I didn't. I never—" Tony choked on his words.

"Tony, help me!" cried Sylvia, lying across the wooden railing, trying to push her way back to solid decking. The wind ripped off her sunglasses and flung them to the sea.

"All you have to do is admit to your crime, and this night will be over!" Brooke roared like a madwoman, which I now understood she was all along. She was a ticking time bomb waiting to go off. I triggered her. My story triggered her.

"None of us did it, you crazy bitch!" Justin's voice came from the salon.

You can't tame a lion with aggression. And tonight, Brooke was a lion out for the kill. Before I had a chance to move or say anything, she flipped Sylvia overboard.

Standing on the deck, I let out a scream, followed by a moment of astonishment. I was at a loss for words. A painful cramp started to develop in my chest. My left arm went numb, and I could feel the blood leaving through the veins in my legs. I thought I was having a heart attack.

The next event that registered with me when Tony snatched a champagne glass from a tray, broke it on the edge of the table, and launched himself at Helen. He tightly wrapped his arm around her neck with a broken piece of glass against her jugular.

"You send help for my sister this instant, or I'll bleed her out!" Tony bellowed at Brooke.

Helen struggled in his hold. She tried to bite Tony's arm, but his grip on her neck was too strong, and her head was clamped tight.

Brooke lowered the gun. "All right! All right! But you need to let her go first."

"Like hell I will! Call the crew! RIGHT NOW!"

Barbara cried out like a bear stepping into a trap. "Enough, please! Enough!" She was pulling on her hair with both hands. Her face was flaming red. She had lost it and was about to explode. "Let her go, Tony! I did it, okay?" she shrieked. "I pushed Julia overboard! Just please stop the boat."

Tony's arm relaxed around Helen's neck. "Mother? What are you saying?"

"It was me, okay? I'm so sorry. I didn't mean to hurt her, Tony, I swear, but she was mean and a narcissist. She was going to ruin all your lives. She knew about your infidelity. She came on that cruise to get vengeance. I couldn't let that happen. But my daughter doesn't deserve to die for my sins."

"You pushed your daughter-in-law into the water?" Brooke held her forehead, her shock etched into her forehead. "For what? So you could keep your undeserved lifestyle?"

"No. No. No. It wasn't for me. I did it for my son, for my children." She moved toward Tony, but he took a step back from her. "She was going to take Sammy and leave you. Leave all of us."

"I can't even…" Tony crouched down and spat saliva on the deck.

"Someone, seize him!" Helen screamed.

"Calm down, Helen," Brooke warned. "Let's just sort everything out first."

Helen's face and chest flushed red from the surprise Brooke's tone must have caused her.

"Please turn the boat around!" Barbara pleaded, looking over the railing into the dark water. "Sylvia had nothing to do with this. We need to go back for her."

I kicked away the broken piece of champagne glass that Tony had dropped and led Helen to a support pillar that stood in the middle of the deck like a sore thumb. She leaned against the structure, rubbing her neck and holding Tony in a piercing gaze.

"Did she beg for her life?" I posed the question to Barbara, holding back my tears.

Guilt sat on her unusually wrinkled and lifeless face. In most cases, I might have felt pity for an older woman, but all I could offer her was my hate and disgust.

"It happened so fast," Barbara said, hyperventilating. "I didn't mean to push her. I-It just...*happened.*"

"She was the wife of your son! The mother of your grandchild! She loved you all and supported all of you for years! How could you?" The injustice of it was cutting me up inside like knives.

"So, what about her drink, then?" Helen's voice startled me. "I saw you taking her drink in a home video. Did you slip something in her drink?"

Barbara rubbed her face. "I did. It was Justin's idea, but it was harmless. We thought if we made her sick, then she wouldn't push the contracts on us. Maybe if we had more time, we could talk some sense into her."

"It's hard to believe that you didn't plan to kill her. Too much of a coincidence if you ask me. What do you think, Jeff?" Helen inquired.

Jeff scratched his head. He had blood on the front of his pants. "I don't know. My brother can piss me off so badly sometimes that it's by the grace of God I haven't thrown him overboard yet."

"Seriously, Jeffrey, that's your answer?" Helen snapped.

He threw his hands in the air. "What do you want me to say? You want me to lie?"

"What am I supposed to tell my son now, Mother?" Tony wiped his mouth, standing up again. "How do I tell him that his grandmother killed his mother?"

"You heard Annie—or London or whatever this woman's name is—Julia didn't die! I didn't kill her."

I caught Brooke walking back into the salon, like the broken woman she was. My heart bled for her. She'd never found Robert's killer, and now it had cost her an act of evil to solve Julia's mystery.

Barbara! I couldn't get the idea out of my head. Yeah, her name started with the letter "B," but I never imagined a grandmother was capable of doing such a horrible thing to her daughter-in-law. By removing Julia, she not only robbed her of her life, she also destroyed her own son's family. How did she get up every morning and look herself in the mirror all these years?

"I did it because I love you. I love you all!" Barbara cried, but her pleading evoked no sympathy in me. "Ever since she entered our lives, she slowly took you away from me. Don't you see what she was doing? She was trying to break our family apart!"

"Mother, that's not love. We don't kill in the name of love. Your love killed my wife and stole my son's mother from him. Julia loved you. She helped all of you, and you killed her."

"What have you done, Barb." Bill looked like a man who just aged a decade in minutes as he stood by the sliding door, supporting Justin's weight.

"I made a mistake, but I didn't kill Julia. She survived the fall!"

For a second time, Barbara tried to excuse her actions by minimizing her role in Julia's tragedy. Yes, Julia did survive the fall, but she suffered a concussion and amnesia. She ended up being a sex slave for more than two years until she died from a combination of malnourishment, unsanitary conditions, and inhuman treatment. She never even had a funeral.

My fingers rolled into balls as the old memories ran through my mind. I readied myself to punch Barbara's teeth out. I was about to lurch at her when a flash of white and blue tore across my vision. Roaring like a lunatic, Helen charged at Barbara and slammed her over the railing.

The sound of Barbara's death cry made my heart skip a beat.

Bill rushed to the railing without a sound.

"What have you done, Helen?" I screamed, joining Bill by the side of the boat. I looked down into the abyss. The water was dark and turbulent. The lights came on below deck, and a pale blue pool of light appeared on the surface. I saw the white-frothed waves falling away from the boat, but not Barbara.

Tony appeared next to me, leaning over and yelling his mother's name in a heart-wrenching voice.

I felt as if my mind had left me, as if my head were nothing more than an empty shell.

"You heard her," Helen said calmly. "Julia didn't die. She was going to get away with murder. I didn't spend three years of my life untangling this mystery to let the killer get away with murder." She stabbed her chest with her finger. "Every waking moment, I thought about what I'd do to the person who hurt her. Do you think that after what Julia suffered through, I'd simply let that waste of space live? Not on my watch, sister."

"But now you're a murderer too! You'll go to jail!" I breathed the words in disbelief. The back of my head was pounding with a sharp pain. Had everyone gone mad in this world?

Helen's eyes shrunk. "Says who? Who will give me up to the cops? You?"

I was too confused to answer. I'd met many different types of evil people, but I'd never seen someone with a complete lack of conscience like Helen. She had no remorse. No regret. Not an ounce of fear.

Tony turned and threw himself at Helen and wrestled her to the ground. Helen cried out in pain, and I screamed, thinking he was going to kill her with his bare hands.

The sound of a gunshot deafened my ears. I looked at Brooke, confused, my ears ringing. She was holding the gun high, pointing it to the starry sky. Her eyes were filled with tears.

Rubbing my ears to regain my hearing, I turned back to Helen who was lying on the ground, her nose bleeding. Tony was sitting next to his victim with his arms resting on his knees and watching the gun in Brooke's hand.

The beep of a handheld radio cut into the stunned silence. "Yes, we're ready," Brooke spoke into a walkie-talkie. "Bring her up."

"What?" Helen shrugged in bewilderment, looking at Brooke as she wiped the blood from her nose in her sleeve. "You did the same thing. You pushed that whiny bitch overboard too."

Brooke shook her head. "Helen, Helen. What am I going to do with you now?"

Helen looked at everybody for confirmation.

Bill passed all of us in morose silence and walked back to the salon where he sat down on the sofa, looking like a man whose spirit had left his body.

Justin held his bandage over his gunshot wound with one hand and kept a fist over his eye with the other as he cried loudly. "Look what you have done! You monster!"

Unsynchronized footsteps thumped up the stairs. I turned to Brooke. "What's going on?"

"Surprise!" she said with a limp flick of her hand, sounding crestfallen.

My chest felt tight, but it was a good pain—a welcomed feeling. I wasn't the only one holding my breath in anticipation. The air was buzzing with hope and uncertainty.

But my body deflated when the two deckhands showed up on the deck with Sylvia wrapped in a cozy thick blanket.

Tony intercepted his sister at the door. "Are you okay? What happened? Where's Mom?"

The deckhand, Ryan, exchanged a silent glance with Brooke. "I saw her go underwater. We'll have to send out a search team for her."

Justin was crawling toward his sister, leaving a smudged blood trail behind him on the wood planks. Bill stormed out of the salon like a locomotive and scooped up his daughter.

"What do you mean she went underwater? Then how is Sylvia here?" Tony roared.

Seeing the manifestation of torment and pain on his face, I felt something snap inside of me. I couldn't help but feel sorry for the man.

"We didn't anticipate a second person. I'm sorry," the deckhand said flatly.

It seemed Tony was slowly coming to terms with the situation, but I read him wrong. He pretended to check on his father when he spun around, jumped at Brooke, and seized the handgun.

Brooke didn't try to stop him.

Sylvia let out an earsplitting wail.

"Tell the captain to send someone into the water to find my mother immediately!" Tony yelled at the deckhands. "Don't look at her. I'm giving the orders now!"

"I'm sorry, sir, but she's gone. There is a large buoy tied to the side of the boat where she landed. I saw her hit her head. She slumped underwater after impact. We looked for her, but we couldn't find her. She never surfaced."

"Then how the hell did you save my sister?"

"That part was planned. We had a net in the water, catching her."

Tony crouched down and started to bang his head with the gun. "Fuck! Fuck!" Then he jumped back to his feet and aimed the weapon at Helen. "I should put a bullet in your head right now," he said through clenched teeth as tears gleamed in his eyes.

"You want to kill me?" Helen scoffed. "Your mother murdered your wife and the mother of your child, not me."

"She is crazy. Her idea of love is twisted, but she is still my mother."

"Tony," I said softly, touching his arm. "It's over." He looked at me, and I gazed back at him. "Please put down the gun. Nobody else needs to die tonight."

Tony's face was going in and out of expression. One second, he knitted his brows and his face shrunk as if he were ready to cry; the next, he stretched his facial muscles and looked at me with wide eyes. Madness was taking hold of him. "I can't...Sam."

I slid my hand down toward his hand. "Yes, think of Sam. He needs a father. He can't lose you too. You don't want to go to prison."

He alternated his attention between Helen and me. When I sensed his hand lowering, I reached for the gun and pulled it away from him. "Yes, see? Everything will be okay."

Brooke got up from her seat and lit a cigarette. "Tell the captain to take us back to shore," she said to the deckhands. "And make sure he calls the Coast Guard and tells them about the man overboard."

"Wait!" Tony called out. "I can't handle another scandal. It would destroy Sam."

"What do you want to do?" I asked, taking a cigarette from Brooke.

"Can I have one of those?"

"Sure. Here." Brooke lit him a Marlboro Light.

Tony took a deep inhale, held it in with his eyes closed, then forcefully exhaled. "Give me a minute to think."

SIX MONTHS LATER

The shirt was stuck to my sweaty back in a most uncomfortable way as I fanned myself, sitting inside the back of a van. I yearned for the cool breeze of the air-conditioning to blow across my face, but the commander gave explicit instructions not to idle the engine. Our objective was to stay unnoticed by the locals.

"Are you all right?" Brooke asked as she set a bottle of Pepsi in front of me.

"I'm getting a little antsy. We're on day three here and still nothing," I said, adjusting my headset because the clamp was digging into my scalp.

"Don't rile yourself up," Brooke said, unwrapping a piece of chewing gum next to me. "We knew this might take days or even weeks."

I took the bottle from the desk, drank from it, and set it aside so that it wouldn't block my view of the street showing on the monitor. "You're right. I need to stay positive."

While the two of us were stuck inside the surveillance van, there was a five-person mercenary team afoot, roaming the streets of Ensenada near the market where Hector used to take Kitana to buy food. Their spy cameras sent signals back to the van. For sixteen hours a day for three days, I'd been slouching in a rotating chair and dripping sweat, scanning the faces of people milling about in the square on multiple monitors. I expected Guerrero, Perez, or Delgado to show their faces sooner or later because the kitchen needed restocking. Our hired guns did the footwork, but I was the only one able to identify the watchdogs from the brothel.

The only thing I feared was the possibility of Ornelas hiring new men to work at the brothel after I left. He may have replaced

Hector with a new guy instead of promoting one of his trusted men for the job. Then we'd be screwed. I didn't know all the players in the cartel that operated in this town. We may have walked by the new guy on day one and not recognized him.

Brooke spared no expense on this rescue mission, but her money didn't stretch forever. We paid the mercenaries by the day, and she had enough money to finance a three-week stakeout.

I started losing sleep over the consecutive unsuccessful days. What if all this effort was for nothing?

It hurt me to think of Brooke giving up her life's work to hunt bad guys with me. Soon after the yacht incident, she'd put her eccentric mansion on the market. It took nearly four months and three price reductions to find a buyer for her home. She had hired a private security detail from the money she received to travel with us to Ensenada and help us free the girls from the brothel. The only problem was that I didn't have an address. I only knew it was near a market with a bookstore where Kitana bought our food and had found Julia's book.

The only time I left the basement was when Hector transported me to Tijuana, but even then, he was instructed to put a bag over my head. All I remembered of the outside was the shepherd dog and the white picket fence. We had very little to go on, but that didn't ebb Brooke's passion for finding the girls.

Brooke stayed with me in the van. She only left my side to get food and drinks. I was once a California girl, and as such, I could handle the heat, but she was dying in the tin can. We spent most of our time talking about our past life in Montclair and our hopes for the future. We agreed that if this mission was successful and my parents' lives were no longer in danger, I would call them in Palmdale. They deserved to know that I was alive and well.

Brooke never missed a day to remind me of my promise.

There was another big event we had to prepare for in due time. Helen's trial was coming up in four weeks. Brooke and I were scheduled to attend as witnesses. We needed to succeed here in Mexico by then so we could return to New York City to support Helen.

Helen was a fool, but she didn't deserve to rot in jail. Barbara's death was a crime of passion, committed in a heated moment. Helen saw it as justice being served, though Brooke warned her not to say that in front of the jury.

When I was a kid and got into trouble at home, I used to say, "But it was an accident," as an excuse. My adoptive mother would reply, "You know what the judge will say? Fifteen years in Chino." That was how she tried to teach me to think before I acted because crimes of passion or manslaughter, they were both punishable by law.

I tried not to dwell too much on what happened on the yacht, but I had a hard time burying my guilt. For the most part, I managed to push the memories to the back of my mind, but the images would frequently come forth into my consciousness without warning.

I felt responsible for Helen's predicament. I was the one who started down a path of revenge and got everyone involved.

Helen was hunting murderers and seeking justice for victims many years before she met me, but that's precisely why she was in an emotionally fragile place, and I should have noticed it. Brooke and I pushed Helen to her limit, yet she was going to be the one to suffer the consequences.

By the time the yacht had returned to shore, the harbor police were waiting for us at the dock. Uniformed men rushed inside the salon and surrounded the vessel. Wherever I looked, stern-faced, intimidating men looked back at me. Where was all this show of force when I was rotting away in the brothel, working as a child sex slave?

When we were still out in the open water, Tony suggested we should find a way to cover up Barbara's death, but Bill wouldn't hear of it. He argued his point so heatedly that he went into cardiac arrest. Helen saved Bill's life by performing CPR on him—it turned out she had worked as a lifeguard when she was in college. Helen's act of courage only complicated things.

By the time Bill awoke in the hospital, the police had already taken everyone's statement. After that, a grieving old man's ramblings weren't worth much.

The story that everyone could make peace with was that Helen and Barbara got in a scuffle, and at one point, Barbara lost her footing and fell overboard. It was a freak accident. According to the internet, boating accidents happened all the time. This way, the truth about Barbara trying to kill Julia would never come out, and Helen wouldn't be charged with first-degree murder either.

That night, we all lost a little and gained a little.

Well, life is rarely fair.

Although Justin agreed not to press charges against Brooke for shooting him, he wanted Helen to pay for his mother's death— even if his mother killed his brother's wife for money. Love is a strange thing.

Brooke negotiated a lesser charge for Helen with Justin and Sylvia. In exchange, they were allowed to keep the original business arrangement they'd had with Julia. But the family trust had to change. Brooke refused to budge on that one, and I fully supported her. I tried to do everything right by Helen, but my focus was on Julia's son. The stability of Sammy's financial future was critical.

Justin and Sylvia took the deal.

The police got their story, and Julia got her justice. But the truth would never make it to the public.

I felt bittersweet in the end. Drowning was too quick a death for Barbara, but at least Sam was protected.

"All your stories sound very similar," the officer had told me after he put away his cell phone, which he had used to record our conversation. "They sound rehearsed."

"I don't know what to tell you," I had said, my face void of expression. "We all witnessed the same event. I imagine our stories would be similar."

My quiet, somber demeanor may have made me look honest, but inside I was dying. This utter madness was not how I expected the puzzle pieces to fall into place. After all the torture we'd put Tony through, he turned out to be innocent. I think I knew it all along. It was obvious. My guilt for not listening to reason was going to spin in my mind for a long time.

"Can I get you something to eat?" Brooke's voice broke through my haze of reminiscing.

"No, I'm good for now. Thank you, though." I stretched and yawned, feeling the joints pop underneath my skin.

I hadn't taken any Vicodin for weeks. I also stopped drinking. Since I had been clean, I was more focused and energetic. I hadn't had any more visions of Julia either. The absence of her spirit made me miss her more—even though she only existed as a fragment of my doped-up imagination.

Once I understood that there was no ghost, only a trick my messed-up mind was playing on me, I started to believe that the letter "B" was something my subconscious conjured up. I may never know what it meant because I never suspected Barbara to be the one who did it. She was the last person on my list. After my horrible experience with my own mother's betrayal, I should have known better.

As my thoughts overwhelmed me, I felt claustrophobic in the small van. "I'm going to get an apple or something. I need to stretch my legs," I said to Brooke.

"Don't wander far," she warned.

I opened the backdoor and stepped out onto the hot asphalt. The blazing sun washed over me and blinded my eyes. I slipped on my sunglasses and headed toward the closest vendor.

The radio beeped behind me. "Team, stand by. Annie is on the move."

"Copy that. This is agent five. I have a visual on her."

Keeping my head down, I put one foot in front of the other, trying to keep a lid on my anxiety. I hated this place more than anything. I'd have never come back if it wasn't for a good cause.

As I passed a pack of flea-ridden street dogs, I pulled my bandana over my nose and mouth to block out the foul smell that hit too close to home. I detected smog mixed with a nauseating stench of fried food, seafood, and urine heightened by the hot, humid sea air.

The market was bustling with locals and tourists, but I was expecting to spot the mercenaries standing post around the square. I couldn't identify any of them. Their blending technique was superb.

At a farmer's table, I picked up an apple and rolled it around in my hand. None of these delicious fruits had ever made it to the brothel's kitchen. I took a bag and started loading it with apples, papayas, mangos, and oranges. The girls would love to have them.

As I was picking the fruit, the combination of a familiar scent and voice seized my body. Guerrero walked by behind me, nudging a red-haired girl to move faster. They came to a halt by the water fountain, where Guerrero lit a cigar. The girl looked to be my age, but I didn't recognize her. She was carrying a wicker basket overflowing with goods.

Where is Kitana? Oh God, please don't tell me I'm too late.

"Guerrero is here," I said into my microphone, shaking. "I'm gonna follow him."

"Absolutely not!" boomed Brooke's voice, loud and clear. "Let the professionals handle it."

"He's with a girl, but it's not Kitana." My voice buckled.

"Señorita, do you need help?" the vendor asked. I turned around, confused. Too many people. Too much noise. And too many emotions.

"I'm going after them!" I ripped the earpiece from my ear before Brooke could respond.

We walked about ten minutes to a small, secluded side street. My heart started to race when I spotted the white picket fence where I used to watch the dog play fetch.

Guerrero didn't appear to be nervous or paranoid. He walked like any other law-abiding citizen would walk. The only telltale sign of trouble was the girl's timid way of moving. Her shoulders were drawn in, and her head was down. She made no eye contact with any passerby as she dragged her feet on the concrete.

They stopped at a small lime-green house and banged on a black metal door. I remembered hearing that door creak open and close. My heart was about to rip out of its cage.

I nervously pushed the earpiece back into place and managed to say in a distracted haze, "I have a location. I repeat. I have a location. Send everyone."

"They're on your six," Brooke replied in a voice swollen with worry. "But don't you dare do that to me again, do you understand me, young lady?"

"Copy that, boss."

I had my eyes on two of our guys. They were quickly organizing the team to surround the building. I didn't want to be in their way and mess up the operation. But I also didn't want to miss my chance to be the first person to comfort the girls.

There was an explosion followed by a massive dust cloud that filled the street. Dogs started barking. A few car alarms went off, blaring out of sync.

The assault was quick and effective. The mercenaries killed three thugs on sight and dragged out eight johns from the building, most of them butt naked.

When the house was secure, the leader of the team escorted me to the basement. A big bowl of emotions swirled inside me as I descended the stairs. This small dark pit had been my home for too many years.

I found the scared girls huddled against each other in the hallway. Many of them cried. Some of them attacked us with forks and shoes in hand.

"It's me, London," I said softly, approaching them with raised hands. Those who recognized me let down their guards and pounced at me with sighs of relief. I held them with all my might as tears washed down my face. It was the happiest moment of my life.

We had all the girls out and loaded in the vans before the local police made it to the scene.

I only knew half of the girls. The youngest was only eight years old. Her Indonesian parents had sold her to the cartel for money to feed their other five kids. Everybody on our team was heavy with emotion as we drove out of the area.

We bumped along the pothole-filled roads toward the US Embassy. It was eerily quiet during the ride. Even the mercenaries, who were some of the toughest men I'd ever met, were at a loss for words.

"I told you I'd come back for you," I said to Najeri. She was cuddled against me, wrapped in a blanket.

"Do you guys know where Kitana is?" I asked the group who was riding in the van with me.

Most of the girls shook their heads in silent disbelief.

"They took her months ago," Najeri said, tears swelling up in her eyes.

I had a hard time swallowing my pain, but I had to stay strong for the girls I did save. "At least you're safe now."

In the waiting room of the embassy, my phone went off. I checked the message.

"Tony again?" Brooke asked.

I nodded.

"He isn't giving up, is he?"

I shook my head.

"Are you going to give him a chance?"

"I don't think that's a good idea. You can't start a relationship with lies. I could never tell Tony that we had him under surveillance for months. Think about it, Brooke, we broke into his home, for Christ's sake. No, we don't have a future together." I put my phone away. "He'll give up eventually," I concluded.

I wasn't sure if I wanted Tony to give up pursuing me. Maybe one day I would be strong enough to face the music and open my heart to a relationship. But that day wasn't today.

On the flight back to New York City, I felt a huge hole in my chest. We'd rescued twenty-seven young girls from the brothel, and this massive accomplishment alone should have brought me joy and pride, but the fact that I'd failed to save Kitana and Julia ate me alive.

I had to find a new goal, because I had been living for revenge and justice for so long that I didn't know how to do anything else. Brooke suggested we start a campaign to bring awareness to child prostitution, but I wasn't sure I was ready to go public yet. I needed to become stronger emotionally before I could stand in the spotlight and talk about my experience. Maybe one day I would be there. But first, I wanted to learn to feel safe again. I wanted to sleep in a real bed without fear and anxiety.

As the flight attendant said after our plane finished boarding: please put on your own oxygen mask first before attempting to help others.

ACKNOWLEDGMENTS

As always, I am incredibly grateful to my avid readers who dedicate their time to read and critique my books, with special thanks to Amanda Johnson, Karen Coffman, Pheadra Farah, Boglarka Mahan, Ellen Wookey who read my manuscript first.

In the past few years, I had the honor to connect with passionate book reviewers on Instagram. To name a few:

Eleni (@lafemmerreaders62), Amy (@novelgossip),
Lisa (@getlostinabookwithme), Dee (@dees.reads),
Janelle (@whatsheseees), Sarah (@sarahandherbookshelves),
KC (@Books.Cats.Travel.Food), Jess (@thegrowinglibrary),
Ellie (@the.raleigh.reader), Ashley (@spinesinds),
BreeAnn (@shejustlovesbooks), Misty (@escapeintothepage),
Sarah (@sarahs.bookstack), Tatum (@titaniumrangel).
Your support is much appreciated.

A special thanks to my editor Kate Schomaker. You brought the best out of *As Sick as Our Secrets* and you polished *This Love Kills Me* to perfection as well. I value our professional relationship more than you can imagine.

To my agents, Sarah Hershman and Tania Rivera, at Hershman Rights Management. I owe you my gratitude for you hard work and dedication.

My profound appreciation goes to Dan, my husband, and our children. You are the reason for everything I do.

ABOUT THE AUTHOR

A former IT engineer and a marketing director, A.B. Whelan is an Amazon top 100 bestselling author of domestic psychological thrillers. She is a James Patterson Masterclass graduate who spends her time raising her children, coaching soccer, and writing books.

She currently resides in California with her family. When she isn't writing, editing, marketing, or researching her next book, you can find her walking her two rescue dogs, socializing online, or doing another DIY project with her husband.

CONNECT WITH THE AUTHOR ONLINE

For early access to new books, giveaways, and more join:
A.B. Whelan's Best Book Friends on Facebook
Author Facebook Page: Author A B Whelan
Instagram: @authorabwhelan
Twitter: @authorabwhelan
Goodreads
Bookbub

Made in the USA
Coppell, TX
13 June 2021

57392432R00192